CHASING TAIL

THE DOGMOTHERS - BOOK FOUR

D1738390

roxanne st. claire

Chasing Tail
THE DOGMOTHERS BOOK FOUR

ISBN Print: 978-1-952196-00-3
ISBN Ebook: 978-1-7339121-9-8

COVER DESIGN: Keri Knutson
INTERIOR FORMATTING: Author E.M.S.

Critical Reviews of Roxanne St. Claire Novels

"Non-stop action, sweet and sexy romance, lively characters, and a celebration of family and forgiveness."
— *Publishers Weekly*

"Plenty of heat, humor, and heart!"
— *USA Today* (Happy Ever After blog)

"Beautifully written, deeply emotional, often humorous, and always heartwarming!"
— *The Romance Dish*

"Roxanne St. Claire is the kind of author that will leave you breathless with tears, laughter, and longing as she brings two people together, whether it is their first true love or a second love to last for all time."
— *Romance Witch Reviews*

"Roxanne St. Claire writes an utterly swoon-worthy romance with a tender, sentimental HEA worth every emotional struggle her readers will endure. Grab your tissues and get ready for some ugly crying. These books rip my heart apart and then piece it back together with the hope, joy and indomitable loving force that is the Kilcannon clan."
— *Harlequin Junkies*

"As always, Ms. St. Claire's writing is perfection...I am unable to put the book down until that final pawprint the end. Oh the feels!"
— *Between My BookEndz*

Before
The Dogmothers...
there was

The Dogmothers Series

Hot Under the Collar (Book 1)

Three Dog Night (Book 2)

Dachshund Through the Snow (Book 3)

Chasing Tail (Book 4)

And many more to come!

For a complete guide to all of the characters in both The Dogfather and Dogmothers series, see the back of this book. Or visit www.roxannestclaire.com for a printable reference, book lists, buy links, and reading order of all my books. Be sure to sign up for my newsletter on my website to find out when the next book is released! And join the private Dogfather Facebook group for inside info on all the books and characters, sneak peeks, and a place to share the love of tails and tales!

www.facebook.com/groups/roxannestclairereaders/

Chapter One

Wait...*what*? Bitter Bark Bar?

Sadie Hartman slowed her step and frowned at the frosted glass etched with three words and two frothy beer mugs. She glanced up and down Ambrose Avenue to make certain she knew where she was. Bitter Bark hadn't changed *that* much in seventeen years, had it?

But...Bitter Bark Bar? Wasn't this...*Bushrod's*?

"You look lost."

Sadie turned toward the male voice, coming face-to-face—no, face-to-chest, and a solid, broad one at that—with a worn leather jacket barely covering the fire department logo on the T-shirt underneath.

"I'm looking for..." She slid her gaze up and...whoa. She was lost, all right. In indigo eyes that crinkled as he smiled. "I'm looking for..." Words. Which eluded her.

"I'm a local. I can help you find whatever you want in this town."

What she wanted was... *Okay, calm down, Sadie. He's just a guy.*

1

And to be honest, he wasn't even a textbook, Hollywood-handsome guy. But there was something about his slightly crooked nose, clean-shaven jaw, and the way those blue eyes reached right into her soul. No, sorry. That wasn't her *soul* that sat up and suddenly craved attention.

He laughed softly at the awkward moment while her thoughts ran amok. With a wink, he notched his thumb toward the door. "How about I buy you a drink at Bushrod's while you figure it out?"

"Yes, Bushrod's! That's what I'm looking for. Where is it?"

"Right here." He glanced at the etched glass. "Oh, they changed the name a while back when the town went through its gentrification years, which followed the lean times but predated the dog period."

"Sounds like I found the town historian."

"No, that's Nellie Shaker, head librarian. I'm just your garden-variety first responder."

Really. Well, she wouldn't mind a barefoot stroll through *that* garden.

His smile widened as his gaze coasted over her face, lingered on her mouth, then settled on her eyes. "But if someone sent you to Bushrod's, this is where they meant. Everyone still calls it that, but Billy, the owner? He wanted the place to sound cooler, hipper, and not so easy to mock."

If anyone understood that, it was a woman who left *Mercedes* behind and recast herself as *Sadie* when she'd left this town.

"I get it," she said, trying not to stare at his face. Or shoulders. Or that little chestnut curl that threatened to fall over his forehead and kiss his brow. But who wouldn't want to kiss that brow? Along with the rest of him.

"So are you meeting someone here?" He gestured toward the door. "Because that drink offer stands."

"Well, it *has* been a long day." A long few weeks, to be honest. A drink was exactly what she needed after a day of licking her wounds and fruitless job hunting on the internet. She'd slipped out for an evening walk in the February air to enjoy the last of winter's chill fading into that clean comfort of spring in North Carolina. But a glass of wine at the local watering hole with Blue Eyes could offer a completely different kind of comfort.

At her hesitation, he lowered his head a centimeter closer as if a whiff of fresh soap from a shower might seal the deal. "I'm sworn to save lives and protect," he whispered, his voice low and just seductive enough to coax nature's finest hormones out of hibernation. "You can trust me. I'm a lieutenant."

She laughed softly. "Okay, Lieutenant. I'm Sadie, and I'll have one drink."

"Sadie? I don't think I've ever met a Sadie. A name as pretty as you are." His mouth slid into a smile that made her feel like he'd waited all day, possibly his entire life, for that drink with her.

"Thanks," she said quickly, not quite sure how to handle a compliment so outright and genuine. But it did make the drink feel like a no-brainer.

In fact, after living in a world where power seemed to be the most effective aphrodisiac, a drink with a sweet, flirtatious Bitter Bark firefighter was just the ticket for her current state of overall disappointment in the human race.

He tugged the door open, and instantly she realized that the name outside might have changed, but inside, Bushrod's was still Bushrod's. Not a thing was different from the last time she'd been here for dinner almost eighteen years ago with her dad, sometime in the summer before she left for college and before he took his poor, broken heart off to Austin. She'd been in Bitter Bark a few times since to visit her grandparents, but she hadn't come to this…joint.

And it was such a joint. Dark and humming with the din of drinkers and a slightly subpar sound system, Bushrod's still smelled faintly of beer and fried food, both of which it served in abundance. The tables weren't full, but peppered with a mix of locals of all ages, from the young Vestal Valley College students using fake IDs to have a drink, to couples grabbing a quick bite on Friday night before hitting the movie theater. The back room echoed with the sound of billiard balls being racked and laughter from a dart game gone south. The place was steeped in a small-town vibe, unpretentious and authentic and as charming as the man who led her to the bar.

He threaded them through tables and past a dance floor that might be packed as it got closer to eleven, but was empty at seven thirty.

The bar was full, though, and her escort seemed to have silent eye contact with the bartender, nodding with familiarity.

"What are you drinking?" he asked Sadie, putting a light hand on her back.

She had skipped the roast dinner her grandmother had made, so she decided to go fairly light. "Just a glass of white wine, please."

A few college girls in front of her burst into a chorus of noisy giggles about something on one of their phones, so loudly she missed his whole conversation with the bartender. But a moment later, he had a bottle of Bud Light, and she had something from a gallon-sized jug served in an inexpensive thick-rimmed glass, so different from the wafer-thin bistro crystal with three overpriced ounces of sauvignon blanc she was used to. And Bud Light was definitely not the craft brew many of the men in DC drank.

But right this minute, with this man, in this bar, the choices were perfect.

"There's probably a table free in the back," he said, angling his head toward a door that led to the game room.

She followed him to a high-top with four stools a few feet from where a couple of guys were finishing a game of pool.

"Welcome to Bitter Bark," he said after she sat, and he took the seat closest to her, tipping the brown bottle toward her glass. "What brings you to town?"

"How do you know I don't live here?"

He gave her a *get real* look, and she expected the *I'm a local firefighter, and I know everyone* response. But he leaned in, quiet while he watched her sip the wine with the tiniest look of envy, like he was actually jealous of the rim that touched her lips.

"I'd never forget you."

The unexpected flirt punched and almost made her choke on the wine. "Oh, you're good, Lieutenant. Yes, I'm from Washington, DC."

"How long are you here?" he asked, somehow managing to infuse those five words with hope, interest, and the subtext that he actually cared about the answer.

"I don't know," she said, sliding into her standard response. "I thought I'd take some time off so I could check in on my grandparents, who live here. They're elderly."

"Who are they?" He shimmied out of his jacket and tossed it on the empty stool next to him, getting comfortable.

She stole a surreptitious glance at his biceps, which were just the kind she liked—strong, noticeable, and well-defined. The kind that came from dragging hoses and climbing ladders, not a $75-an-hour personal trainer spotting him on the bench press.

"Your grandparents?" he urged, a hint of a smile that made her wonder if her "surreptitious glance" had been anything but.

"Oh, I had to think of Nana and Boomie's names for a second," she said quickly. "Margaret and James Winthrop."

"Oh, sure. They live on the corner of Jessamine Court, don't they? The property with the gardens and all those live oak trees?"

She smiled. "Wow, I forgot what life is like in a small town."

"Jim Winthrop had to have a pacemaker put in about a year ago, and I was the EMT on duty when his wife called for help. I was with him in the ambulance."

"Aww." She reached out and touched his forearm, which was strong, thick, and dusted with hair. "That's so sweet. Thank you. I remember when he had to go to the hospital and Nana was so upset."

"Is he okay?" He seemed genuinely concerned. "I

could have sworn I saw him at the hardware store last weekend."

"He's fine," she said, taking a deep drink of the wine to cover how much she just wanted to stare at this real-life hero who took Boomie to the hospital and went to hardware stores on the weekend.

"But you're in Bitter Bark to take care of him?" he urged.

She was in Bitter Bark to take care of *herself*. But that would beg questions she didn't want to answer, so she went with the same line she'd told her grandparents, which was honest—and purposely vague. "I needed a break from the grind of politics."

He lifted his brows. "You're a politician?"

"A former...aide." She took a sip, keeping the full title to herself. She didn't need to impress him with the fact that she'd been the deputy chief of staff for a congresswoman. It would just invite questions she didn't want to answer about that congresswoman. And what did Nana always say? *If you can't say anything nice, say nothing at all.* And she sure couldn't say anything nice about Congresswoman Jane Sutherland at the moment.

"My job was not nearly as heroic as yours," she said. "Tell me about life as a firefighter. It can't be all shirtless-calendar photo shoots and kittens stuck in trees."

He gave a slow smile and eased the tiniest bit closer. "It's hours of boring broken up by moments of adrenaline rushes."

"How often do you get to save someone's life?"

"When I get those kittens out of trees," he teased. The joke, or the way he said it, reminded her of

Roxanne St. Claire

someone, but she couldn't imagine who. It certainly wasn't any of the power players in DC who flung their Armani suit jackets over their shoulders, loosened their ties, and expected women to swoon.

"What else do you do?" she asked, magnetically drawn to his mouth. Was she staring at it too openly? Probably, but *come on*. That thing was a work of art.

"Well, occasionally I help stray out-of-town knockouts find their way up and down Ambrose Avenue."

"Knockout?" Smiling, she drank again, surprised she'd nearly downed the entire contents of her glass. "Whoa, there wasn't much in there."

"That's how Billy makes money," he said, maybe not kidding. "Another?"

"No, I shouldn't."

"But you are walking back to the Winthrops' house? You're staying with them?"

"I'm staying in the garden shed Boomie converted into a little bitty guesthouse, where I am currently sleeping on a pullout sofa with a beautiful girl named Demi."

His eyes widened. "That sounds terribly...interesting. And kinda hot."

She laughed as the very first tingling effects of the wine danced along the edges of her nerve endings, brushing away a few inhibitions and making her want to *be* terribly interesting and kinda hot to this delicious firefighter. "Demi's my cat."

"Is she named after that famous actress married to Bruce Willis?"

"They split up a million years ago," she said, kind of liking that the personal lives of celebrities obviously held no interest for him. "Are you a cat person, Lieutenant?"

"Only when I have to save them from those treetops," he quipped. "But I guess I'm a little more of a dog guy. Right now, I don't have either one, but there are a gazillion dogs in my family. My uncle literally owns a dog farm."

"A dog farm? That's a new one on me. Demi hates dogs," she said. "Well, she hates everything, to be fair. She has…issues. But then, she had a rough start."

"Tell me." He put his elbow on the table and dropped his chin in his palm, staring at her like she was without a doubt the most fascinating person he'd ever met, and he was hanging on her every word about her cat. Once again, she had that flash of familiarity, but then, he was sort of the quintessential small-town guy she'd known growing up—uncomplicated and free of an agenda.

Oh, sure, he probably wanted to get her into bed, but in some weird way, she respected that level of pure honesty. In DC, at least in Sadie's experience, sex frequently fell a distant fourth after power, status, and access.

"How did you find this little Demi?" he prodded, tapping her knuckles lightly so little sparks of contact crackled between them.

"Well, I found her in an alley, soaking wet, behind a dumpster." She looked down, not wanting her expression to show how the memory of that night hurt her—gutted her, actually.

"I can't imagine *you* in an alley."

She couldn't have imagined being there, either.

One minute, she'd been getting in Nathan's Buick SUV to head off to yet another DC function…and the next, she'd made him pull over and drop her off and get out of her life forever.

"Okay, you're in an alley. Were you…dumpster diving?" he prodded.

She smiled at the joke, but not the memory of standing in the rain, finally knowing the truth, facing the inevitable loss of both her job *and* her man, broken by betrayal and as soaking wet as the cat she heard crying in the night.

But there was no way she was ruining this lovely exchange by telling this man how she had discovered her boyfriend was sleeping with her boss, crumbling not only her well-crafted life, but her already shaky faith in people she'd thought she loved.

No, not tonight. Tonight, she had faith in the firefighter…and a little wine buzz.

"Actually, I was waiting for an Uber," she said, which was absolutely true. "And I heard this high-pitched cry. I couldn't help it, I had to go see, and there she was, this orange street cat, wet and alone and starving."

"Oh, who's the hero now, Sadie?" he asked, lightly touching her knuckles again and sending a shiver through her whole body. "So you just picked up the cat and took her on your date?"

She blinked in surprise. "I never said I was going on a date."

"I imagine a woman as beautiful as you would have nothing but dates."

She rolled her eyes. "You're really on your game, Lieutenant."

"Not a game, Sadie." He eased a tiny bit closer. "Unless you want to play."

Heat coiled through her, and she tried to cool it off with a sip of wine. Everything felt fiery and taut in her body, so she let out a slow, calming breath and slipped out of her jacket. "I guess it depends on what we're playing for."

He pointed to the pool table, free now. "Winner buys the next round?"

"I don't want another drink."

"Winner gets a phone number?"

She fought a laugh as she pushed off the stool. "How about we just play for bragging rights?"

He instantly followed. "Boring."

"Not if you win."

"Which I will." He pulled a cue stick from the rack, handing it to her along with a piece of chalk.

"Are you sure?" Maybe it would be a good time to tell him that her father had a pool table, and they'd spent hours together in the basement, playing while he practiced the next day's poli-sci lecture on his young, rapt audience.

"Positive. But I have to warn you, Sadie..." He closed his fingers around hers as they exchanged the chalk, his hand warm and strong and callused like she'd expect from the work he did. Nothing like Nathan's. God, he was the antithesis of Nathan Lawrence. "I don't lose."

"At anything?"

"Not if I can help it."

She chalked the tip and tipped her head toward the table for him to rack. "There's a first time for everything, then."

He didn't move, though, looming over her at easily six-one or six-two, with a sexy, sly half-smile as he held her gaze. "Then let's play for a first."

"Your first loss?"

He dipped a centimeter closer, locked on her eyes, somehow drawing her whole body toward him. "Our first kiss."

Heat blasted through her, sudden and powerful enough to weaken her knees.

"That way," he whispered, tapping her chin with the chalk square, "it's a guaranteed win for both of us. Doesn't that seem fair?"

Right that moment, nothing seemed fair. Not how achingly bad she wanted to kiss this stranger, not how sexy his lips were, and certainly not how the only place she could bring him to take care of the burn in her body was a converted garden shed in her grandparents' backyard.

She swallowed and drew back, lifting her stick a bit. "Are we calling shots?"

His eyes flickered with surprise. "You're calling them all tonight. I'm just going along for the win... Sadie."

Her name slid through his lips like he liked the sound and taste of it, like he wanted to whisper it in her ear, like it was his new favorite word.

"Okay, you can break."

He still didn't move to the table, and neither did she. They were inches apart, and the whole place seemed to fade into the background, the music, the voices, the scents and sights disappearing as every one of her senses focused on the man in front of her. They didn't say a word, but looked right into each other's eyes for a few seconds, and each passing heartbeat made her lower half melt a little more. The palpable pull of attraction was sexy and intense, making her blood hum and her throat dry.

The arrival of a group of men, laughing as they entered the room, forced them apart.

"Take it slow, Mahoney," one of them called, lifting a beer. "You're on duty in the a.m."

He barely glanced over his shoulder to respond. "Screw you, Probie."

"Not a probie anymore."

Sliding into a booth, the men resumed their conversation, but the interruption had broken the tension...and cleared her head.

"Sorry," he muttered, turning his laser-sharp gaze back to her. "Where were we?"

But she just stared at him, an ancient file opening somewhere in the recesses of her hormone-fogged brain. "Mahoney?" she asked in a hushed whisper. She knew a Mahoney from Bitter Bark. That kid who'd joked his way into the class presidency. That football player named—

"Connor Mahoney," he said. "But you can call me Lieutenant."

Seriously? Connor Mahoney? She let out a soft, rueful laugh. "You have got to be kidding me."

"Not kidding about anything." He frowned, searching her face. "Should I be?"

"Connor Mahoney." She shook her head, half smiling over the irony of it, half wanting to kick herself for not realizing who he was. The chestnut hair might be shorter now, but still thick and shiny. The blue eyes might have a few laugh lines, but they could still send a message without a word. The shoulders were broader, the jaw a little more square, and the mouth not as youthful. "I don't believe this."

He looked utterly baffled. "Do we know each other?"

"I know you." He was the swaggering quarterback who charmed and disarmed and deflowered half their class. The cocky prankster who ran for class president *on a bet he made with his football buddies* and then beat the far more qualified candidate.

A hot kiss and flirtatious games with the small-town firefighter were one thing, but she wasn't so lonely for a local boy that she'd make out with the fake-humble victor who'd been instructed to shake the loser's hand and *hadn't remembered her name.*

"But...do I know you?" he asked. "Oh man. Do we have...a past?"

"Not what you're thinking, Connor," she said lightly, snapping the cue stick back into the wall rack. "We never dated. We never flirted. We never had sex. In fact, you never knew I existed except for about a minute when you had to congratulate me on a great campaign." She lifted a brow. "Ring a bell?"

She could tell from his completely blank expression that nothing was ringing at all. "I have no idea what you're talking about. I've never met anyone named Sadie in my life. Sadie...Winthrop?" he guessed, using her grandparents' last name.

"Mercedes," she said, holding out her hand for a formal shake and hating that little thud of disappointment when he showed exactly zero recognition. "Mercedes Hartman. Your formidable opponent for class president of Bitter Bark High."

14

"Mercedes." He took her hand, but didn't shake it. Instead, he enveloped her fingers and drew her closer. "Wow, you've changed."

With a soft snort, she slipped her hand from his. "You don't remember me."

"I'm sorry. I don't." He gave an apologetic shrug. "It was a long time ago, and that election was not...that big a deal to me."

"It *was* a long time ago and not that big a deal to me, either." Not today, anyway. The day of the defeat? She closed her eyes at the unexpected punch of an old and ugly memory of Connor sauntering across the cafeteria the next day and mocking her.

She turned to their table and reached for her jacket. "I honestly haven't given you a moment's thought since then. But..." As she slid her arm into a sleeve, she let her gaze drop over his body, and damn, it was tempting to just laugh off the past and get back to the present.

But Sadie Hartman was a woman of principles. Wasn't that why she was standing in a dive in Bitter Bark instead of an upscale cocktail lounge on Capitol Hill? Her *principles* had forced her to run far and fast...and they were going to lead her away from the fry-your-eyes firefighter who'd thought everything was a joke in high school and probably hadn't changed one iota.

"So, thanks for the wine, Connor. See you around."

"Seriously? You're going to brush me off for something that happened, like, seventeen years ago? Something I don't even remember?"

"I'm not..." Yes, she was.

"Being honest," he finished for her.

"Okay, it's stupid, I'll give you that. But not only did you win with exactly zero qualifications, you...you..."

"I what?"

"You called me Ear Girl." Her face warmed at the memory. *Ear Girl.*

"Ear? Oh...yeah. The ear posters," he muttered as at last something came back to him. "What did they mean again? You listen to everyone?"

"It was my campaign slogan," she admitted with a sigh. "Experienced. Approachable. Responsible."

"Oh, yeah." He tried to cover a laugh. "But everyone called you Ear Girl."

She gave an easy smile, too, because it was funny now, considering how sophisticated she'd become at campaigning. But she still wasn't going to give him the satisfaction of a game or a kiss or anything. On *principle.* "So Ear Girl is calling it a night."

He shook his head as if he just couldn't believe this turn of events. "Let me walk you."

"Not necessary. I'm going right around the corner."

"I know, but..." He picked up his jacket, and she put a hand over his.

"No. Thank you."

Instantly, he dropped the jacket, but gave her a side-eye. "You didn't recognize me tonight, either."

"I know, but I should have." All the charm and playful banter, the electricity and zing, the seductive whisper of her name. That was what Connor Mahoney did to girl after girl after girl. Was that the kind of guy she wanted to be with after what she'd been through? Not a chance. "I really should have, because in all these years, you really haven't changed at all."

"How can you be so sure?"

"You still don't take anything seriously, do you?" It was a guess, true, but based on the millisecond of a response in his eyes, she knew she'd hit the mark.

Before he could answer, she gave him a quick wave, turned, and made her way through the bar and out the door, never once looking back.

Chapter Two

"It's official." Connor dropped the *Bitter Bark Banner* on the dining table where three other firefighters were scarfing down scrambled eggs and bacon. "Blanche Wilkins is retiring as mayor of Bitter Bark."

"'Bout time," Ray Merritt muttered through a mouthful of toast. "She's never been half the mayor her husband, Frank, was. But then, who could be?"

"Careful." Pouring a cup of coffee at the counter, Connor's older brother spoke softly with the voice of authority these men were all used to hearing from Captain Declan Mahoney. "Connor and I are kind of related to Blanche, Ray."

"How so?" Cal Norton brushed a crumb from the uniform shirt the recently promoted probie wore with such pride. Connor glanced at the kid, who'd unwittingly and prematurely wrecked what was shaping up to be a mind-blowing connection the night before. But he couldn't completely blame Probie. Once Sadie found out his name, she'd have bolted. But maybe he'd have gotten that kiss and convinced her not to run.

"My cousin Shane Kilcannon is married to Frank and Blanche's niece, Chloe," Connor explained.

"Oh, Chloe's the one that came up with calling the town *Better* Bark for a year," Ray said. "Put this town on the map for dog lovers."

"But tourism is down a little." Mike Skinner's thick fingers held a bacon strip he used to point to the others. "Not to mention that the teachers haven't had a pay increase in two years. Ambrose Avenue has six new potholes every winter. The lights are falling off the trees in Bushrod Square—"

"And all the first responders need a raise," Ray interjected.

Rounding the table to get his own cup of coffee, Connor felt the heat of his brother's intense gaze cutting through him. Declan didn't say anything, which wasn't unusual, but Connor shot him a sideways glance. "What?"

"I thought you were going to run," Declan said.

"For mayor?" Cal interjected with wide-eyed interest. Or maybe it was abject shock.

"I flirted with the idea," Connor said.

"What—or *who*—haven't you flirted with?" Ray cracked.

"He was certainly working some smokeshow at Bushrod's last night."

"Shut up, Probie," Connor fired back, but without much bite. Cal had had no idea that calling Connor by his name last night would be the equivalent of aiming a hose at a six-alarm blaze. And Connor sure as hell wasn't going to admit it.

"A new one?" Ray snorted. "Shit, Mahoney, you really are not the mayoral type. A mayor should be settled and stable."

You still don't take anything seriously, do you? He tried to shake off Sadie's parting shot, like he'd been since that *smokeshow* beelined out of Bushrod's. But he couldn't quite forget the stinging observation.

"He killed it at the bachelor auction, though," Cal said.

"Precisely." Mike punctuated that with a gulp of coffee. "Stick to what you know, LT. Women."

"Spoken by a man who hasn't had a date in three years," Connor shot back. These guys loved to needle him, but the truth was they were mostly married or sadly single, two things Connor would never be. Marriage wasn't in the cards, and there was *nothing* sad about his single status. Well, not counting last night, which might not have been sad, but sure had been infuriating and incredibly confusing.

He had no idea where his physical yearbook was, but he'd found the online version last night and still couldn't remember the girl, even after looking at Mercedes Hartman's imminently forgettable senior picture.

But Sadie? Oh, Sadie. Now *she* was a woman he'd remember. With that coffee-colored mane surrounding delicate features and a set of dimples that went straight to his heart. Eyes that warmed to whiskey-gold when he got too close and a body that managed to be slender and curvy and would no doubt fit him perfectly.

There was nothing forgettable about Sadie...which was a damn shame, because the only thing he should be doing is forgetting her. She'd made that perfectly clear. Unfortunately, he was doing a crappy job of it. In fact, all morning he'd had one thought: Should he try again, or take the L and move on?

God, he hated defeat.

And speaking of defeat, how could he be held accountable for who he'd beaten for class president? He'd decided to run two days before the election because some of the guys on his team bet twenty bucks each that he couldn't win. The only thing he knew at the time about his opponent was that she had ridiculous campaign posters with pictures of an ear. That was it. He honestly had forgotten Mercedes Hartman existed, probably by fifth period the day after the election.

And if that's what ticked her off, he got that, he really did. Calling her Ear Girl in front of their classmates had been a dick move by a seventeen-year-old who'd made a lot of them. But, for crying out loud, they were in their thirties now, and life had moved on.

So should he try again?

"Sorry, Connor, but I just don't see you as mayor." Mike lifted a beefy shoulder used more for hauling the line into a fire than having a woman hang on it. "You can't run a council meeting on jokes and motivational football quotes."

Connor rolled his eyes as he drank some coffee. "Come on, man. How hard could the mayor's job be? First of all, I love this town right down to my last strand of DNA, and I'm good—no, wait, I'm *great*—with people."

"*Female* people," Ray stage-whispered to Cal.

"All people. I can cut a few ribbons, throw down the gavel at town meetings, give the nod to the dates of the next Paws for a Cause fundraiser and still get my hours in here. Anyone with half a brain and a decent personality could do it. Hell, a dog could do it." He gave a soft snort. "In this town? A dog *should* do it."

"Then why aren't you running?" Declan asked.

This time, he shrugged with practiced nonchalance, knowing better than to color the truth with this man. "You know, Dec, I got the same reaction when I floated it past everybody at Christmas." Dec knew, of course, that *everybody* meant their sprawling extended family. "Pretty much mockery all around when it came to the idea of *Mayor* Connor Mahoney. And you *know* how I feel about losing."

Declan gave a bittersweet smile. "I know how Dad felt about it," he said softly. "'Doesn't build character. It makes you weak, son.'"

Connor didn't bother to argue with the words they'd heard their whole young lives until they lost that man who'd loathed losing and fear and negativity and anything else he thought made a man *weak*. As the oldest, Declan had heard it constantly. And as the football player in the family with Dad as his coach, Connor could recite every platitude the man liked to spew during practices. "Well, I'd hate to let down his memory with a defeat at the ballot box."

"Maybe you'd win."

"My unpaid focus group"—he gestured toward the table—"says differently." And he could still hear Joe Mahoney's voice in the car on the way home from practice.

You play to win, Connor, not to lose.

Dad might be gone twenty long years now, but the sentiment had guided Connor through life, helping him easily know when not to get into a position of weakness.

Declan picked up the newspaper from the table to read the headline. "God, they really are still invoking the name of Saint Frank Wilkins. Poor Blanche had such huge shoes to fill when she took over the job after her husband died."

"She's done a decent job," Connor said. "Tourism has tripled."

"Thank Chloe for that." Declan stuffed the paper into Connor's hand. "And personally, I think you'd make a great mayor."

He *would* make a great mayor, and the idea had been nagging him since he'd heard the rumors of Blanche Wilkins's retirement. As it was, he was stuck on the same professional firefighter rung and ready for a new challenge. His only possible promotion had him running smack into his own brother and two other captains firmly in place in Bitter Bark.

He'd have to leave town to move into another job, and he'd cut off his damn arm before he did that. He loved this town and wanted only to give back to it, which he'd done for years at this station. Running for mayor felt right to him, but apparently not to anyone else.

Just like Sadie said, no one thought he took anything seriously, which wasn't true, but changing people's minds in a small town was no mean feat.

"A great mayor?" Mike cleared his throat to line up his next joke, but Connor warded it off by waving the folded newspaper.

"Declan spoke like a *real* brother," he said, shooting a warning look at his fellow firefighter. He skimmed the article again, his gaze dropping to the last paragraph he hadn't read yet. "Good God, I hope this is a mistake. Mitch Easterbrook might run? He'd be the worst mayor ever."

"Oh, he's gonna run," Ray said. "And no one has the balls to oppose him."

"The guy is a pompous, arrogant ass who siphons money from people at the worst time in their lives." Mitch Easterbrook was the definition of unethical, despite the veneer of self-righteousness the funeral director wore like one of his thousand-dollar suits. "He can't run for mayor."

"Oh, he is." Ray nodded with the authority of a man married to the owner of a hair salon. "Barb does Mrs. Easterbrook's highlights every three weeks. She's already planning an over-the-top victory party at their mansion."

Connor grunted in disgust and pity, remembering the woman who was *not* Mrs. Easterbrook, whom an EMT crew once found in Mitch's bed while on a medical call to that very mansion.

"And he'll win," Mike added. "'Cause the undertaker knows where the bodies are buried."

While Cal snickered at the dumb joke, Connor dropped the paper and, he hoped, the conversation. As much as he hated the idea of Mitch Easterbrook as mayor of Bitter Bark, Connor couldn't beat him without some kind of miracle. If his family and coworkers were already laughing at the idea, the whole town might, too, especially with the budget Easterbrook would—

The electronic screech of an incoming call cut off every thought and word as they all froze for a millisecond to listen to the dispatch.

"Engine One, Ladder One, Rescue One. Lost child, 609 Sweetgum Springs Road."

Connor didn't hear much past *lost child*, knowing exactly how that dictated which vehicles would go—all of them if they needed rescue gear and medical—and what to wear. A lost child meant search and rescue, so he grabbed a neon vest because Sweetgum Springs meant they could be in thick woods east of town. He also snagged fire boots since they were water resistant, and the creek there could reach five feet in spring.

The dispatch repeated the information, and every man and woman on duty moved with choreographed grace, processing the orders Declan barked out regarding vehicles, drivers, and personnel. But over his brother's authoritative staccato, the words *lost child* echoed in their heads. Move, move, *move*. Minutes counted. Seconds counted. *Everything* counted.

He hauled up to the passenger side of the ambulance, driven by Tasheema Soni, the paramedic on his crew he admired most. As always, Tash was silent and drove like she was on a racetrack, which was key since there were always the idiots who hit their brakes in the middle of the road or were driving with earbuds in. But his cool coworker was unfazed and focused. Of course. Lost child? This mother of two looked even more determined than ever.

They rolled out behind Declan and his crew in the lead SUV, not waiting for the engine and brush pumper he knew would follow. They needed every person in the station and all the medical and rescue equipment on those trucks.

"Not a good place to lose a kid," he mused, narrowing his gaze at a minivan that swerved in a moment of panic when they approached, but finally managed to get out of the way.

"Rushing springs and miles of woods? All those cliffs and ravines?" She shook her head. "No, it is not."

"Did you hear the call come in?" Connor knew Tash frequently monitored the dispatch center and sometimes knew before the captain or crew exactly what they were dealing with on a medical emergency.

"Father home alone with a three-year-old. Took his eyes off the kid for one minute, which, lemme tell you, is all it takes. He is freaked the hell out."

Connor huffed out a breath, listening to the radioed progress of the trucks behind them, the vehicles in front of them, and the updates for the county sheriff and local police. After a minute, another dispatch came through from the Bitter Bark Police on-site, and Connor closed his eyes to get every word while the ambulance careened out of town toward Sweetgum Springs.

"Boy, age three. Last seen in a red sweater, gray pants, and navy blue mittens. Disappeared from backyard. Father searched for an hour before calling the mother at work, who immediately called 911."

Connor felt every muscle and brain cell suck in the adrenaline, mentally reviewing his equipment, ready to fight a fire, save a life, or…find a three-year-old in a red sweater, gray pants, and navy blue mittens.

Navy mittens. Navy mittens. He focused on that one detail as he used the app on the ambulance tablet to track the other vehicles and look at the hilly terrain of Sweetgum Springs.

"Damn, those woods are dense," he muttered,

scanning the satellite image of the area around the target address. A new housing development backed up to the several square miles of woods full of hills and gullies. A winding creek cut through the center, fed from the snow currently melting at peak rate right now.

"An hour?" Tash shook her head. "Come *on*. Who waits an hour to call 911?"

"The guy frantically searching for his kid, sure he'll find him any second?" Connor suggested.

Tash shot him a look. "If it was my husband? He'd be the one needing a paramedic right now."

Connor didn't even smile as they pulled up behind the captain's SUV, not at all surprised to see Chief Winkler, head of the Bitter Bark FD, deep in conversation with two county sheriff deputies as an ad hoc command center was being set up.

Tasheema and Connor leaped out of the ambulance and headed toward them just as the engine came screaming in and the crew emptied out. Not far away, a young couple huddled with a deputy sheriff, the woman wiping a constant stream of tears, the man talking with his hands, pointing at the woods behind the clapboard house with faux Craftsman columns.

"The boy's name is Dylan James O'Keefe," Chief announced as he turned an electronic topographical map for all of them to view. "Blond hair, thirty-four pounds. Wearing a hooded red jersey, dark gray sweatpants, navy mittens. Last seen at approximately 9:45 a.m. in his backyard, near the fence along the woods. Captain Mahoney will break you into teams of two, and you'll take the closest six sections of the grid." He tapped the screen and leaned back, listening to the deputy on a cell phone next to him. "More rescuers are on the way from Holly Hills, and Simons Mill is sending search dogs," he called out. "Let's not need them, people. Move! Find Dylan!"

In a matter of minutes, with little fanfare and zero confusion since Declan called the team shots, the twosomes were formed and fanned out. Connor and Ray Merritt hustled over a wooded hillside, heading toward the ravine area they'd been assigned.

Connor had one thought pumping through his head with the blood and adrenaline. *Red hoodie. Gray pants. Navy mittens.* That's all he had to see. Had to.

The minute they were in the thick of the trees, the cloudy day seemed totally sunless, making it even more difficult to see, even though they both carried flashlights to shine into the darkest parts of the woods.

"Dylan!" Connor stilled, waiting three seconds to listen for any sound. *Red jacket. Gray pants. Navy mittens.* "Dylan O'Keefe!" *Red hoodie. Gray pants. Navy mittens.* "Dylan!"

He repeated the name and words like a mantra, lifting branches, checking under bushes, vaguely aware of Ray not thirty feet away, doing exactly the same thing. They moved south, pushing through bare trees, using their gloved hands to create visibility, listening to the others calling the child's name and waiting, silent, expectant, full of hope.

He clung to that hope as they half slid down the side of a muddy hill toward the sound of rushing water.

"Creek's high," Ray called. "I'll go downstream. You search here."

Connor held up one hand in acknowledgment and squinted upstream through a thicket of pines near the edge of the water.

"Dylan! Dylan O'Keefe!" *Red hoodie. Gray pants. Navy mittens.* "Dylan!"

He didn't even breathe, forcing himself to hear over the water, to block out anything but a three-year-old's voice, crying, calling, or…

Barking?

The rescue dogs hadn't come out yet, had they? Command would have radioed. A stray?

He muted the comm device that hung around his neck, needing to block out every other sound but the one he'd heard. He leaned into the soft breeze, away from the stream, listening for…

A bark. Again. Once, twice, insistent. That was no coyote. A wolf could bark, but it was rare and just didn't sound like that. That had to be a dog. No one had mentioned the family having a dog, so what was one doing out here?

He got his footing in the mud and climbed over rocks and a rotted, fallen tree, sensing but not knowing that the sound came from the other side of those pines. He resisted the urge to call for the child, not at all sure what he'd find when he came around the green thicket.

He aimed his flashlight, took a step closer, heard another single bark.

Come on now, Dylan. Red hoodie. Gray pants. Navy…

He stared at the shredded, soaking-wet mitten on the ground, blinking in disbelief. He looked at the ledge maybe fifteen feet above him, spying its mate hanging from a root that jutted out.

Did he fall off that cliff and into the water? Just as he opened his mouth to call for Ray, a golden head with two pointy ears and topaz eyes appeared in the pines next to him and barked right in his face.

"Whoa there." Connor reached out a hand, not at all sure what to make of the creature as it came out of the pines. The dog had the face of a Staffy, the body of a Lab, retriever paws, and a tail that had to come from a…Husky? "Hey, Frankendog. You see a little boy around here?"

He barked again and jumped, slapping massive paws on Connor's chest to bark right in his face. As Connor backed up, the dog put his nose down and lifted the mitten in his teeth, water dripping from the wool.

Holy *shit*. "You have?" Without thinking, he rubbed the dog's head, giving him praise and encouragement. "Where?" He flicked the mitten the dog held tight in his teeth.

The dog looked up, and Connor followed his gaze to the other mitten, dangling above them.

"Did he come from up there, buddy? Did he fall? Where is he?" He stood, and the dog instantly turned and darted back through the pines.

Connor followed, vaguely aware of his face being scratched by needles. He barely took three steps before the dog stopped and chewed on the mitten like it was lunch, staring behind the bush. Connor launched closer, shoved the branches to the side, and saw the tiny body. The hood of the dark red, wet jacket had fallen over a soaked blond head down in the dirt.

He squeezed the button of his lapel mic and dropped to his knees to put a light hand on Dylan

O'Keefe's drenched back. He'd been in the creek. He'd been in the water, and the dog…

"We got him," he announced into the device. "Area six. Mahoney and Merritt, at the creek."

Almost immediately, he could hear Ray reading off detailed coordinates as his footsteps grew louder behind Connor. But Connor ignored everything and leaned over the child.

Please, kid. Please. Please.

Lightly lifting the wet hood, he carefully placed his ear to the child's mouth and felt the tickle of a warm breath.

Oh, thank *God.*

As Connor straightened to radio the crew, the dog next to him licked his cheek, a long, slow, grateful slurp.

"Good work, bud." He looked into the green-gold eyes and could see relief pump through the dog's mismatched body. He pulled him in for a hug. "Damn good work."

"Media wants you, Lieutenant Mahoney."

Connor put down the water bottle on the bumper of the engine, squinting up at Chief Winkler. "Me? Dec's the captain."

As soon as he spoke, the dog lying next to him on the grass picked up his head, keeping his gaze on Connor, his precious navy mitten under his giant paw as if he feared someone might take the proof of his moment of glory.

"Well, they can't interview the dog." Chief kept a

wide berth around the beast who growled warily at everyone but Connor, whose side he hadn't left even during all the action of getting Dylan warmed, treated for hypothermia, and taken to the hospital with a second ambulance crew. "So I guess you're the next best thing, since you found our hero."

"No one's showed up yet to claim him?"

Chief shook his head. "No collar, no tag, no chip. Put him on the news, and if his owner's around, he'll come."

Something told Connor this boy had no owner. He was rough, filthy, starving, and smelled like he dined on dead animals. Connor had already caught him gnawing on a stone twice. The dog backed away from anyone who came close, unless they had a treat, then he jumped and slammed his paws and barked in their faces.

But Connor could have sworn the mutt gave a smug look to the two Belgian Malinois that showed up all polished and chomping for a rescue. *You can go home, boys,* his look said. *Carcass Breath already did the heavy lifting today.*

"Come on, Connor." Chief gestured him toward the small group of local reporters and handheld cams that had gathered sometime in the last hour or so. "You love the media. You were born for this, LT."

He kind of was, he mused as he pushed off and popped to the ground, tilting his head toward the dog. "Hey, bud. Your adoring public awaits."

The dog stood and gave a marvelous full-body shake, his torso shimmying from his barrel chest that showed plenty of ribs to that ridiculous tail that curled up and around like an apostrophe over his ass.

"Let's go make the ladies swoon, Frankendog."

Instantly, the dog leaped up, throwing his body weight at Connor.

"Hey! No jumping!" Connor ordered.

The dog hung his head, and Connor realized he was reacting to his tone, not his words.

"Oh, buddy, come on." He crouched down and put his hands on the big yellow head, but the dog jerked back. "It's okay, man. You're the hero today. Easy does it. I didn't mean to scare you."

Connor tucked the navy mitten in his pocket and put a strong hand on the dog's head. Together, they walked across the O'Keefes' front lawn. The dog stayed right next to him, matching his pace and looking up with a mix of hope and fear in his golden eyes.

"You know what?" he said to the dog. "Nobody claims you, you're mine. I'll take you out to Waterford Farm and put my dog-training cousins to work. How's that sound?"

"Lieutenant Mahoney!" A young man holding a microphone and shoulder cam broke from the small pack to reach him first. "Jack Wells, stringer for the ABC affiliate in Charlotte. Can you tell us what happened? How did you find Dylan O'Keefe?"

The others moved to catch up with him as if Connor were some kind of celebrity and they were a pack of paparazzi. Instantly, the dog growled.

"Back away, ladies and gents. Our boy needs his space. We do not know if he eats journalists."

They laughed nervously and made a cautious semicircle around them, while Connor kept a steady, ready hand on Jumpin' Jack Flash.

"I didn't find Dylan," he finally said to the man

33

who'd asked the first question. "I found this guy right here, who led me right to the boy."

"Do you think the dog pulled the kid from the creek?" a middle-aged woman he recognized as a reporter for the *Bitter Bark Banner* asked.

"No question about it." He smiled down at the dog and rubbed his head. "I'm sure the scene analysts can tell you more, but Dylan's sweatshirt had a few rips in it consistent with this dog's teeth."

"But he didn't bite the child?" someone called out.

"He dragged him from the rushing creek water using his mouth and instinct," Connor said. "And he wouldn't leave the boy until help came." He couldn't help smiling at the dog as he snagged the mitten from where it stuck out of Connor's pocket and swished his ridiculous tail as he gazed up, waiting for praise, which Connor heaped.

The whole group laughed and shifted every camera to the furry star.

"What kind of dog is it?" the TV guy asked.

"What kind of dog *isn't* he is probably a better question," Connor shot back.

"Who owns him?"

"We're trying to find out."

"How did you feel when you found the child?"

"Like there really is a God."

"What's the dog's name?"

Connor looked at the mutt, rooting around for a good, heroic name, like Underdog or Supermutt or MittenMan, but he was just...Frankendog. "Frank. I'm calling him Frank."

More muffled laughter. "Frank?" the *Bitter Bark Banner* reporter asked, with just enough edge in her voice to put him on alert. "Why would you call him Frank?"

Was Frankendog politically incorrect? Would he offend anyone with that joke? Not that he cared, but the department did, and Chief Winkler was on the sidelines watching this.

"Is he named for someone special?" she pressed, her eyes narrowing a little, making him suspect she might pounce on the name because of some kind of negative connotation to a monster.

"Yes, he is named for someone special," he said, rubbing his hand on the dog's head to buy some time as a line from that morning's paper flashed in his head. Hell, this lady might have written it, for all he knew. "I named him after Mayor Frank Wilkins, one of the greatest leaders Bitter Bark ever had."

"Oh…" Heads nodded, cameras rolled, and pens scratched on notebooks.

The reporter broke into a genuine smile. Yep, she must have written the line.

Another man with a shoulder cam moved in, this equipment larger and more expensive-looking than the one used by the Charlotte stringer. "I'm shooting B-roll for cable news feature departments," the man said. "This story has a lot of potential for a national feel-good piece. Anything you want to say to the country about this dog?"

Connor looked right into the camera and slowly lowered himself to a crouch next to the dog, draping an arm around his neck to show him love and also make sure he didn't body-launch at the costly camera. "Frank is smart, strong, fearless, and gives a damn about his fellow man. He's what Bitter Bark, North

Carolina, is all about. Good people and good dogs."

The reporters reacted with a smattering of spontaneous applause, taking some more pictures and notes. The *Banner* lady stepped closer and studied him, then the dog, for a moment.

"Named for Frank Wilkins, huh?"

"I'm a fan of the former mayor's," he said, standing back to his full height.

"Me, too." She tucked her notebook in her bag and eyed the dog, keeping a respectable distance. "Well, you've got my vote, Frank. Pretty sure you've got the whole town on your side after today." With a nod, she walked away with the other reporters, leaving him to turn and look into the dog's freakishly intelligent eyes.

"You got her vote." He blinked at the dog and inched back. "Holy…wait a second. Frank! That is the *best* idea."

Frank barked once, sharp and loud, knocking that fuzzy tail so hard from side to side his whole butt wiggled. Connor got down on his haunches and ruffled the dog's head and gave him a quick kiss on the fur. "How would you like to be mayor of the world's greatest town, Frankendog?"

He picked up the mitten from the ground and rolled it in his big teeth like he was literally chewing on the idea.

"After what you and I pulled off today? We could sail into the mayor's office together, riding the hero wave. You get the glory, and I'll do the job."

Frank gnawed an actual hole in the mitten, giving a wary eye to one more person trying to take a picture.

"Okay, maybe you're not mayor material yet, but my cousins can train any dog to do anything." He threaded his fingers into the dog's furry neck and let their noses touch. "Let's drop-kick old Mitch Easterbrook into the jaws of defeat. With your name on the ticket, there is no way we can lose."

Frank dropped the mitten, smacked his paw on top of it, and lifted his head for more love.

"I'm taking that as a yes."

Chapter Three

Sadie blinked, trying to clear her eyes and head, but the LinkedIn screen full of job postings still all blurred into one big uninspired mess. Research assistant. Speechwriter. Special projects coordinator. Senior office manager. Blah, blah, blah, *blah*.

Not a single position that would be right for the former deputy chief of staff and legislative director for a United States congresswoman. Not one that would renew her faith in the people who made up the world of "government" she'd once believed in so fervently.

Trust and idealism—and her heart, to be honest—had been dealt a crushing blow by the people she'd trusted most. She rolled over and pushed away thoughts of the man and woman who dealt that blow.

"Coffee," she muttered. "I cannot hunt for a new job or a fresh start in life without coffee."

She stretched her foot over the blankets and used her toe to stroke under Demi's chin, waking her slowly. "But I do *not* want to walk into Nana's sewing club meeting alone and face those ladies and all their questions."

In the month she'd been here, Sadie had managed

to avoid most of Nana's friends, thus avoiding the questions.

Why did you leave your big Washington job? *Because my boss and my boyfriend had an affair.*

What was it like working for Jane Sutherland? *Amazing...until it wasn't.*

Might she be president someday? *God help us...yes.*

She rolled over and groaned. She couldn't avoid people forever. "At least if I bring you, Demi, I have a distraction."

Demi slowly rose to all fours, making a striped orange arch before gazing across the sofa bed with an expression of pure disgust. It sure hadn't taken this cat long to establish who was the boss in this relationship. And after that weepy road trip from DC to Bitter Bark together, their roles were set.

"I know, I know. You hate to be used, and there *is* a coffeepot ten feet from me in that little kitchenette because Nana and Boomie are the world's kindest people and have stocked this guesthouse to meet my needs, but..." She leaned closer. "Nana has that espresso maker I gave her for Christmas and...*latte*, Demi-cat. Mama needs a latte, and we are a long, long way from a Starbucks."

Demi jumped off the sofa and sauntered to the window, her lean body moving like the catwalk was literally named after her, and she was selling something other kitties could only dream of having. With one graceful leap, she got on the sill, moved the lace curtain with her nose, then stared out at the driveway, barren garden plots, and wraparound porch they'd have to cross in order to get that latte.

Then she turned and delivered an Oscar-worthy *you've got to be kidding me* look with slanted, judgy green eyes.

"You're unbelievable, you know that?" Sadie whispered on a laugh. "I saved you from a life of crime on the streets of DC."

Demi turned away.

Okay, then. There was only one thing that worked with this cat, Sadie had figured out in the very short time she'd owned her. Reverse psychology and temptations. A simple plea was never enough.

"So stay here." Sadie closed her laptop. "I know you don't care that Boomie made a bowl of Catnip Crumble for The Others. "

Demi yawned, making sure she communicated her utter indifference to treats, the sweet old grandfather who loved to share them, or his three lively cats who were fascinated by Demi.

"I'll just go alone..." She rolled off the sofa bed and took a step toward the door, and Demi just watched, clearly waiting for the stakes to go up. "But rumor does have it that the Pins 'n' Needles ladies often bring yarn."

She turned back to the window with a yawn. Yarn was so...pedestrian.

"And they bring..." Sadie walked to the door and twisted the knob, taking a breath. "Plastic grocery bags." She sang the words and fluttered her fingernails against each other to imitate the sound the bags made in a happy cat's paws.

Instantly, Demi leaped down from the windowsill and bounded to the door, so light on her paws it was like she was flying.

"You're not as complicated as you like to let on, kittah. And we might have to find a new bribe when those bags are finally illegal." Except some people in Congress were too busy banging their staffer's boyfriend to focus on making new laws.

Damn, she had to let go.

It had been almost a month since that wretched night in Georgetown. A month since she inhaled that disgusting perfume in Nathan's car and saw the guilt on his handsome features. A month since he admitted he was sleeping with her boss.

Actually, the words he'd used were *in love with her*. And "*there's more to this than you can understand, Sadie.*"

What was to understand? Jane was gorgeous, respected, and a powerhouse in DC, already anointed and likely to be on the world political stage for her whole career. And Nathan was smart, successful, handsome, and the ideal partner for an unmarried congresswoman.

Oh, God, it hurt to lose them both.

The only thing that could heal Sadie's wound would be a new job and new life, which was why, after a conversation with Jane, she'd quit her job, thrown some clothes in a bag, grabbed her brand new cat and a few personal items, and took off for Bitter Bark. Here, she knew no one but her dear grandparents and no one likely remembered her.

Bitter Bark was a stopping point, a place to regroup and find a job. Then she'd go back and officially move out of her apartment in DC and start over somewhere new.

But if she stayed here much longer…then she'd be

unpacking and living in her misery. Those words of advice, given to her many, many years earlier, always floated into her mind when she got too settled in a bad place. And she always heeded that advice.

"Come on, Dem." She opened the door. "We don't unpack and live in misery. We move on and thrive."

Demi took three steps, then whipped her head around and hissed as two older women climbed out of a Buick the size of the *Titanic*, followed by two little dachshunds, one tan, one...wow. *Fat* was the first word that came to mind. *Chunky*, *round*, and *chubalicious* were a few others.

The dogs heard the hiss and started to bark, but the taller, dark-haired woman held tight to the leash. "Whoa, pups."

"Oh, Agnes, she's here! Finally! We've hit the jackpot," the tiny Q-tip-top whispered just loud enough for Sadie to hear...and wonder what jackpot they'd hit. "It's Margie's granddaughter. The one from Washington, DC, remember?" The older one glanced at Sadie and leaned into her friend's ear to whisper something inaudible.

"Oh, of course." She might not have been much younger in years, but the dark-haired woman had clearly taken good care of her skin and maybe had indulged in a few injections. She waved to Sadie. "No worries, dear. Pyggie and Gala are harmless."

Please, God, don't let the fat dog be named Piggy.

"Well, my cat's not a fan of dogs," she told them.

The little white-haired granny came closer, a yellowed smile making her bifocals crooked, the chilly spring wind blowing her coat open to reveal black slacks and a polka dot cardigan.

"Mercedes Hartman, as I live and breathe." Her brogue was rich and musical. "Your grandmother told us all about you comin' to Bitter Bark all the way from the big city."

Thank God Sadie hadn't told her chatty grandmother *everything*.

"You're the politics girl, right?"

"I don't think that's the way she wants to be described, Finnie," the other one said quickly. "Some young women find it offensive to be called a girl."

"No offense taken," Sadie assured her. Nana's club was mostly made up of sweet old ladies who were certainly allowed to think Sadie qualified as a *girl* at thirty-five, and her position in DC had certainly been political enough. "I go by Sadie now. And this is..." She looked down to Demi, but all she saw was the tip of an orange tail flicking from inside the doorway.

"Fraidy-cat," the little white-haired lady—Finnie—joked.

Sadie laughed, closing the door when the tail disappeared, because two dogs would wreck poor Demi completely. "She really doesn't like dogs. Even two as cute as these." She bent down to greet the two doxies, getting wagging tails and a few friendly barks. "Hello, you little darlings. Piggy?" She gave the chunky one a stroke and looked up with a question in her eyes.

"Short for Pygmalion," the younger-looking woman explained. "And the other is Galatea. I'm Greek."

"That's adorable."

Just then, the back kitchen door opened, and Nana stepped out, wrapping a thick sweater around her generous bosom. "Oh, there you are, Finnie. Agnes.

And you've met my sweet granddaughter. Mercedes, er, oh, she's Sadie now."

Sadie gave Nana a quick smile, loving her for always remembering the preferred name. It was something that her mother, who was Nana's daughter, refused to do during any of the rare three-times-a-year conversations they had.

"And, Sadie, this is Finola Kilcannon and Agnes Santorini. We like to call them the Dogmothers."

Sadie chuckled at that as they all walked toward Nana's kitchen. "You two are just oodles of cute," she said, holding out a hand to shake theirs. "So nice to meet you."

"But I met you years ago, lass," Finola said. "I believe you went to high school with my grandson."

Sadie rooted for the name her grandmother had just used. "Kilcannon? Oh yes, Garrett Kilcannon was in my class."

"I was referring to my daughter's son *Connor Mahoney*."

She kept her expression fixed, not reacting any differently to that name, the one she'd tried for the past ten days to wipe out of her memory. No, it wasn't the *name* that had fueled her fantasies. She could forget his name...but hadn't quite wiped out the rest of him.

"Of course," Sadie said as they entered the warm kitchen together, the delicious aroma of coffee and pastries almost covering the memories both old and recent of Connor Mahoney. "I actually bumped into him at Bushrod's right after I got here."

The two women whipped around to share a look, like they were thinking they should have known about this meeting.

"And how did that go?" Agnes asked after a beat. "Did you two get on well? Reminisce? Set a date, er, I mean, another date?"

Cute and…meddlesome. "It was nice to see a familiar face," she said easily.

"And a fine-looking face it is, donchya think, lass?"

Cute, meddlesome…and as subtle as a two-by-four. "He's as good-looking now as he was in high school." There was a non-answer that the communications staffers would be proud of. But she could not resist adding, "When he beat me for class president." She put a hand on Agnes's shoulder. "So, I'm afraid your matchmaking would be an uphill battle."

"Matchmaking?" She put her hand on her chest. "Is that what you think we're doing?"

"I was there, lass," Finnie said before Sadie could answer.

"At Bushrod's?"

"At the campaign speech you made in the high school auditorium. Yours was stirring."

She tipped her head with a self-deprecating smile. "I don't think the student body was too stirred."

Finnie inched closer and peered hard at Sadie. "You're even prettier than I remember."

Sadie had to laugh. How could she not with these two? "I finally peaked at thirty," she joked, rooting around for a change of subject. "So, I heard Garrett did really well with a dot-com company. PetPic? The one that sold to FriendGroup."

"Garrett's fine," Finnie said. "He's married, but *Connor* isn't."

Well, that was a relief, considering how he'd flirted

with her. "Nana, do you mind if I make some espresso?"

Little Old Irish Grandma was having none of a polite subject change, though. She simply leaned closer and used all of her four-eleven, hundred pounds of determination to get in between Sadie and her coffee. "Connor is a firefighter and EMT now."

"A lieutenant," Agnes added, as if this were somehow a godlike accomplishment that probably helped him collect phone numbers and trophy panties. It damn near got hers.

"He mentioned that." She added a smile at the other woman, hoping maybe she could see Sadie wasn't biting their bait. "So, Agnes, are you an embroiderer and cross-stitcher, too?"

"Please call me Yiayia, and this is Gramma Finnie. I just come for the gossip and pastries." She frowned a little, not too deeply, thanks to Botox. "Connor's in politics, too, you know. Just like you are."

Politics? "He is?" She couldn't hide her surprise at this news and cursed herself because the grandmas clearly read that as interest.

"Oh, he is now," Finnie exclaimed, clapping age-spotted hands in front of her chest.

Sadie eyed the espresso maker behind them, imagining that she could just lift the tiny one and move her out of the way.

"You'll read all about it in tomorrow's paper," Finnie continued. "Frank is running for mayor, which is the sweetest and most brilliant idea, and everyone is so excited about it."

Sadie inched back, trying to put two and two together and coming up with... "Frank? Another

Kilcannon or Mahoney?" She remembered that there were a lot of them.

"Not exactly," Agnes said. "But it's the biggest news in Bitter Bark. You've been here a few weeks. How could you miss all the hoopla about Connor and the dog?"

"Oh, yes." She had seen the gushy front-page coverage, and Nana and Boomie had practically burst when he was on CNN crowing about the town and a dog who'd been involved with a child's rescue. None of it helped kill those pesky fantasies. "But I've been so busy."

Nana put a loving arm around Sadie's shoulders and guided her closer to the espresso machine, because she was a queen that way. "Frank is the dog, honey."

"And not just any dog, lass," Finnie added with a gleam in her blue eyes. "He's a national hero! And so is Connor."

"Yes, I heard."

"He's a stray," Agnes added.

"Frank or Connor?"

The woman gave a sharp laugh, then looked at Finnie. "She's perfect, really. Pretty, funny. I like a funny woman."

Oh boy. Sadie had walked right into that. "So, help me understand this, because I'm confused. The *dog* is running for mayor?"

"Oh, it's been done before," Agnes assured her. "There's a golden retriever with the title in California and…"

"A Great Pyrenees on his fifth term in Minnesota," Finnie finished. "Connor found about six more all over the world. So, why not the hero Frank? It's such a clever way to bring attention to our little dog-lovin' town."

Even if it made a mockery of the political system, she thought. How like the man who ran for office on a bet, without a single campaign promise or motivation other than to impress girls.

"Well, I'm sure he'll win," she said, taking the little coffeemaker from the stand. "He apparently wins at everything."

"He does," Finnie agreed. "But Frank has required some extensive training, though I say he's made great progress. Connor has had Frank at Waterford Farm every day for almost two weeks."

"Waterford Farm." She remembered that's where the big Kilcannon family lived. "Is that the dog farm Connor mentioned?"

"It's the largest canine rescue and training center on the East Coast now," Agnes said, sounding a little like she'd memorized the marketing materials.

"And Frank's really comin' out of his shell, like so many strays must," Finnie said. "He's only a little scared of strangers. He does still like to eat rocks and jumps on Connor every time he sees him, but that's just love."

"Well, he better not love the voters, because they might not like being jumped," Sadie teased as she filled the pot with water.

"Oh, he doesn't jump on anyone else," Agnes said. "But he does love Connor."

"Who doesn't love the lad?" Finnie cooed. "He's such a wonderful boy."

"Connor or Frank?" she asked again, giving Agnes a playful wink.

"They both are." Agnes put her hand on Sadie's shoulder. "And they could use a campaign manager, among other things. Like a wife."

"Agnes!" Finnie tsked. "Have some tact."

"There's not time for tact, Finola. This girl's going to make her coffee and disappear."

That was the plan. But instead, she gave the sweet ladies a smile and an A for effort. "A campaign manager, huh?" She let the *wife* part go. "For a dog?"

Suddenly, there were two Dogmothers on either side of her.

"Connor is going to be the mayor," Agnes said softly. "The dog is more or less a symbolic thing."

"Mmm." She tapped the filter and resisted the urge to remind them that government didn't actually work that way, but whatever. It was Bitter Bark, North Carolina, not Washington, DC.

"Bitter Bark was named *Better* Bark a few years back, lass. Didya know that?" Finola asked.

"Nana mentioned that to me."

"'Twas a wee bit of a symbolic thing, you know," Finnie continued. "But it helped put the town on the map in a very competitive tourist market. And best of all, our coffers grew along with our reputation as the most dog-friendly town in North Carolina."

"Then a dog for mayor is a great idea." The coffee hissed in the pot, drawing her closer.

"You should help him," Agnes plowed on. "Your nana said you don't have a job at the moment, but we know you worked for that wonderful congresswoman. Jane…Jane…"

"Sutherland," she supplied. And the congresswoman was anything but wonderful.

"And you aren't, you know..." Agnes tapped the ring finger on her left hand.

"Agnes." Finnie shot her friend a deadly look of warning, then turned back to Sadie. "What she's sayin', lass, is that you're not distracted by, you know, love. At the moment."

"Love," she said, looking from one to the other with a deep sigh, hoping they got the message, "hasn't been kind to me." Before they could make promises about their handsome blue-eyed grandson, she added quickly, "And honestly, neither has politics."

"Oh, lass." Finnie put a parchment-soft hand on her cheek. "When life plows your field, your soil is ripe for the plantin'."

She laughed and put her hand over the little grandma's. "I'll remember that."

"What my Irish friend is saying is that you should give both love and politics another chance." Agnes leaned in closer. "Ever since your nana talked about you at our last meeting, we had, you know, a *feeling*. And our track record is, if I might say so myself, quite good."

She looked from one to the other. "I really don't want to run a campaign for a dog," she said, knowing damn well their *feeling* wasn't about her working for the man. "I think the idea is precious, but..."

"'Tis Connor folks will vote for," Finnie said. "Assuming they don't vote for Mitch Easterbrook."

Sadie almost choked. "Mitch Easterbrook?" The name tasted foul on her tongue, especially because it was never spoken in this house. "The undertaker?"

"The very one, lass," Finnie said. "A man of questionable character and ill repute."

For a moment, she couldn't breathe, inching back as if she could get a little bit farther away from the idea of Mitch Easterbrook. Questionable character and ill repute? That was one way of describing him. Another would be: the bastard who seduced her mother, wrecked her parents' marriage, and broke up a very happy little family.

"He cannot be mayor of Bitter Bark," she whispered to herself.

"Exactly!" Agnes practically shouted the word. "Which is why Connor and Frank so desperately need you."

"Connor can't beat a guy who has that much money and power," Sadie said. She knew how campaigns worked and what Easterbrook was made of—pure, unadulterated corruption and a buttload of money.

Agnes nodded furiously. "See? You already know what he's up against. You'll be such an asset to his campaign. His whole life, actually."

Sadie blinked at her, not really hearing this last pitch because her mind was whirring. Connor could lose—especially with the dog idea. Yes, it was newsworthy, but when people walked into that voting booth, would they pull the lever—or fill in the box, in this case—for a dog and his cute firefighter or a man who had every outward appearance of a leader? Mitch was very…persuasive.

Just ask Elaine Hartman.

"Something needs to be done," she said under her breath, inching away from the coffee as that need literally pushed her to the door. "Mitch *can't* be allowed to win."

The two women practically burst with excitement.

"You'll be such an asset to Connor's campaign!" Finnie exclaimed.

"He'll need all that help with speeches and things." Agnes tried to lift her brows. "You know, over long dinners."

Finnie clasped her hands and looked to the sky like her prayers had been answered. "Oh, lass, I remember your speech in that auditorium was so magnificent it stayed with me all these years. Something about... hearin' with the ear...I can't quite remember."

"E-A-R," Sadie said, not embarrassed now but confident in the knowledge that she'd come so far since then. Plus, as campaign slogans for high school presidents go, it wasn't awful. People sure as heck remembered it. "Experienced. Approachable. Responsible."

"And you spoke with so much passion and purpose," Finnie added.

Oh yes, she had. Every word had been meaningful, every promise easy to fulfill, every need in the school outlined with a brilliant plan to fix all the problems. Who cared what her slogan was? She was truly going to improve things.

But Connor Mahoney went up there in his football jersey, cracked a few jokes, and winked at the girls. Nothing had really changed since then. This time, he was campaigning with a dog, but the stakes were so much higher. Maybe he'd win...but maybe he *wouldn't*.

"I have to do something about this," she said, conviction rising up through her whole body, like a fire that had suddenly be reignited. A fire that had been doused that day when Jane Sutherland looked over her desk and faked an apology that stank like the spicy waft of her Shalimar. Sadie could still see Jane's hand trembling, the pen in her fingers shaking as she tried to act like stealing Sadie's boyfriend was no big deal.

It sucks, honey, I know. And he'll always care for you, but Nathan and I have something...different. It isn't like we have any control over that kind of chemistry. You'll move on, I'm sure. Now, do you have the latest poll numbers ready...

And in some ways, Mitch Easterbrook was made of *exactly* the same stuff. He didn't care about people, not really. But he could put on one hell of a show.

"We absolutely cannot take a chance Connor would lose," Sadie said softly.

"Amen and God bless you," Agnes said, putting a hand on Sadie's shoulder. "Go now. He's campaigning at town hall."

"He's there until five," Finnie added, nudging her from the other side. "I think he's keeping an eye on the office, just to see if someone else throws their name in the hat. Today's the last day to register as a candidate."

"The last day?"

"Ladies!" Nana called as she opened the back door with two more friends in tow. "It's time to start the stitching! Oh, Sadie, you never got your coffee." She gave slightly accusing looks to the two old ladies flanking her.

The two dogs they'd brought barked and came bounding into the kitchen at the new arrivals, distracting everyone.

"It's fine, Nana," Sadie said as she made her way toward the door, everything, including her precious latte, long forgotten. "I have something I have to do."

Agnes and Finnie exchanged a look that could be described only as victorious.

"Thank you, Dogmothers," she said to them. "It might not be exactly what you imagined, but…"

"Just go, lass. We know you might not fall in love, but the Irish say, 'You only regret the chances you didn't take.' You take this chance and see what happens."

"Oh, I know what's going to happen." She certainly wasn't going to fall in love. But Mitch Easterbrook would lose the election. And right then, standing here in this kitchen where so many tears had been shed by her, her grandparents, and her father, all because of that awful man and her mother, his loss was all that mattered.

She blew them an impulsive kiss and darted out the door to get that new job and new life she needed so much.

Chapter Four

Frank didn't exactly love campaigning. But he was a smart dog and a quick study who learned that letting strangers pet him always earned a treat. If he swished his tail and didn't back away and growl, he got two. And if he posed for a selfie with his constituents, Connor brought out a Beggin' Strip, and a dog who'd spent God knew how much time alone in the woods would literally sell his soul for some fake bacon.

"Good boy," Connor praised and treated after a group of people walked away, headed around the corner to the Town Clerk's office to register to vote in the election coming up in just under a month, on the lucky date of Saint Patrick's Day. "You're awesome, you know that?"

His bright pink and ridiculously long tongue hung out as he eyed Connor's midsection, no doubt ready to show his love with his usual upward vault.

"No, no, Frankendog," Connor whispered, reaching into his pocket for a tiny treat that he was now never without. "Sit like a good boy. Here comes…" He glanced at the huge double front doors as one opened slowly and late afternoon sunshine poured in to silhouette the person entering town hall. He blinked into the light at the shape of a woman moving with purpose toward him. And as the door closed and her body was no longer backlit, he saw her face. "Here comes trouble," he finished on a whisper, slipping the treat to the patient dog. "The kind I really, really like."

Sadie Hartman looked around to get her bearings, obviously not familiar with the inside of town hall. It gave Connor a minute to observe the way her long hair-of-many-shades spilled over a white jacket like chocolate and caramel syrup over vanilla ice cream. She wore a tight skirt and heels, a businesslike look that was insanely hot, and a little more makeup than she'd had on the night they met. Didn't need it, but he still wanted to kiss that color right off her pretty lips.

Oh man. The jolt to his libido was powerful and sent a few aftershocks to his chest. This wasn't run-of-the-mill sexual attraction. There was something about this woman that got under his skin. Not that he'd say no to what his hormones were hyped for, but remembering how easy it was to talk to her, the intelligence in her eyes, and the soul in her laugh made him want more than sex. At the very least, he wanted another chance.

Ear Girl was way too enthralling to give up without a fight.

"Come on, Franko." He tugged at the leash. "Let's go make her forget she lost an election eons ago. And remember just how much she wants to kiss the guy who's gonna win this one." He threw a look at the dog. "I mean me, not you."

As they approached, Sadie stared right back, long enough for Connor to mentally note that she didn't seem the least bit surprised to see him standing there with a dog. He didn't know if time exactly stood still or heavenly hosts sang in his head, but the silent seconds of eye contact were electrical enough to make the hairs on the back of his neck dance a little, while his whole gut tightened.

"Well, if it isn't Mercedes Hartman."

She smiled and wrecked him with those dimples. "And this..." She gestured to Frank. "Must be our local hero."

So she'd been following the story in the news. That gave him a shot of hope as Frank took a step backward and kept cautious eyes on her.

"He's too humble to admit it," Connor said. "But yes, this is Frank, saver of children and town hall greeter. Say hi to the pretty lady, Frank."

"Hello, Frank. Aren't you a handsome guy?" She took a step closer to reach out a tentative hand. "May I?"

"He's shy, but he won't bite."

"Oh, hi, shy guy." She rubbed his head, and Connor reached into his pocket for one more of the Milk-Bone Mini's. "Give him one of these, and he'll get a little friendlier."

She took the treat and held her hand open for him, unfazed by that big tongue on her skin.

"Look at that," Connor said, leaning closer. "You got him eating out of the palm of your hand...just like me."

She straightened and laughed, pushing some of that glorious hair over her shoulder. "Is that so, Lieutenant?"

He put his hand over his chest with a slight thump. "She remembers me."

"Who could forget you?"

"You, apparently, after seventeen years of carrying a grudge."

"Not grudge-carrying, I promise. It's the future that I'm thinking about."

Yes. He took a step closer, locking on her golden-brown eyes and lowering his voice. "You just made my day."

"How's that?"

He let out a sigh, knowing that sometimes you had to show your hand to win the next one. "Because I haven't stopped thinking about you since the night at Bushrod's, Sadie. I fully confess I considered taking Frank on a walk past your grandparents' house a few too many times in the past week."

"Creepy."

"In a totally non-creepy way. I wanted to see you again."

"And here I am."

He smiled and let his gaze drop over her business attire. "What brings you to town hall, Mercedes?"

"Please, it's Sadie now." She petted the dog again, quiet for a moment. "Unless you prefer Ear Girl."

"Only if it makes you smile."

She rewarded him with a dimpled grin. "I should be able to laugh at my past mistakes," she said. "I hope I didn't overreact."

More hope zinged up his chest. "Maybe a little, but after hours of consideration and the promise of a do-over, I'm certain I'm the one who owes you a seventeen-year-old apology. How about if I buy you dinner and grovel for a solid hour, with heartfelt assurances to only call you Ear Girl if I'm nibbling your actual earlobe?"

Her smile wavered, but he saw the warmth hit those whiskey-colored eyes. "Um...no. Thanks. I don't think that under the circumstances..."

The circumstances? She *really* couldn't let go of that class president race. "Frank," he said sotto voce to the dog. "Help me out here. Impress the lady and make her reconsider. Do the tail move, big guy."

Frank wagged his mighty tail, making them both laugh.

"He's cute, but..."

"He's running for mayor," Connor told her before she could slip away again. "Surely that touches the heart of a woman who's worked in government and politics."

She lifted her chin, an almost defiant look in her eyes. "I've heard."

"You have?"

"I admit I thought it was...odd."

He laughed. "Bitter Bark's a dog town now, Sadie. It's perfect. And as mayor, my boy Frank is going to put the fun back into functions and fundraisers."

She inched one shapely brow up. "How...fun."

He had to laugh, liking her dry wit and the tease in the subtext. "You know, since you've been living out of town, you have to re-register to vote."

"I have maintained a residence here for seventeen years," she said.

He frowned. "I didn't know that."

"My father actually..." She took a breath and waved her hand. "Long story short, my dad moved to

Austin when I left for college, so he put the house in my name and rents it out. That way, I kept state residence for UNC, and we saved a bundle in out-of-state tuition. So technically I am a resident."

He nodded. "But are you currently registered to vote?"

"I don't think so, but I do intend to fix that. I guess I should do that first."

"First? Before…"

She looked around. "Do you know where I'd go to do that?"

"Around that corner in the Office of the Town Clerk." He pointed in the direction. "Do you have proof that you own the property?"

"Yes." She tapped her bag.

"And a phone number?"

"I need a phone number to register?"

"No, but I need it to call you." He smiled. "And make that dinner date. I'm free tonight."

"Connor." She said his name on a sigh, as if it wasn't the first time she'd thought about him. He liked that.

"Sadie." He matched the tone and sigh, making her smile. "Look, if you're involved and not single or not at all interested…" He held up a hand of surrender. "I will back off. But if not, I'd really like to see you again. I'd hate to think an election I won in high school ruined my chances now when we're both adults."

She scanned his face, obviously considering the offer, that whisper of a smile threatening to bring back those precious dimples.

"It's just one date, Ear Girl." He lowered his voice to add, "He said with nothing but affection and interest."

She laughed. "You are smooth, Lieutenant, I'll give you that, but…"

"But not your phone number?"

The smile faded. "You're running for mayor."

Why would that matter? "Um, not technically. Frank is. I'm merely his chief of staff. I speak for him." As if on cue, Frank came closer, looking for a treat, so he gave a bark *and* a tail swoosh, doing his job as a furry wingman and earning a soft, sweet, genuine laugh from Sadie that was music to Connor's ears.

"Sounds like he's speaking for himself," she said, giving the dog another pat on the head. "Is it really…legit?"

"The dog running? Yes, he meets the qualifications. My cousin is a vet, and she signed off on his age at about six years old, which means he's forty-two in dog years, and I'm now his official owner. I'm a lifelong resident of Bitter Bark, so he is a resident, too. The Election Committee overwhelmingly approved the idea because, as you know…" He inched a little closer, drawn to her and the subtle fragrance of lemons and flowers that clung to her. "He really did save a boy's life recently. I happened to be the EMT on scene, but it was all Frank."

"So what's Frank's platform?" she asked.

The question surprised him, mostly because it was asked with complete seriousness, which wasn't something *Frank's platform* usually got. "More public water bowls in Bushrod Square, monthly dog parades, and all pet taxes at the local hotels have to go to the county shelter." He fired off the spiel without hesitation, but then, he'd said it twenty-seven times today. "His agenda is to spread joy and wag tongues and tails. Oh, he guarantees all poop will be promptly picked up."

But maybe his jokes had lost its zing, because she didn't seem more than mildly amused. "And you think that'll get him a victory on Election Day?"

Behind him, some kids squealed at the sight of Frank, but when he glanced their way, a woman hushed the boys, and her friend raised her finger to silently say they'd wait for him.

"I think the fact that this town got fat and happy on dogs over the past few years is all he needs to get the job done," Connor said.

She lifted an uncertain brow. "I'm sure there's more to the job than…water bowls and poop pickup. I imagine the people of Bitter Bark care about managing the budget, setting the calendar, and handling emergency management issues."

Was she testing him or interested in what the mayor of a town like this did? Or just lingering to spend more time with him? The last one, he hoped. "Well, you know, the budget of a town like this manages itself, the calendar was set a year ago, and as you know, I'm a firefighter with the Bitter Bark FD, so emergency management is kind of what I do."

"I bet it's a little more complicated. In fact, I know it is."

"Hey, if you're offering to give me political pointers, I'll take them. Over dinner?"

She laughed softly at his persistence. "Political pointers from Ear Girl?"

"Experienced. Approachable. Responsible." He

gave a hopeful look. "It's brilliant. Can I borrow it for my campaign?"

"It's all yours."

"Great. Then can Frank count on your vote?"

She raised both brows, almost as if sending a warning. "I think that depends on who else is on the ticket."

"Well, see, that's the thing." He leaned in a centimeter, close enough to see the sun on the lightest strands of her magnificent hair. "The other guy is bad, Sadie. In every way. Bitter Bark would never recover from someone as crooked as this guy being the mayor."

She nodded, holding his gaze with a question in hers. "And you really think you can beat him?"

"I believe I mentioned the other night that I don't generally lose."

"And I believe I mentioned that there's a first time for everything."

"Frank!" one of the kids called, making Frank cower a little closer to Connor.

"Your shy guy needs to go greet his townsfolk," she said, nodding toward the waiting group.

He turned and signaled to the kids. "One sec, you guys," he called, then put a hand on her back to guide her. "Frank, let's take the lady to register."

But she dipped out of his light touch and shook her head. "Oh, no, that's fine. I'll handle it."

He had to let her go, but did he have a shot or was he just making a fool of himself? "Are Frank and I getting blown off?"

She pointed to the kids and moms. "Your adoring public needs you, Connor."

He didn't normally pursue a woman who wasn't interested. That was definitely what his dad would call going after a loss. But there was something about her, something so damn irresistible, he broke his own rule.

"Can I have a second chance, Sadie? If the answer is no, I won't ask again, I promise."

She didn't say a word, drawing out some of that blood-humming eye contact so long he could almost hear her say the word *yes*.

Next to him, Frank pressed into his leg like a kindergartner on the first day of school. As the kids got closer in a pack, he let out a low growl that Connor knew needed attention and treats.

"Listen, Sadie—"

"Your constituents await, sir. You wouldn't want to lose their vote in your effort to get mine."

"Frank!" The kids finally escaped their moms and lunged toward Frank, who instantly vaulted at Connor like all he wanted was to be picked up and protected.

"Whoa, easy, boy." He got him down, reached for a treat, and when he turned back to Sadie, all he saw was a flash of her hair as she disappeared around the corner.

Gone…for now. She hadn't said *no* to the second chance. Not yet, anyway.

But Frank needed his full attention as the group came on strong, not expecting that this big, strange-looking dog would react like they were a pack of wolves coming at him. Maybe some had out in those woods.

Connor instantly went into Frank-management mode, holding the dog, getting down to his level, giving him treats, and watching the kids get a kick out of Frank slowly trusting them to pet him.

The moms got pictures, then a few more people joined the group, and Connor got back in mayor mode, the well-practiced phrases pouring out.

Ceremonial mayor...put the fun in fundraisers... public water bowls...spreading joy...I was just there, but Frank's the hero...can he have your vote?

Two more groups showed up and then a features photographer from the *Banner*, who wanted to take Frank outside on the stairs for a picture. That took a little convincing and a lot of Milk-Bones, but they got the shot. Best of all, the photographer said he had it on good authority that the editor of the *Banner* was most likely planning to endorse Frank.

An hour later, he was finally free to look for Sadie Hartman, but she wasn't in the town clerk's office, which was empty except for the woman behind the reception desk, currently on the phone.

Huffing out a breath, he turned and almost slammed right into Blanche Wilkins.

"Oh, Mayor, I'm so sorry."

"Don't be, Connor. I was just dropping this off and hoped to find you." She looked up at him with bright blue eyes, crinkled at the sides from sixty or so years of smiling. "You'll be at the Election Committee meeting tomorrow, right? We'll finalize the slate of candidates and set a schedule for events and debates."

"Of course," he said. "Tomorrow at ten in your conference room."

"Yes." She was fighting a smile. He could tell by the light in her eyes.

"Does that look mean you have good news?"

She bit her lip and nodded. "I think it's good."

"Easterbrook dropped out? No doubt he heard Frank's getting the *Banner* endorsement."

"No, he didn't drop out. But the slate has changed."

He drew back, surprised. "It has?"

She looked down at a piece of paper he recognized as the official declaration of candidacy. "A young woman who grew up here in Bitter Bark and is back with big ideas and tremendous experience."

Seriously?

"Sadie Hartman," Mayor Wilkins said brightly, handing him the paper to read even though he didn't bother. Instead, he just mentally reviewed all the questions she'd asked him earlier and her interest in the mayor's job, and the whole time…she was planning to be his opponent.

"I actually think you went to high school with her."

"I did," he said slowly, shaking his head a little at how he'd been duped. "We ran against each other for class president." He lifted a brow. "For the record, I won."

But could he be so sure this time? Not to mention, he could kiss that second chance goodbye. He didn't know which turn of events ticked him off more.

"Oh, she'll be a formidable opponent." Mayor Wilkins tapped the paper in his hand. "Just look at that résumé. She's recently moved here from DC, where she was the deputy chief of staff to Congresswoman Jane Sutherland from Texas. She worked on several difficult national campaigns and has a law degree from the University of Virginia. Oh, and just tons of big ideas, too."

"Is that so?" Funny how she'd boiled all that down to *aide* when he'd asked her what she did. Or how she let him beg for a second chance when she planned to come in here and put her name in the hat. "Then what's she doing running for mayor of Bitter Bark, North Carolina?" Besides wrecking his campaign *and* his ego. "Don't you have to live in Bitter Bark to be mayor of Bitter Bark?"

She tapped the paper. "She's held the deed to a house in Ambrose Acres for many years, and that qualifies her as a resident."

"She hasn't actually resided *in* the town, though, which would be what the word *resident* means."

"True, but she grew up here, and her passion is small-town politics." Mayor Wilkins practically crooned this news. "I have to say, her enthusiasm reminded me of my Frank when he first ran for mayor and held the position for seven consecutive terms."

"He was a great mayor." And *this* Frank was supposed to be his four-legged namesake.

Her smile grew again. "Oh, I knew I could count on you to be a complete professional about it. I still have faith in you, but Mitch is planning an aggressive campaign, and if he wins…"

She didn't say the words, but he could read her expression. Mitch Easterbrook would be a disaster for Bitter Bark.

"Mitch has issues," he finished for her.

"And you know I want you to win."

He looked down at Frank. "You do remember he's running for mayor, not me?"

"Then you'll have to speak on his behalf, unless you want to drop the whole 'Frank as mayor' thing." She lifted her brows, almost as if she was suggesting he do just that.

"Would you prefer that, Mayor Wilkins? Even after reading about the other four-legged mayors around the country and what they can do for tourism and spirit?"

She sighed. "Oh, Connor, I am well aware of what dogs have done for this town. Before your cousin's wife came here and put 'Better Bark' on the map, I was this close to having to resign for all the fiscal problems we were having. So I'm the last one to scoff at a canine idea that's out of the box. But that said, the job isn't quite the day at the park you seem to think it is."

"I know that. I joke about it, but I know it's a serious job."

"Good, and what I prefer doesn't matter," she added. "It's your decision all the way."

Before he could respond, her phone dinged, and she reached for it, checking the screen and letting out a soft grunt of frustration.

"Anything I can do to help?" he offered.

"No, unless you want to attend the Finance Committee meeting and face down six different subcommittees who all think their budget is the one that can't be cut. Or you could complete the four staff evaluations I need to write tonight." She shook her head, obviously not serious about the offer, but the message came through loud and clear. "I better go, but I wanted to make sure you weren't blindsided when you walk into the meeting tomorrow."

Oh, he was blindsided all right. "I can handle whatever gets thrown at me."

Just then, a group of about six people came into the office, laughing and talking. They startled Frank, who instantly jumped up and pawed at Connor's waist and hips. "Even Frank," he added on a laugh.

Mayor Wilkins laughed, too, shaking her head. "I'm glad to see you're both being such good sports about it. May the best man or woman...or *dog* win." She gave a quick nod and hustled off, obviously too distracted to remember she'd given him the candidate's filing paper.

He glanced at it, skimming all those lofty titles and positions and education.

Why would this hotshot want to move from the Beltway to Bitter Bark and be the mayor?

There was only one reason: revenge for the class president defeat. Wow.

He walked over to the desk and handed the woman behind it the paper. "Pretty sure Mayor Wilkins meant to leave this with you."

Leading Frank outside, he stepped into the sunshine, pausing at the top of the stairs to survey Bushrod Square and consider canvassing for votes he'd need more than ever.

But his gaze landed on a woman in white, with burnished brown hair fluttering in the wind as she walked with purpose across the square.

"C'mon, Frank. Let's go chat up the competition."

Chapter Five

After finishing her paperwork and the meeting with the mayor, Sadie crossed Bushrod Square with a sense of satisfaction and a hint of terror as the questions poured over her. Was this the right thing for her life? Could she beat Mitch Easterbrook? Would she be a good mayor? And why, oh, why, did Connor Mahoney have to be even hotter than he'd been in high school?

That was the one question that she couldn't begin to answer. Honestly, couldn't he have gotten fat? Bald? Boring? Arrested? Why hadn't he peaked in high school and then gone downhill from there? Wasn't that the way it was with the über-popular kids in movies and books, leaving room for the nameless, faceless idealists to have their day in the sun?

Sadly, that was not the case with Connor Mahoney.

"Excuse me? Ms. Hartman?"

She immediately recognized his voice behind her, and if she hadn't, the dog bark would have been a dead giveaway.

"Sadie?"

She slowed her step, wondering if he'd be furious,

curious, or amused by this turn of events. Or, knowing Connor, would he pile it up with the other reasons they should go out together?

"Come on, Ear Girl. You know I know."

Sadie turned, pushed her hair back to get a good look, and watched the man and his dog stride toward her. No, he certainly hadn't peaked in high school. It might have been this morning, because how could the man get any more confident, sexy, or masculine? His long, powerful legs ate up the walkway, while his dog-of-many-breeds trotted as close to his owner as he could get without actually being carried.

"You know I know...what?" she asked. Except, she *did* know. She could tell by the look on his face, which wasn't quite as playful as it had been inside the town hall.

"The good news," Connor said as he came closer.

"I didn't expect you to think it was good."

He gave a casual shrug. "Frank thinks you'll be a worthy opponent and hopes you don't split the vote so the wrong guy wins."

"I intend to get the vote, not split it." She reached out to pet the dog, who backed away and got behind Connor. "Sorry, Frank. I hope you understand."

"Wanna talk about it?" Connor asked.

"What's there to talk about?"

"Oh, I don't know." He came within a foot of her, looming at a good six feet and change over her five-and-a-half-foot frame, putting her eye-to-broad-shoulder, and letting her get a whiff of that clean, soapy scent and undercurrent of frustration. "How about why you didn't mention your plans back there?"

"You didn't ask." A lame answer, but the truth was

she hadn't wanted him to use some magical persuasive charm to talk her out of the idea.

He slid his hands into the pockets of his khaki pants, the position casual and easy, like his tone. But the tension in his jaw and the darker tone to his blue eyes told her he wasn't feeling casual about this.

"So you let me beg for another shot with you when you knew all along you were there to put your name on the ballot?"

"I haven't qualified yet," she said. "Mayor Wilkins said they would vote on it at the Election Committee meeting in the morning."

He snorted. "A dog qualifies, and come on, Sadie. It's not like you have a crappy résumé. It's not every day a town like Bitter Bark gets a former deputy chief of staff for a Texas congresswoman wanting to run for mayor. Why'd you leave that cushy job, anyway?"

She let out a mirthless laugh. "It wasn't cushy." Brushing back a strand of hair that blew in her face, she looked up, making contact with those insanely blue eyes. "Honestly, Connor, I didn't mention my plans because I hadn't yet registered and didn't know if Mayor Wilkins would even consider my application."

"Consider? The mayor is drooling." He looked skyward for a second. "So at least I'm not the only one."

She let a smile pull at her lips, because, honestly, there wasn't much else a woman could do when a man as hot as Connor Mahoney stood like a chestnut-haired firefighting god in front of her and admitted she made him drool. "Hey, don't be too hard on yourself. I'm the one who practically threw myself at you at Bushrod's."

"Not exactly."

"I was about to."

He dropped his head back and grunted. "I will make Probie pay for that."

"Don't be mad at your coworker. I would have found out your secret identity sooner or later, Lieutenant."

"But I might have gotten the first kiss in by then and sealed the deal."

She laughed. "I do like your confidence."

"So you like something?"

She gave him a side-eye as they walked, going along with Frank as he sniffed along the grass. "Plenty of things. But now...we're opponents." She shrugged. "Things have changed."

It was his turn to scrutinize her with a long look, then he stabbed his fingers in his short hair, running his hand over his head like he couldn't quite make it work to figure things out. "Are you still pissed about high school? Is that why you decided to run?"

"Run from you that night or run for office now?"

"Both."

She smiled at his quick comeback, but wanted to be completely honest. "That night, I ran on principle. Not holding a grudge, but you did embarrass me pretty bad."

"I'm really sorry." There was no way the apology was anything but genuine.

"Then all is forgiven. But about the mayoral race? I'm running because..." She didn't want to reveal the story of her mother and Mitch Easterbrook. The seasoned politician in her knew better than to give the competition that kind of information.

Mitch, in some weird way, could be trusted to be quiet about it, since having had an affair with a married woman almost twenty years ago could only hurt him. But if Connor—or anyone in town—heard the story that her family had kept buried and thought she was running against Mitch out of pure revenge? Or that she was somehow as tainted as her mother? No matter how it came out, it could only hurt her. The truth was she was running because she knew Mitch was scum and shouldn't hold the job.

"Wow, this is taking a long time," he joked. "You really need to work on your canned answers, Madam Candidate."

She smiled. "Okay, I'm running because I think I could do an amazing job and because I lived here for a long time and think highly of the town."

"Whoa, that *was* canned, like a freaking sardine."

"But it's true."

"Really, because you *lived* here was past tense. And you think *highly* of the town?" He gave out a little dismayed snort. "Bitter Bark's in my blood, Sadie. I went past 'thinking highly' of it when I was six years old and had my first pastry at Linda May Dunlap's bakery. Which is still there, if you're interested."

"Then why are you using a gimmick to get elected?" She gestured at Frank, who responded by coming closer to Connor and nudging his nose into his knee.

"How can you look at this adorable beast and call him a gimmick?"

She laughed. "You have me there. Though, full disclosure, I'm a cat person. And you're right, Frank has a very, uh, distinctive look."

"Hear that, Frankie? The lady called you distinctive. I hope that's not a euphemism for ugly."

"Connor!" She gave him a little jab with her elbow. "I didn't say that. He's quite handsome. Also, naming him after the late mayor?" She made a thumbs-up sign. "Someone's giving you genius campaign advice."

He looked away, past her, swallowing as if he wanted to say something but held back. Frank took a few more steps, heading back to the grass and trees while they walked.

"Well, you know this town is all about dogs," he finally said.

"Yes, the Better Bark campaign."

"My cousin's wife's idea, by the way." He leaned a little closer, letting their arms touch. "Who also happens to be the director of tourism *and* Mayor Wilkins's niece."

"A little nepotism never hurt anyone," she teased. "Funny, your grandmother didn't mention that."

"Gramma Finnie?" He stopped and frowned at her. "When did you talk to her?"

"She was at my nana's house for a sewing club meeting." She lifted her brows to deliver the next bomb. "She and her friend sent me to town hall to be your campaign manager."

His jaw loosened. "My...her friend..." Then he shut his eyes and shook his head. "Oh no. That's not why they sent you."

"I got that, too." She laughed. "They fancy themselves matchmakers?"

"No fancying. They believe they are the yentas of Bitter Bark and have a few successes under their belts to prove it. I'm sorry if they were..." He shook his head. "No. Never mind. I'm not sorry. They have impeccable taste, and you should date me."

"You never quit, do you? We're opponents, Connor. We can't date."

"Who made that stupid rule?"

"It's not stupid. It's for the safety and security of the campaign."

"Still stupid." He looked past her at Frank. "Oh no." Jerking to the side, he launched toward the dog, seizing his head and sticking his finger in his mouth. "No, Frank. No eating rocks." He knocked a few to the ground. "Bad habit he picked up in the woods," he said, trying to open the dog's jaw wider. "Don't swallow that, Frank!" He stuck his finger in deeper and got chomped a bit, but he didn't give up until he got the last rock out of the dog's mouth.

"Would it hurt him if he swallowed it?"

"Depends on the size. Most likely, he'd pass it. But if a sharp edge got him, he'd need an X-ray to make sure he's not bleeding." He patted the dog and guided him back to Sadie. "No rocks, Franko. Bad boy."

Instantly, Frank folded on the ground and hid his face behind a big paw.

"Oh, he doesn't like to get reprimanded," she said with a little coo in her voice. "He's like a gentle giant."

"That's for sure." Connor knelt next to him with no regard for his khaki pants, just the dog he stroked with a tender touch and large hands. "He looks tough, but scares easily. And he doesn't trust anyone but me. It's okay, Frank. You didn't swallow anything."

"Then he's lucky he found you."

"I'm lucky I found him," Connor said. "He gave me the incentive I needed to run for mayor. Well, for him to run." He looked up. "Which reminds me, except for your canned answer, I still don't know what your incentive was."

Mitch Easterbrook. She shrugged. "I love politics."

"And hate me."

The words cut more deeply than she expected them to. "I don't hate you, Connor. Oh my gosh, I'm sorry you think that."

"So you don't still hold it against me that I won your office on a bet?"

"I don't," she said. "And that's not why I'm running."

"Then why is a big-time congressional staffer and deputy chief of staff sniffing around the mayor's office in a town the size of Bitter Bark? I really want to know."

"Sniffing? Says the man with a dog on the ticket."

"Don't use jokes to get out of answering," he warned. "That's my technique. Get your own. And I'm serious. What takes a person from Capitol Hill to Bushrod Square?"

"A long and complicated road."

He stood, holding her gaze with one that demanded an answer. "I'd love to hear about it."

And something deep inside her knew she'd love to share it. He'd make her laugh and see it all differently, and then he might kiss away all the hurt.

"You're going to have to answer the question sooner or later," he said after her long hesitation. "So, practice on me."

She sighed and glanced around again. "Bushrod Square," she said instead. "It's the one thing that doesn't change about Bitter Bark, you know? But I see it could use a little sprucing up. What are Frank's plans for increasing the maintenance budget?"

"Don't change the subject, DC."

"I didn't. I turned the question around. It's *my* technique."

"Good to know. My guess is you left Washington for a reason, and it's a doozy. You know I'm not going to sleep until I know. So I'm going to ask one more time. Will you let me take you out so you can tell me your whole story, and I can make up for not only beating you for class president, but also for stupidly not paying attention to you when I had the chance? Because I know that's kind of irking you, too."

Damn it, he was right. And the word *yes* was right there, ready to roll out in a single breathless whisper. But something stopped her. Resentment from the past? Fear that he really could get the whole story about Nathan and Jane over dinner and the Mitch Easterbrook saga for dessert? Or then, when it was all done, that she'd fall into bed with him.

Oh, Sadie. Catch yourself before you get smashed into a million pieces again.

"You know what's the first thing you learn in DC politics?" she asked.

"How to lie?"

She brushed off the joke and refused to let him know how true it was. "Not to date"—anyone—"your opponent."

"But you're not officially announced as a candidate yet. So we could squeeze in one, quick…" He leaned just a little closer, near enough that she could see the speckles of navy in his blue eyes and the golden tips of his thick lashes. "Dinner."

"As if you'd stop at dinner," she whispered.

"I'd stop where you said stop." He drew back. "And when you say stop. So, if you want me to stop asking you out, just say so, and I will. Until you do, I'm going to keep trying."

She opened her mouth, but damn, she just couldn't say the word. Because if she weren't running against him for mayor...then she might give in to all the electricity shooting through her body. Broken hearts be damned. He'd be good for the body, if not the soul.

"I'll see you tomorrow, Connor." As she backed away, still holding his gaze, he broke into a grin, and Frank took a few steps closer to her, taking a quick lick of her knuckles. "Oh! I wasn't expecting that."

"Neither was I," he said, smiling at the dog. "I guess he really is my wingman."

She rubbed the big dog's head. "As if you need one. See you tomorrow, Lieutenant."

"You bet, Ear Girl."

Chapter Six

"Look at that." Shane Kilcannon crossed his arms and watched Frank circle the Waterford Farm training pen, led in a slow walk by his brother Garrett. "Damn, I do good work."

"You?" Connor snorted. "I haven't done anything for two weeks but dole out treats and sweet talk."

"It's working."

"Maybe." Connor pressed his elbows into the wire fence separating him from the pen and Shane, taking a deep breath of early spring air that always seemed to smell a little better out here in the homestead that his uncle and cousins had transformed into a haven for dogs and people. "Frank still sleeps six inches from my face, follows me into the bathroom and shower, and has gnawed the crap out of my electrical cords and a pair of sunglasses. I almost wrecked my truck trying to get a dime out of his mouth the other day."

"But you did it, which is all that counts."

"Wasn't going to let him swallow it, but damn, it worries me that he could eat something that could kill him."

"I get that. But remember, the dog could have gone days or more at a time without food out there in the woods," Shane said. "You keep him fat and happy, and he'll stop eating things he shouldn't. But Frank's real problem is he has trust issues." Shane nodded at Garrett as he and the dog came closer. Garrett gave a signal, Frank stopped, then started walking again. "See that? See how he stopped when Garrett signaled? That's progress, man."

"He does that all the time with me."

"You're his savior, and after two weeks of food and affection, he trusts you. But someone likely dumped that dog in the woods and not as a puppy, or he'd have never survived. That means he knows love and he knows loss. Eventually, he'll be a great dog, you'll see."

"He's already a great dog," Connor said. "But how long will it take for him to trust anyone but me?"

"Hard to say." Shane frowned and ran a hand over his whiskers. "But it might not be before Election Day, if that's what you're worried about."

Connor gave a look that said it was exactly what he was worried about. "It would be nice not to have him cower from voters."

"Especially now that there's a new candidate on the slate and all." Shane gave his signature know-it-all grin at Connor's surprised expression. "Hey, I'm married to the director of tourism, remember? She said the new-candidate gossip spread like wildfire, if you'll excuse the firefighting pun."

Garrett and Frank trotted over to where they stood, and Connor laughed when Frank pounced on the fence, trying to get to him.

"No jumping, Franko."

"It's really hard for him," Shane said, giving the dog a gentle rub on the head. "That's kind of his way of saying he loves you."

"When a simple bark would do," Connor said, stepping into the pen when Shane unlatched the gate. He crouched down to Frank's level to avoid the next jump. "Good job trusting Garrett, big boy. Try that with all the voters now."

Garrett laughed. "Yeah, 'cause they all might vote for Ear Girl."

Guess they'd all heard the news. "You remember that?"

"Oh, hell yeah. I was right there. You totally mortified that poor girl in the cafeteria like the smug, sore winner you are. Or..." Garrett tipped his head. "Used to be."

Connor curled his lip as he straightened, kind of hating his seventeen-year-old self. Of course, he had an excuse, blaming the death of his father when he was sixteen for turning him into a teenage ass-pain. And these two, his closest cousins in age and friendship, knew that.

"Hopefully, I'll be a little more gracious in victory this time," Connor said.

"If you have a victory," Shane said, earning a dark look from Connor.

"You'll win if she bases her campaign on some other inane body part," Garrett said. "Those ear posters were bizarre."

"First of all, *Frank* is running for mayor," Connor reminded them.

Garrett looked skyward. "Right."

"And second of all, there's no body part on her that could be called 'inane.' Hell, I think it's fair to say even her ears are hot now. I don't really remember her from high school, but holy crap, the woman is a dime and a half."

"And of course, you reduce a female to her lowest common denominator and your conquest to get her in bed," Garrett said. "Are you ever going to change?"

"Jealous much?" Connor's quip came easy. Easier than trying to convince his cousin that Sadie was different and getting her into bed wasn't…okay, it *was* what he wanted, but it wasn't the *only* reason he'd been making a fool of himself around her.

"Are you kidding?" Garrett looked hard at Connor. "Do you have any idea how happy I am since I met Jessie?"

"Same with Chloe," Shane chimed in.

"Yeah, yeah. I got it." Connor held up a hand. "Went to all three hundred family weddings and twelve christenings in the last two years."

"Whoa." Shane wiped his mouth with the back of his hand, barely covering his smirk. "Someone's pissed about a little more competition on the ballot. She could take votes from Mitch, too, you know. You should be glad she's running."

"She's going to take votes from both of us," he said. "She's smart and knows politics, and the whole town is going to be dazzled by her résumé and… dimples."

"Only you are dazzled by her dimples," Shane cracked. "The rest of us just want a really good mayor."

Lola, Garrett's tan and white Aussie, came

hurrying over from the other side of the pen. When Garrett greeted her with a gentle pet, she dropped to the grass and turned over, paws and tongue out, making them all laugh.

"Now how do you get that kind of trust?" Connor mused. "Frank wouldn't do that in his most unguarded moment."

Garrett obliged the dog with a two-handed belly rub. "She didn't show up this way," Garrett said. "In fact, she didn't let anyone near her until Jessie arrived to change both our lives."

"So I need…Jessie?"

Garrett chuckled, but Shane eyed the dog, thinking. "He might just need a lovey."

"A lovey?"

"It's parent-speak," Garrett explained. "A thing of…comfort. A stuffed animal, a soft blankie."

Connor felt his face twist up at his cousin. "Did you just say blankie?"

Garrett shrugged, unapologetic.

And Shane rubbed Frank's head. "Sometimes a dog who's been through such a rough patch needs something, or someone, that grounds him and makes him comfortable. When he finds that, he could change, you'll see."

"How will I know who or what that is?"

Shane shrugged. "You'll just know." He grinned and pushed off the fence. "But brace yourself, you'll be dragging that thing everywhere you go and kicking yourself if you leave it in a restaurant."

Connor thought of the mitten that Frank loved, but then he turned at the sound of a vehicle pulling into the driveway, spotting the ancient refurbished dog van that belonged to his cousin Molly and her husband, Trace.

"Looks like we got a crowd for Wednesday night dinner," Connor mused, checking out a few of his family members already gathered on the wide wraparound porch that hugged the yellow farmhouse.

Even from this distance, he could hear chatter and laughter. He saw Gramma Finnie and Yiayia in their rockers, his little cousin Pru, and a few of the new babies making noise. The side door banged as people went in and out before the informal dinner that was always served on Wednesdays at the home his uncle Daniel billed as "a hundred acres of happy."

Not one of the extended family would disagree with that description, especially now that Daniel Kilcannon had healed from the loss of Aunt Annie and married a woman who'd added her own crew and a Greek grandma into the mix.

"Yeah, I'm starved," Shane said. "Chloe's in the kennels with Ruby. I'm going to get her, and I'll meet you over there." He headed toward the long clapboard building that housed all the Waterford training and rescue dogs, while Connor and Garrett started toward the house.

Instantly, Frank rushed to his side, his fur brushing the jeans Connor had changed into for this afternoon training session. "Come on, bud, it's dinnertime. Just don't eat any wires or loose change."

"No worries," Garrett said. "Patrick is walking now, did you see?" He beamed at the toddler taking steps in the grass near the porch, but still holding tight to his mother's hand. "Jessie has been through this entire house and babyproofed it again, even though

Fiona's been toddling for a while now. I imagine with Danny and Annabelle crawling, it'll stay that way for a long time."

Without waiting for any kind of response, Garrett picked up speed, and he and Lola hustled toward Jessie and Patrick. He swooped the little guy into his arms and gave Jessie a kiss on the lips. Once more, Lola fell to the ground and rolled over, submissive and unafraid.

"Take a lesson, my man," Connor murmured to Frank. "We love dogs around here. But…Dogmothers?" He raised his voice and got the attention of both the older ladies and the teenager sitting at Yiayia's feet and playing with the two dachshunds who were never far away.

"What is it, lad?"

"Thanks for the help." He slathered a few layers of sarcasm on the sentence.

Yiayia's rocker stilled as her unnaturally smooth face lit up. "She's your new girlfriend?"

"Sweet Saint Patrick, that was fast." Gramma Finnie chuckled.

Pru reached her hand up to get a high five from them. "Dogmother record. I'm calling it."

"No. She's my new opponent for mayor."

"Opponent?" Yiayia dropped back like the weight of this news was too much for the old Greek matriarch. "She wasn't supposed to be *against* you. At least, not in that way."

"She was signin' up to be your campaign manager, lad." Gramma Finnie tipped her rocker all the way forward. "That was the plan, not anything else."

"Well, your plan blew up." He crossed his arms

and leaned against the porch post, vaguely aware of Shane and Chloe coming up behind him from the kennels and Uncle Daniel, Aunt Katie, and God only knew how many others listening on the other side of the kitchen screen door.

When neither his grandmother nor her Greek partner-in-crime said a word, he took the last step and narrowed his gaze on the tiny Irish woman who was as wily as she was strong.

"Finola Kilcannon. You meddled, and now I could lose the election."

Eyes the color of summer skies sparked as she took a slow, deep breath. "Oh, lad. 'Twas your heart we wanted you to lose, not the race."

Yiayia reached out to put a hand on his arm. "We only meant to help you because she's so pretty and has all that political experience, and we had been talking to her nana about her for a while. Then we met her, and she seemed so pretty and eager and...pretty."

"You like pretty," Gramma added coyly. "And so we suggested the lass be your campaign manager."

He felt his eyes shutter closed, knowing there was no reasoning with an eighty-eight-year-old Irishwoman on a mission to marry off every single grandchild while she still had breath in her body. Still, he had to try.

"You two have to stop sticking your noses in everyone's personal lives."

"'Twould be like holdin' our breath, lad."

He heard the laughter from behind the screen door and more from his cousin Shane, who joined them on the patio with Chloe, who held their six-month-old, Annabelle.

"All of town hall is buzzing with the news," Chloe

said, dodging the grabby hands of her baby, who managed to pull a sizable strand out of Chloe's always-neat ponytail.

"Happy buzzing?" Connor asked.

"Well, Aunt Blanche isn't *un*happy to have another candidate."

"Wait a second," Pru said, sitting up straight, a frown pulling her young features. "Your aunt Blanche is *happy* about Connor having more opposition? What's up with that?"

"Exactly!" Yiayia interjected. "What kind of family traitor is this mayor?"

"She's happy because she wants someone to beat Easterbrook," Connor said. "And I don't think she's thrilled with the idea of Frank the Dog stepping into the shoes of Frank the Mayor."

Chloe sighed, brushing back that loose hair. "You're right," she said. "Aunt Blanche is torn, obviously. She would love family in the office, and you are that, through me."

"Through me," Shane added.

"'Tis all family," Gramma reminded them. "And we help each other."

"By sending me a really strong opponent?" He shot her an accusatory glance.

"By sending you a…"

"Wife," Yiayia said.

He choked hard, ignoring the snickering from the others. "For God's sake, ladies. No more matchmaking. We're adults. We can handle our own lives."

Gramma Finnie crossed her arms in front of her polka dot sweater. "Then what's takin' you so long, lad?"

"I was on the job already, Gramma. If you'd just let things be, I'd have had a better chance with her *and* the election. I'd already met her a few weeks ago."

"And had, what, exactly zero dates with her since then?"

He huffed out a noisy breath and shook his head. Did he really have to get romance advice from them? Here and now?

But Gramma Finnie ignored his not-so-subtle message. "We thought if she was your campaign manager, you two would have...what was that thing, Pru? The thing you mentioned in your modern literature paper?"

"Forced proximity."

"That sounds illegal," he shot back. And fun.

"Well, they did the frenemies thing with Alex and Grace," Pru said. "And that worked."

"And friends turned into a couple with Cassie and Braden."

"What are you even talking about?" Connor asked.

"Tropes and themes," Pru said. "We're studying them in my English class, and my teacher says as long as we can find them in literature, it doesn't matter if we use Shakespeare or romance novels, so you can guess which one I picked." She lifted a paperback next to her, showcasing a photoshopped calendar shot of a shirtless guy on the cover.

"You're allowed to read that trash in high school?"

Her back straightened. "It is not trash, Connor Mahoney." She fired the words at him. "These are stories about empowerment and love."

"And...frenemies?"

She shrugged. "That's just one trope. There's also hot neighbor next door, fake fiancée, best friend's little sister. The Dogmothers can give them all a try."

Everyone else thought it was hilarious, but irritation marched up his spine and settled into a low-grade headache at the base of his brain.

"You are all out of your ever-lovin' minds." He leaned closer and sliced all three of the meddlers, including the teenage one, with a warning gaze. "How about you just let me play *The Bachelor*? How's that for a trope?"

"That's a show, dummy, not a trope," Pru said. "The trope would be…love in a month? Insta-love? Reality show? There's a lot of ways you could go with that."

"How about going this way…*out* of my love life, please?"

"I'd hardly call it a 'love' life, lad."

"More like a love-'em-and-leave-'em life," Pru muttered.

"And a lonely one," Yiayia added with a dramatic, sad sigh.

He just stood there for a moment, then let out a soft laugh of disbelief. "Okay, you work your…your *tropes* on someone else. Now she's my opponent in the race and…"

"And that screws up your chances of *ever* going out with her," Garrett finished.

He glanced at his cousin, hating that he was right. He didn't want to miss out on a chance with Sadie, but it might be too late. And God knew he'd given it his best shot. "Pretty sure that ship has sailed."

"Ships can be turned around," Gramma Finnie said. "It takes a strong wind and a keen sailor, but it can be done."

"Honestly, you are relentless."

"I like relentless. Has a nice ring to it, donchya think?" Gramma pushed up her old bones and put a gnarled hand on his arm. "Come now, lad. Let me pour you a Jameson's. You look like you need one."

Chapter Seven

It wasn't Capitol Hill, that was for sure.

Still, walking up the steps to Bitter Bark's town hall had a certain charm to it, especially when Sadie turned and looked out over the square where the giant statue of Thaddeus Ambrose Bushrod stood sentry over the small town he founded in the mid-1800s.

As she entered the town hall and crossed the marble lobby to the elevator, she remembered the highlights from her long conversation with Nana and Boomie last evening, discussing all the town history that they knew. Of course, the discussion slid into personal pasts, how they'd moved here in the early sixties and Boomie got a job managing the local market. But when Elaine Winthrop Hartman was mentioned, the old sadness came over Nana, and they called it a night.

Which only steeled Sadie's resolve to beat the man who was so much a part of that heartache. Obviously, he wasn't the only one to blame for the broken marriage and family. But Sadie had spent so much of her life blaming her mother, it actually felt comforting to redistribute some of that old resentment to the man who helped make it happen.

But today, she had to put the old hurts out of her head and force herself to think about the Election Committee meeting that was starting in a few minutes. This would be the first time she'd seen Mitch Easterbrook since the whole affair blew up and Mom moved as far away from Bitter Bark—and her family—as possible. She had to be strong and on her game.

Plus, there would be another man in the room putting her off-balance. Sweet and sexy as he was, Connor Mahoney was still her opponent—well, his dog was—and he might try to trip her up. She already knew the words *local hero* would be in every message he sent to the voters of Bitter Bark.

She was the outsider. He even called her *DC*.

Except when he'd said it, instead of an insult, he made the initials sound like a term of endearment and kind of made her toes—

"Hey, DC."

Curl.

She turned and offered a smile, which faltered and slipped at the sight of Connor in a white dress shirt that fit his broad shoulders like it had been tailor-made to melt over his muscles. He wore a narrow, understated striped navy tie...and Frank wore one of almost the same color and pattern.

She looked from one to the other and sighed out a laugh. "Honestly, no one else stands a chance against this guy."

"All part of my campaign plan," he said. "Also what happens when you have dog groomers in the family."

"Hello, handsome." She reached for Frank's head, but the dog backed up and stared nervously at her.

"Frank, when a lady calls you handsome, you smile and say 'thank you.' Also, you could add, 'You look gorgeous, too.' Watch and learn, doggo." He took a slow appraisal of her dove-gray jacket and skirt, lingering on her no-nonsense pumps, then moving his gaze back to her face with a light in his eyes. "Although gorgeous would be an understatement."

She smiled as the elevator doors opened, and he gestured for her to go first into the empty car. "You should give flirting lessons to all the poor guys who are clueless about it."

"It's not flirting," he said with the slightest hint of disappointment in his voice. "I'm just naturally charming. And…" He leaned his head a little closer. "Brutally honest. God, you smell good."

She just laughed and shook her head. "Is this part of your plan, too?"

"To compliment you out of the race? Maybe." He winked. "Or maybe I really think you smell good and see no reason not to tell you."

The elevator bounced as it came to a stop, making Frank bark.

"You tell her, Frankendog."

"Frankendog? I thought he was named for the former mayor."

He opened his mouth to respond, but the doors whooshed open, and Mayor Wilkins was standing there with a file folder against her chest.

"Oh, there you are! Perfect. The Election Committee is in conference room two. I have to run down to the second floor for a second."

They exchanged places with her, letting Mayor Wilkins into the elevator as they stepped into the hall.

"Frankendog?" Sadie repeated when the doors closed, and they were alone again, her voice rising.

At the tone, Frank backed up, then dropped his head with a whimper.

"Oh my God, I scared him." She instantly bent down to pet him, but he cowered close to Connor. "I'm so sorry."

"It's okay, Sadie." He reached for her hand to straighten her and look into her eyes. "And yes, truth be told, I named him that without thinking. The minute I did, I realized it might be politically incorrect or offensive to someone somewhere, so I made up the Mayor Frank thing on the fly. Will you use that against me in a campaign message?"

"Not if you don't mention my cat was found outside a DNC office and that's why she's named Demi-cat. You never know how that's going to go over."

His jaw loosened. "Okay, we both have secrets." With a quick smile, he offered for her to go ahead of him to the conference room, where two men and two women—none of whom were Mitch Easterbrook, thank God—were chatting at the table. Maybe he wouldn't show. Maybe, when he heard Sadie was a candidate, he'd dropped out.

"There's our local hero!" The woman with wavy hair and plastic-rimmed glasses rose from her seat and reached for the dog. "I saw your picture on the front page of the *Bitter Bark Banner* this morning! Looking so good at the top of the town hall stairs."

Frank looked a little horrified at the attention, barely moving when Connor led him around the table.

"Hey, Nellie." Connor reached to shake the

woman's hand. "He takes a minute to get used to people," he added quickly. "By the way, nice job on the Saint Patrick's Day decorations at the library. You do this Irish boy proud."

The woman, somewhere in her mid-fifties, blushed like a teenager being asked to dance. *Because Connor Mahoney had that effect on all women*, Sadie mused.

"Nellie Shaker, this is Sadie Hartman, our newest mayoral candidate. Sadie, Nellie is our—"

"Head librarian and historian," Sadie finished, remembering what Connor had told her that first night outside the bar. "And also on the Election Committee?" she guessed as they shook hands.

"Actually, no. I was asked to be here today." A frown pulled behind Nellie's plastic glasses. "You don't know why?"

Connor and Sadie glanced at each other, then shook their heads.

"Bitter Bark history test?" he guessed.

But no one else at the table was smiling as Nellie threw a look at the others. "They don't know?"

"Know what?" Sadie asked.

"You'll see." The man sitting next to Nellie stood and extended his hand to Sadie. "Ricardo Mancini."

"Oh, you own Ricardo's." She recognized the name and the signature white hair. "It's always been one of my favorite restaurants."

"I'm so sorry I don't recognize you." He looked intently at her, a light New York accent coming through in every word. "I thought I knew all my regular customers."

"Well, I haven't been there in many years, but..." Because she hadn't lived here since she was eighteen and was trying to act like a regular. "But I actually had my first date at Ricardo's."

"Ah, well I love to hear stories like that. Did that romance last?"

"Truth? No. I don't remember his last name," she admitted, making them all laugh. "But I will never forget the lasagna."

Connor gave her an easy smile and a wink. "Good save. And do you know Linda May Dunlap? Just mention the raspberry croissants, and you're golden."

"I had one two days ago when I was in your bakery with my grandparents."

"I saw you there," Linda May said, shaking Sadie's hand. "I wish I had known then you were so interested in running for mayor."

Was that a little dig at her spontaneous decision? Before she could answer, a young man at the end of the table stood to greet them. "Gavin Stocker, vice president of the Bitter Bark Chamber of Commerce and head of the Election Committee." He offered a firm handshake that matched his clipped hair, sharp tie, and zero-nonsense attitude. He actually looked like he'd stepped out of Nathan's lobbying firm. "Welcome to Bitter Bark, Ms. Hartman. We are thrilled to have someone of your qualifications on the ballot."

"Ouch," Connor joked, taking a seat. "Dog's been dissed."

"Not the dog," Gavin said, barely under his breath.

Connor chuckled, but Sadie could practically taste the tension between the two.

"All righty, then." Mayor Wilkins careened into the room, looking a little more frazzled than she had yesterday. "Mitch is here."

Ice slid through Sadie's veins as she turned to the tall man in the doorway. His hair was more salt than pepper now, his torso a little thicker than she remembered, and his face bore a few more lines, but all she could see was the man who played such a pivotal role in shattering Sadie's world.

Next to her, Connor grunted softly, all humor disappearing from his expression.

The rest of the people in attendance just kind of gave tight smiles, as if they all felt the same way about him. After an awkward beat, Connor pushed his chair out and stood, a little taller than Mitch and so, so much classier when he extended his hand.

"Mitch. How are you?"

"Mahoney." He shook his hand, but he stole a glance at Sadie, then pointedly ignored her. "How are things at the fire department?"

"Fine. I think you know Frank, our hero dog and your other worthy opponent."

He looked down at the dog, who had most of his body on top of Connor's shoes. "With all due respect to your clever and newsworthy idea, I'm not going to dignify Frank with an acknowledgment."

Disgust crawled up Sadie's spine. He hadn't changed. He was still awful, only now he had a paunch and gray hair. *Oh, Mom. How could you have been so stupid?*

"Then how about Sadie?" Connor said, as if he wouldn't let the guy get away with dismissing her, too. "Will you dignify this opponent with your acknowledgment?"

The question sent a zing of appreciation through her, but no small amount of fear. How was Mitch going to handle their past? He *had* to remember exactly who she was.

He merely nodded at her. "I don't have any opponents," he said as he walked straight to the empty chair at the head of the table, which, of course, was where Mayor Wilkins should have sat.

"Now that's confidence," Connor joked as they all sat down.

"Ah, actually..." Mayor Wilkins took an empty chair next to Nellie, and the two women shared a meaningful glance. Only, Sadie had no idea what the meaning was.

"Is something wrong with my application?" she asked. "Was it approved?"

"It was," Linda May said quickly. "We would have loved to have you on the slate, but..."

"But what?" Sadie and Connor asked the question in perfect unison, which did a little to erase her sudden feeling of being very much alone and on the outs in this room.

"Now, listen," Mayor Wilkins said, her voice tight and her cheeks flushed, "let's calmly tell Connor and Sadie what's going on."

"Then do so, Blanche," Mitch said to her impatiently. "I have another meeting shortly."

With a sigh, the mayor tapped the table with her fingers. "The Election Committee meeting is officially called to order."

With her chest growing tighter with each passing moment, Sadie glanced at Connor, sitting to her right. His gaze was moving around the table, his jaw clenched, his shoulders tense. He didn't like this any more than she did, that much was obvious.

"I'll take it from here," Gavin said from the other side of the table. "Ladies and gentlemen, as some of you know, the Election Committee has been in conversation all morning with Mr. Easterbrook, and that's why we've called in our town librarian, Nellie, to verify the fact that…"

At the dramatic pause, Ricardo Mancini barely concealed his eye roll and a huffed breath, and Linda May bit her lip and stared at her blank notebook, visibly swallowing whatever it was she wanted to say.

"Oh, for God's sake, just say it," Mitch demanded. "You can't run. Neither one of you. You're both out of the race."

"*What*?" Once again, they spoke in the same tone and with the same incredulity.

Mitch just looked at Gavin and nodded. "Tell them."

Gavin cleared his throat, shuffled some papers, then adjusted his horn-rims. "I have in front of me a copy of the original founding charter, penned by Captain Thaddeus Ambrose Bushrod on October 22, 1867, after he claimed the settlement of Bitter Bark, North Carolina, as a village to be governed under him. In it, he states the requirements of any man who would, I'm quoting now, 'henceforth hold the title of governor.'" Gavin looked up. "Which, in case you don't know, was officially amended to include 'mayor' by Thaddeus Bushrod's son in 1902, with the express stipulation that all other requirements for the governorship would hold for the mayor."

Connor slowly leaned forward and directed his gaze to Gavin. "And your point is?"

"His point is that old Thad had a different vision in

mind for mayor than you, your dog, or this girl." Mitch still didn't look at her, but Sadie felt Connor bristle.

"She's actually a grown woman," he said to Mitch.

Sadie let out a little sigh. "Thank you," she said under her breath.

Mitch flicked his fingers at Gavin. "Of course. Keep going."

Sadie sat straighter as slow rage marched through her whole body. Next to her, she could practically feel the same thing happening to Connor.

"The bylaws and requirements to hold the office are numerous, and they do include a required thirty signatures from 'well-respected citizens of the town,'" Gavin said.

"That's it?" Sadie leaned forward. "I need to get thirty signatures?"

Connor nodded. "You do, and I'll help you get them," he said.

Her heart flipped at the concession and the sudden shift the room had taken from "us against each other" to "us against them."

"There's more," Gavin said. "In addition to the signatures, each candidate must meet personal requirements that ensure they are reputable individuals who honor God and family."

"Is this about the dog?" Connor asked. "Because I sat in this room with you, and everyone there agreed, voted, and passed the ordinance—"

"Statute," Mayor Wilkins corrected.

"Whatever. You all agreed that Frank would be a ceremonial mayor for publicity and town morale and that I would act as his chief of staff. In that role, I, not

Frank, needed to meet the legal requirements of any mayoral candidate, which I do. If needed, I can have an additional thirty signatures by noon. Is there anything else?"

"Yes," Gavin said. "I'm not done reading."

Connor waved his hand in that direction. "By all means, let's hear about the rules and regs from two hundred years ago."

"One hundred and fifty-three," Mitch corrected. "And if proven governing documents are good enough for our country, then they are good enough for Bitter Bark. Gavin? Read section four, article two, please."

He took a breath and looked back at the paper in front of him. "Section four deals with the reputation, moral aptitude, and community standing. Article one states that the candidates will be members in good standing of a church."

"Old school, but fine," Connor said. "I was baptized and confirmed at St. Gabriel's." He turned to Sadie. "You?"

"My family went to First Baptist, steps from the front door of the building we're in."

"And," Gavin continued as if they hadn't spoken, "they will be members of 'local families of good repute.'"

Connor leaned back with a huffed breath. "Mine takes up half the town, and our reputation is rock-solid," he said. "And Sadie's grandparents are well known and respected."

Oh God. Oh *God*. Was Mitch going to throw her parents' divorce on the table? *A divorce he caused by sleeping with my mother?*

She held her breath as Gavin leaned forward, his

gaze moving around the table as he lifted the paper with a slow intake of breath. "Article two states that 'any candidate must be married, widowed, or betrothed at the time of the election.'"

For a moment, no one said a word.

"*Excuse me*?" Sadie barely whispered the question.

"You heard him," Mitch said. "Married, widowed, or betrothed."

She choked a disbelieving laugh, relieved that the ugly past hadn't been brought into it. "Well, can't you change that? I have to believe a simple vote from the town council to add a codicil that is in keeping with twenty-first-century social norms shouldn't be that difficult."

"No." Nellie, the librarian, swallowed as the room turned its attention to her. "No codicils can be added to Captain Bushrod's town charter. The bylaws and constitution, yes. But not Captain Bushrod's personal charter. It was in his will that it can never be amended except by a blood relative and there are none left."

"But this document is a hundred and fifty years old," Sadie insisted. "I mean, I'm surprised a woman can even run under those constraints."

"There's nothing about gender," Nellie said. "But the charter is truly etched in stone."

"Literally," Sadie grumbled. "During the actual Stone Age."

Nellie gave a conceding tip of her head. "For the most part, it's sound and holds up to today's laws. But the charter was signed by the first town board of governors and has been upheld since that day. We have never had a mayor who wasn't married or, in Blanche's case, widowed."

"And since neither one of you are..." Mitch's mouth turned down as his shoulder went up. "You cannot be on the ballot."

Fury snapped at Sadie. "That's the most ridiculous thing I've ever heard, and trust me, I've heard a lot in politics. What's it going to take to get this changed?"

"It can't be," Mayor Wilkins said.

"Even if we put it to the citizens? There must be some way to amend the charter by a public vote." Sadie looked from one face to the next, all blank, disappointed, or, in Mitch's case, smug.

All but Connor, who was silent, looking down at the table.

"Are you going to just sit there and accept this?" Sadie asked.

Very slowly, he lifted his gaze to meet hers, his blue eyes as serious as she'd ever seen them. "Could I talk to you outside for a moment?"

He was dropping out of the race. Seriously? He didn't have the backbone to flatten the very first roadblock? She'd expected so much more from him, but maybe if it couldn't be solved with a disarming smile or a cute dog, then he'd quit.

Disappointment seeped into her veins. She didn't want Connor to be a quitter. In fact, his tenacity was one of the most attractive things about him. Oh well. Wasn't the first time she misjudged a man.

"Sure," she said, pushing her chair back.

He surprised her by taking her hand as she rose, his fingers warm and strong.

"Nellie." He reached into his pocket and pulled out a small plastic bag. "Give Frank as many of these as he needs if he gets upset. We'll be right back."

Sadie gave him a confused look, but let him lead her out, closing the door behind them.

"Connor, I—"

"Shhh. I have to ask you an important question." He glanced into offices as they passed, each occupied. "Somewhere private."

They reached a steel door at the end of the hallway, a square window showing it led to the dimly lit stairwell. He pushed the door open and guided her into the chilly area.

"What is it?" she asked. "Why are you out here instead of fighting those ridiculous, insane, stupid—"

His mouth came down on hers, stealing her breath and words, stunning her, and jolting her whole body with the electrical charge when their lips made contact.

"What..." She pushed him back, gasping for air. "What in God's name are you doing?"

"I thought we should kiss."

"*Now?*"

"At least once before we get engaged. Will you marry me, Sadie Hartman?"

Chapter Eight

The thing Connor liked about Sadie, besides pretty much everything, was how easy it was to know what she was thinking just by watching her expression change. And this was like taking in a feature film.

As his words hit, her wide eyes blinked with astonishment, then dismay, and then utter disbelief. Her delicate jaw dropped a bit as she realized he wasn't actually kidding, then her pretty lips formed an O as his brilliant logic registered. And then, very slowly, delicious dimples deepened with a smile, and she dropped her head back with a hearty laugh.

"I totally underestimated you, Mahoney."

"Is that a yes?"

The laughter faded as she drew back, sliding out of his arms, staring at him.

"Good idea, huh?"

"Good?" She put her hand on her chest as if she had to catch her breath. "Uh, ridiculous, but A for creativity. That's some…thought process you've got going on in there."

"Honestly, it wasn't me. Something my cousin Pru

said yesterday gave me the idea." What had she called the trope? Fake fiancée? "But it's a brilliant solution, and you know it. It'll shut Easterbrook down *and* shut him up, which is all I ever want to do to that scumbag."

"He is a scumbag," she muttered, making him happy she could see that, too.

"So, say you'll be my fiancée and stick his article two where the sun...shut him up for good."

"Not gonna lie, as political campaign strategies go in the face of absurd two-hundred-year-old small-town laws? It's genius, but..." She drew a little bit farther back. "You can't think for one minute that we could pull that off with any credibility."

What he liked, all the way down to his toes, what that she didn't dismiss the idea out of hand. "Why not?"

"Uh, because it's a lie?"

"So make it a truth."

"Connor." She laughed softly, shaking her head. "It's preposterous."

"No more than a dog running for mayor."

"Which, if you have your way, means I'd be engaged to your dog."

"You could do worse," he joked. "Come on, Sadie. Hear me out. They don't know what our relationship is. You could have come back to Bitter Bark because we've been carrying on a torrid long-distance romance and finally want to live in the same town."

"Torrid?"

"I don't do tepid."

She put her hands on his chest as if she wanted to push him away, but left them there for a second, looking up at him. "I can't lie. It goes against everything I stand for."

"You want Easterbrook as mayor?"

She shut her eyes as if the very idea sliced her.

"Talk about not having principles," Connor said with a scoffing laugh. "That man's never met a principle in his life he hasn't violated every day of the week and twice on Sunday." He shook his head. "Obviously, you can see the guy's a bona fide asshole."

"That's being kind."

"Right? And trust me...he's even worse than you know," Connor ground out, forcing himself to say no more. He had no right to reveal things he knew as an EMT who'd been called to that bastard's house when a woman had damn near overdosed on a mix of alcohol and antidepressants. Mitch had tried to pass her off as a family friend—who apparently slept in the master bedroom while Mrs. Easterbrook was conveniently getting her eyes done at some spa in the Caribbean.

No, he wouldn't share that, but anyone who'd ever had to use Easterbrook Funeral Home came away with lighter pockets and a heavier heart. "He can't win, Sadie."

"I know," she said, gnawing on her lip. "That's the whole reason..." She swallowed. "No, he cannot win. I agree. One of us has to run and beat him."

"Exactly. And with this rule, *neither* of us can run, and no one will have the nerve, or even the time now, to launch a campaign against him. I'm gonna be straight with you, Sadie. I want to win. I do. I love the idea of being mayor, but I'd risk losing to you if it means keeping him from having that much power in

Bitter Bark. And with two of us on the ballot, he has an even smaller chance of winning. So let's get engaged."

She gave a little shiver at the words. "What happens…after the election?"

"Gavin said the candidate has to be married, widowed, or betrothed *at the time of the election.* Nothing about an amicable breakup a few days or weeks later."

"'The candidate' meaning Frank?" she asked. "You still want to use him as a gimmick?"

He took a breath, thinking hard about it, weighing Frank in the whole mix. "You know, the dog *is* a gimmick, I'll give you that, but I believe in him. Bitter Bark grew exponentially the year we were Better Bark, and turning this place into a dog haven was a very smart move. I think people know that and love the idea. I'm betting on him to do great things for this town."

"*If* you win."

"I can't win if I can't run, and neither can you. Unless you have another fiancé you can pull out of your hat in the next five minutes. If not, say yes to my proposal."

She stared at him, still, thinking. "I really despise unethical behavior in politics."

"I just asked you to marry me. Who's to say that's 'a lie'? It's a question, answer, and a…state of our relationship."

"Relationship?" She gave him a dubious look. "We barely know each other."

"Insta-love."

"Excuse me?"

"Another one of my little cousin's great ideas. Come on, Sadie. We don't have much time before they rubber-stamp that jerk right into the mayor's office."

Her eyes narrowed. "We can't let that happen," she agreed. "But this is so fraught with crater-sized holes."

"Tell me one and watch me fill it."

"How about that we've failed to mention this to anyone?"

He shrugged. "Keeping it quiet. Lots of people do. Next?"

"What about the God knows how many women you've dated in the last few months while we're supposedly having this torrid-not-tepid long-distance romance? It makes you look like…a cheater."

"I'm not and never have been. Not to mention, I haven't had a date in more than a month. Frank's the only company I've had in bed for quite some time. Anything else?" He searched her face, seeing the torture as more questions formed, and he suddenly guessed one that he didn't like at all, but had to ask. "Do you have a boyfriend back in DC?"

"Not anymore," she said. "But I haven't been single very long, and plenty of people in Washington know that."

"But you are now." He had to be certain of that before he took this any further.

"I am."

"Then does the word *whirlwind* mean anything to you?"

"With the town's most infamous love-'em-and-leave-'em guy?"

"That's just folklore and a reputation I let grow

because it's funny. Look, have I been in a long-term relationship? No, I don't do them, true. But who's to say that if the perfect woman waltzed into my life..."

"Perfect?" she snorted softly.

He touched her cheek, grazing his knuckles along her jaw, making her eyes shutter. "Damn close, Ear Girl."

Fighting a smile at that, she studied him again, her features softening to a new expression, one that gave him real hope. She was seriously considering this.

"Won't people think it's weird that we're engaged and running against each other?" she asked. "What couple does that?"

"The couple that wants to win," he replied. "We tell them that this way, one of us is sure to be mayor, and the other will support him or her completely. It's a fantastic hook. The media will eat it up. In fact, this idea will steal all the spotlight from Mitch, and we'll campaign on our own platforms. No animosity, no arguing, no dirt. Just a clean campaign that'll make people want to vote for Frank—"

"Or me."

He smiled. "But not Eastercrook."

She huffed out a breath. "God, I hate him."

"That didn't take long."

"I...we...knew him before."

Of course, she had lived here long enough to know the guy's rep, and he could tell by the surrender in her voice and softness in her shoulders that she was coming around to his idea.

"Then..." He took her hands in his, lifting them to his chest. "You want me to get down on one knee? 'Cause I will."

A little color drained from her face. "You've got a dog running for mayor and a fake engagement between two opposing candidates. Let's skip the pretend proposal."

"Is that a yes?"

Once again, she bit her lip and looked at him, searching his eyes as if she could find answers there. "It's not a no."

"What does that mean?"

"It means I'll go back into that room and announce that we just got engaged, but I will not pretend that it's anything other than a statement about that archaic rule and how stupid it is. I will be 'betrothed'—which sounds more like the meaningless business arrangement it is. I won't act like I'm madly in love with you. I won't tell stories about some whirlwind long-distance relationship. I don't want to lie, but I'll do what I have to in order to keep that man from running unopposed."

He looked at her for a long time, nodding slowly. "Okay, then," he finally said. "We're engaged. I thought it would be scarier than this."

"I thought it would be more romantic than this." She held up her left hand. "I even thought there might be jewelry involved."

He sucked in a quick breath. "We need a ring."

"It's not necess—"

"Oh, hell yeah, it is. It makes it official and believable. So, come on, I have an idea." He started to tug her to the door, then stopped and turned. "One kiss before we do this? You know, for authenticity and to seal the deal?"

She stared at him for a moment, no doubt winding

up her next retort to shut him down and remind him that this bogus idea was so far from authentic that it crushed her honest-to-the-core soul. And, for God's sake, there would be no *kissing*.

But then she stepped closer, put her hands on his cheeks, and pulled her face to his. Without a word, she leaned into him and kissed him square on the mouth.

Her lips were warm and soft and felt like they melted under his. Angling his head, he took more, unable to stop himself from wrapping her in his arms again. She let out the softest, sweetest whimper in her throat, sliding her hands around his neck and holding tight while they both got lost in the sensation.

"What on earth is going on?" The door flew open and hit the wall with a crack, revealing Mayor Wilkins, who stood with one hand on her hip and a packet of papers in the other, staring at them like a high school principal catching teenagers making out in the janitor's closet.

"We're kissing, Blanche," Connor said, still holding Sadie and loving that she didn't whip away and try to pretend they weren't.

"And we're waiting," the mayor shot back, looking from one to the other, her expression one of disbelief. "Are you ever coming back, or has Easterbrook scared you away?"

Sadie turned and slid her arm around Connor's waist. "We'll be right there, Mayor Wilkins. We were just...ironing out some details of our campaigns."

She used the papers to swipe up and down at them. "Is that what you're calling this?"

"Give us one minute, Mayor," Connor said, holding tight to the woman next to him. "We just have one more minor detail to agree on, then we'll meet with the committee."

"One…more…" She narrowed her eyes. "What kind of detail?"

"The kind that people discuss when they are engaged," he said.

"*Betrothed*," Sadie corrected.

Blanche gasped. Her hand fell from her hip. And her jaw dropped so hard it could have hit her chest. "Oh…oh. *Oh.* You wouldn't."

"The law is ridiculous," Sadie said. "Sometimes you have to fight a ridiculous law with an outrageous idea."

"That's just…" The mayor looked from one to the other. "That's not…" She let her shoulders drop. "That's actually…" She sighed, frustrated and obviously weighing every word. "Quite inspired."

"We can't let him win," Connor said softly. "You know that, Blanche. You know it in your heart. You know how your late husband would feel."

"Frank would twirl in his grave if that man sat in the mayor's seat at town council meetings," she said softly.

"We feel the same way," Sadie said. "He can't win, so we're fighting his old-school rules with our newfangled idea."

"But…" Blanche lifted the papers in her hand. "You need to know that I just spent ten minutes reading that charter very carefully, and right under article two, it says…" She looked at the paper and squinted, then shoved the packet toward them. "I forgot my glasses."

Connor took the papers and skimmed the words and numbers, looking under the detested article to read out loud.

"'Any individual in any position of governance who willfully and knowingly commits an act or omission not in accordance with the commandments of this charter will forfeit their position immediately.' What the hell does that mean?"

"I think," Sadie said, turning the paper to reread it, "it means if the elected official is caught lying, he or she must step down immediately." She looked up at him. "Pretty sure that pretending to be engaged would be considered 'an act or omission not in accordance with the commandments of this charter.'"

"Then...we don't pretend, Sadie." Connor looked hard at her.

She stared at him, a storm of emotions in her eyes. "We don't?"

"Or we are so convincing, no one can possibly accuse us of committing an act not in accordance with the charter." He put his finger under her chin and lifted her face to him. "Can you do that?" Especially after that "meaningless business arrangement" speech she just gave.

"To beat him, I can."

"Okay, then," Blanche said, sliding the papers from Connor's hand. "I'll give you two a few more minutes. And as far as I'm concerned, we didn't have this conversation." Without another word, she backed out of the stairwell, letting the door clunk behind her.

For a long moment, they stood silent, still arm in arm. Very slowly, he turned to face her, easing her body into his. "Come on, Ear Girl. There are worse ways to win an election."

She stared up at him for a long time and finally, slowly nodded.

"Is that a yes?" he asked one more time.

She didn't answer, but got up on her toes and put her lips on his again for another long and sweet kiss. He held her tighter and closer, letting their bodies press and find the natural curve where they both fit.

Blood thrummed in his head as he tasted her lip gloss and inhaled that soft, sweet, citrusy scent of Sadie. She gripped his arms and slid her hands up to his shoulders, angling her head, deepening the kiss, letting heat build. Then she drew back with her eyes still closed and her lips parted.

"Yeah," she said on a strangled breath. "I can fake...feelings."

But they both knew the truth. Nobody was faking anything.

Chapter Nine

"If you lose that ring, Connor Mahoney, Shane will kill you, and I'll hide the body." Chloe pointed at Connor as they were leaving her office on the third floor. Like Mayor Wilkins, Chloe had been surprised by their "announcement," but when Connor explained the situation and asked to borrow her engagement ring, she didn't hesitate.

"You'll get it right back," he called as they headed out of her office to return to the conference room. "I promise."

Sadie looked down at the impressive oval solitaire on her left ring finger, knowing its worth from the endless conversations she'd had with her ex about diamonds. Not one on her finger, of course, but his expertise on the subject had been remarkable.

"You sure this isn't going to blow up in our faces?" she mused, still a little dizzy from that last kiss.

"What's the worst that could happen?" he asked as they slipped back into the stairwell and headed up to the fourth floor.

"They throw us out of the race completely? Oh, and I could lose this rock."

"Please don't."

She slowed her step and took a steadying breath, but he turned to her, putting a warm hand on her cheek. "You ready, future Mrs. Mahoney?"

The words and gesture, meant as a joke, literally made her a little off-balance.

"Maybe save the affection for when we're in public."

"Says the girl who just kissed the daylights out of me. *Twice*."

"I don't generally buy things without trying them on. *Twice*."

"And I fit like a dream."

She snorted softly. "Shut up." She pointed to the closed door of the conference room. "It's show time."

He draped an arm around her and planted a kiss on her cheek that was unnecessary, but gave just the boost she needed. "Let's crush the competition."

They both took a breath as he opened the conference room door. "Sorry for that—"

Frank lunged at Connor, letting out a few desperate barks demanding to know where he'd been, swatting at Connor's stomach, and whipping that tail like a big, hairy windshield wiper.

Connor laughed and eased him back down to the ground. "Easy, bud. Easy. And sorry for the delay, everyone. Sadie and I had to agree on something."

"To officially withdraw from the race?" Easterbrook asked, impatience and irritation imprinted on his scowling face. "Gavin has the paperwork ready."

"No," Sadie said. "To go public with our news." Without a word, they joined hands and raised them so the diamond could sparkle in the sunbeam that poured in through the window.

"Sadie and I are…"

He lifted a brow at her, letting her do the honors of dropping the bomb.

"I believe the word Thad Bushrod used was *betrothed*," she said, smiling at him.

"What?" The reaction reverberated around the room in a chorus of voices at various pitches and levels of astonishment, including from Frank, who barked at the general commotion. But no one was louder or angrier than Mitch Easterbrook, who launched out of his chair and turned as white as his crisp, collared shirt.

"What the hell do you take us for, Mahoney?" he demanded, addressing Connor exclusively. "Idiots?"

Frank barked and crawled under the table.

"A lot of things, Mitch, but not that." Connor dropped to his knees to comfort the dog. "And congratulations would be nice."

"Congratulate my ass," Mitch hissed. "This is a farce, just like your dog running for mayor."

"You're the one who brought in antiquated rules," Sadie said, gesturing toward the paperwork in front of Gavin. "And we're willing to comply with them."

"So which one of you is out of the race?" Easterbrook asked.

"Neither one of us." Connor stood and put his arm around her again. "Frank is running, with me as his chief of staff, and Sadie is running as she announced. We're both running."

"Against each other?" Easterbrook's voice rose.

"That's usually how engaged people spend their time," Connor joked, getting a few laughs from everyone except Mitch.

As the others muttered comments to each other and

themselves, Mitch gathered up some papers, flipping through them frantically, tapping his finger on some words Sadie assumed were the ones they'd read in the stairwell. "You *will* forfeit."

"We will not," Connor lobbed back.

Easterbrook slammed the papers down and stared hard at Sadie. "I should have expected something like this from you."

The force of his words and the unbelievable nerve it took to speak them made her take a step back.

"Watch it," Connor ground out, tightening his grip on her, but narrowing his eyes in warning.

Mitch ignored him, staring hard at Sadie. Could anyone else see the challenge in his eyes? Was he daring her to go public with what she knew about him? Because Mitch Easterbrook also "knowingly committed an act" not in accordance with the "be of good repute" part. He had to know she had that on him.

"So you come waltzing back to town after almost two decades and think you can turn things upside down with some...*fake* relationship?"

She lifted her chin defiantly, hoping he could read the warning in her eyes. He definitely had more to lose than she did. "Do not push me."

The entire room went dead silent, and she could feel Connor's questioning gaze on her, but she refused to back down. Mitch finally retreated, getting his papers and shifting his blistering stare to Connor. "Typical of you, Mahoney. Everything's a joke."

Connor flinched so slightly that no one else might have even noticed, but Sadie did, and her own accusation came to mind. Easy to see why Easterbrook thought that, with the canine mayoral candidate and those quick one-liners, but the man who made impassioned speeches about the town? She was going to give him the benefit of the doubt.

"The joke is you thinking you could run for mayor unopposed," Connor said, his voice low and steady. "So we will see you on the campaign trail."

"Oh, speaking of," Mayor Wilkins said. "We need to set a date for the first debate."

"I don't care what day or time it is," Mitch muttered, rounding the conference room table. "You're going down, Mahoney. You and your dumb ideas and your stupid dog and your...your..." He threw a glance at Sadie.

"I would be very careful with your next word," Connor said softly.

Mitch shuttered his eyes, then marched to the door and slammed it as he walked out, leaving the room in stunned silence before it suddenly erupted with questions, comments, and a few very noisy barks.

Then Mayor Wilkins extended her hand to Sadie. "May I be the first to congratulate you, my dear?" She gave a wistful smile. "And you, Lieutenant Mahoney."

The rest of the room chimed in with their congratulations, none that heartfelt, all a little skeptical. Gavin simply flipped through some papers in front of him, which Sadie assumed were copies of what Easterbrook had.

"He's right, you know," Gavin finally said softly, his words quieting everyone down. "This is a creative solution, obviously, but if it's just that, then he can make a compelling argument for a forfeit if either of you wins. And he will."

"Let him try," Connor said confidently. "We're in one hundred percent agreement that this is real."

"And if you dissolve the relationship after the election?" Gavin asked.

"Not a chance." Conner pulled her closer. "Right, honey?"

She just smiled at him like he hung the moon, because…show time.

Then she turned to Gavin. "If you would be so kind," she said. "Can you tell me if, other than a betrothal and thirty signatures from locals, there is *anything* else I need to do to formalize my run for mayor? Blood from a stone? Family tree tattooed on my arm? Two chickens sacrificed in Bushrod Square?"

Gavin ignored the chuckles around the room and gave her a dark look, obviously not convinced by their act. "The signatures need to be turned in to the Election Committee by the end of the day on Monday," he finally said. "Other than that, we just need to pick a date."

"For…the wedding?" Linda May asked brightly. "'Cause I'll do the cake for free."

"For the debate," Gavin clarified with a frustrated sigh, not thrilled that everyone was playing along.

"As quickly as is reasonable," Mayor Wilkins said, shooting a look at the door. "I have a feeling Mr. Easterbrook will be stirring up some, uh, controversy, so the sooner you two get out in front of Bitter Bark and present your platforms, the better." She opened her calendar. "I suggest next Thursday. That gives you time to prepare and share your…news. But the signatures have to be in, Sadie."

"My family alone will get you most of them," Connor said.

Sadie frowned and glanced at Gavin. "Family members of the opposing candidate? Let's be sure there's not some rule that can be used to trip us up."

Gavin looked up from his papers, then shook his head. "There's no reason you can't have those signatures from Connor's family. As long as they've lived in Bitter Bark for ten years."

Connor nodded. "We can get everything you need from Mahoneys and Kilcannons and finish up with my coworkers at the fire station. And your people, of course."

She had no people. Just Nana, Boomie, and Demi now. "I'll start with my grandparents this afternoon," she said, wanting very much to tell them the engagement news before they heard it through the Bitter Bark rumor mill. "Is that it?"

"That's it." Mayor Wilkins closed her calendar and let out a long sigh, looking at both of them. "I will tell you that I have my informal briefing with the press tomorrow, and I expect they'll have a lot of questions. It's not a press conference, but it might behoove you two to campaign in the square or near town hall tomorrow to get your message to the media."

"Thanks, Mayor," Sadie said.

She nodded and added, "I hope you two know what you're doing."

So do I, Sadie thought.

A few minutes later, they took the elevator down to the main floor with Gavin, Nellie, and Linda May, who chatted about getting back to the bakery before the lunch rush, no doubt so she could serve up some gossip with her croissants.

Frank stood inches from Connor, staring up at him and swishing his tail. Gavin scrolled through his phone, silent. When the car clunked to a stop, Nellie put her hand on Sadie's elbow to hold her back.

"Can I talk to you privately for a second?" she asked.

"Of course."

As they all stepped out of the car, Sadie held up a finger to Connor. "Gimme a minute, okay?"

"Sure, I see Shane just came in, probably on his way to have lunch with Chloe. Frank and I'll be right over there."

With a nod, she turned to the librarian, who inched her off to the side, pushing some hair behind her ears and taking a breath before she started.

"For what it's worth," Nellie said, "between you and Connor, I'd really love to see you win. I mean, having Frank as the 'mascot mayor' would obviously be great for our town and tourism, but to be honest, we have some serious problems in Bitter Bark, and it might take a serious person to fix them."

Sadie nodded. "I agree, Nellie. We may be, you know…engaged." The word still felt strange on her lips. "But I doubt we'll approach the mayor's race the same way. I don't think Connor and I will have similar platforms or styles at all."

"You shouldn't. He's running on the whole dog thing, which, believe me, did benefit a lot of store owners and built tourism. But that brought new issues, and no one wants to address them because it sounds like they're anti-dog or anti-Bitter Bark or anti-something."

"What kind of issues?"

"Could you come to the library this afternoon?" Nellie asked. "I can fill you in on everything you need to know before you talk to the media tomorrow. We have traffic issues, a little crime, and rents have gone sky-high because now we've got so many tourists. It's not always a good thing for a small town."

Sadie absently rubbed her fingers over the diamond engagement ring that belonged to...the director of Bitter Bark tourism. "Okay," she said, sneaking a peek at Connor just in time to catch his eye and see him lift his brows in question as he tugged Frank to a stand. "I can meet you this afternoon."

"Good, because we need a fresh perspective and some of your amazing experience."

"Thank you," Sadie said, reaching out to touch the woman's arm. "That means the world to me." She glanced at Connor, who was talking to another man, but caught his eye once again. "I better go," she said with one more quick squeeze of solidarity. "I'll come by the library later."

Nellie nodded and said goodbye, freeing Sadie to join Connor, who held her gaze and damn near flattened her with a smile as she approached. "Have you met my cousin Shane Kilcannon?" Connor asked, reaching for her hand in the most natural way, pulling her close as if, well, as if she really were his fiancée.

She instantly saw the resemblance between the cousins, with similar-colored hair and the strong jawlines. Shane's eyes were much more green and practically dancing with humor that seemed to hum through him.

"Hello, Shane." She shook his strong hand and held her other one up to show the diamond ring. "I don't know if we knew each other in the past, but I, uh, am wearing something I assume you paid for."

"Connor just told me. Defeating Easterbrook is a worthy cause, and I know my wife will get it back."

"Right now," she said, tugging at the gorgeous solitaire that already felt oddly comfortable on her finger.

"You'll just need it tomorrow for the media," Shane said. "Guard it well, and I'll get it from Connor after that."

"Really?"

Shane shrugged and took a step away. "It's all in the family."

"And mine is amazing that way," Connor added.

"Speaking of amazing, I'm off to see my wife." Shane nodded his goodbye and headed to the elevator, leaving Sadie standing with her...fiancé.

"Wow," she whispered. "What a morning."

He scanned her face, looking hard at her. "One question before you take off?"

"Of course."

"What is your history with Easterbrook?"

She just stared at him, speechless.

"Sadie. You're the one obsessed with honesty. Now would be a good time to tell me the truth, don't you think?"

On a sigh, she nodded. "Do you want to have lunch?"

"I'm free until a twelve-hour shift starts at five. Come on." He put his arm around her and tugged

Frank's leash. "He's not the best restaurant dog, though. Let's grab some pizza at Slice of Heaven and eat in the square."

She followed him to the door, dreading the confession, but knowing she had to make it.

Chapter Ten

Connor didn't press the subject. They had enough to talk about without demanding her Easterbrook explanation right out of the gate. At the pizza place, he chatted with the owner's niece, Beck, making Sadie laugh when he explained she was yet another wife of yet another Kilcannon cousin.

Once they had their pizza, they took Frank to the square and found a secluded table. They were two slices in before he leaned in and finally got back to what had been bothering him since the moment he saw Sadie look at Mitch Easterbrook.

"So…you *do* know our opposition, I take it."

She sighed and set down her slice, wiping her hands on a paper napkin. "We go way back, I'm afraid." She bit her lip and looked down, staring at Frank, who snoozed under the table, his chin firmly resting on Connor's foot to be sure he didn't move. "And it's not that complicated a story, especially if you know the kind of guy Mitch is."

"I know he sits on the hairy edge of sleaze, gouges grieving people for money, and…" He lifted a shoulder. "Treats his wife like crap and tries to appease her with money."

She cringed. "Yeah, it's kind of the 'treats his wife like crap' part I know." She finally looked up at him, almost taking his breath away with the pain in her eyes. "This is really hard to say," she whispered.

He reached over the pizza box and put his hand on hers. "You can trust me."

Her expression was nothing but doubt, but she nodded. "Okay. I'll just say it. He had an affair with my mother. I don't know a lot of the details, but it was a dark time. My parents divorced because of it, and my mother moved across the country. My dad and, oddly, my mother's parents, Nana and Boomie, raised me from then on."

"Oh God." He huffed out a breath. "Now I hate him even more."

"Get in line," she said with a wry smile. "He's mine to hate, and I think I've proven that I'll do just about anything to keep him from being mayor of this town."

"I'm sorry you had to go through that." He didn't know what else to say, so he just added some pressure to her hand. "How old were you?"

"Fourteen. Just old enough to understand that my mother was horrible, but not really why."

"Do you understand why now?" he asked.

"She's never told me outright what happened, and my dad rarely talks about it. But she was a social climber and wanted more than a professor of political science at Vestal Valley College. Mitch had money and power and a family name that meant status in Bitter Bark. And I guess…" She curled her lip. "He was considered quite handsome. My mother got swept away and seduced, plain and simple, not that she was innocent in the whole thing. She bears half the blame, without a doubt."

"But I can still understand why you'd hate Mitch."

She nodded. "Mitch, no surprise, wouldn't leave his wife. But I get the impression he led my mother on for quite some time, making her believe he would divorce for her. Of course, he didn't."

"God, Sadie. That's awful."

"No one knows but my family, so at least my mother didn't become gossip fodder. My dad stayed in Bitter Bark for me, really, because I grew up here, and I've always been really close to Nana and Boomie. But the minute I graduated from high school, my dad took a job at UT in Austin, and he's there still, happily remarried. My mom's living with a painter in Oregon."

"Do you talk to her?" he asked.

"Three times a year, on her birthday, my birthday, and Christmas." She tried for a casual shrug, but he suspected there was nothing casual about her feelings.

"You're left to extract vengeance on the villain who caused it all."

She considered that for a long time. "My mother was equally responsible. It takes two to cheat." Her voice went flat and dead. "You'll never find me blaming only the man in that case. So I wouldn't call this vengeance as much as a determination to stop him from having that much power."

"Well, it does explain a lot, and thanks for sharing with me. Not that I needed reasons to loathe the man any more than I already do. If it's any consolation—

though I'm not sure it will be—your mother wasn't the only one."

"I figured that."

He studied her for a moment, filing away all she'd just shared, always wanting to know more about her, and wanting to ease the conversation into something that would erase the hurt in her eyes.

"So, does the poli-sci-professor father get credit for your career choice?"

"Along with Mr. DeFord."

He frowned, thinking. "Mr....the civics teacher at Bitter Bark High?"

"Junior year, third period?"

"What?" He blinked at her. "We had a class together? How could I not know this?"

"Because you were in the back with the cool kids and jocks."

"Nah. It was third period, you say? Then I was starved for lunch."

"You were starved for someone named Erin McFarland, who sat next to you, if I recall correctly."

He hissed in a soft breath. "Oh yeah. Maybe a little."

She had to laugh at his honesty. "It's fine. I loved the class, though. That teacher and my dad were huge influences, making me love politics and government and the system that works for the people. There have been other people along the way…" She looked off for a moment, smiling, thinking of someone. "You never know who's going to inspire you."

He fisted his hands and rested his chin on them, staring at her. "I'm so impressed by you."

"Well, you sure weren't in Mr. DeFord's class."

"I was an idiot."

"Kind of," she agreed, making him drop his head back and grunt. He *had* been an idiot in those days. Burning with anger at what the world had taken from him, full of pent-up resentment, trying to prove something even though the only person he wanted to amaze was…gone.

He shook off the thought. "Well, I'm impressed now," he said. "And I still can't figure out how you didn't get snagged and bagged by now, but—"

"Snagged and bagged?" She choked. "Are you kidding?"

"Hey, I'm the un-PC guy who named my dog Frankendog. How did you manage to stay single all this time, Sadie?"

She shifted a little uncomfortably. "I told you I had a boyfriend in DC, but we broke up."

"Is the breakup the reason you left DC?"

She looked down at the pizza, silent.

"Whoops. Sorry." He plucked a pepperoni from one of the remaining slices. "That bad, huh? Don't want to talk about it?"

She closed her eyes. "You'd think that *one* sob story about a cheater would be enough for an afternoon."

He dropped the pepperoni before it went into his open mouth. "No."

"Yes."

"He cheated on you?"

"With my boss," she whispered.

"What the…holy shit, that *sucks*."

She laughed lightly. "Yep. It does. It's totally… mortifying."

"Nothing to be mortified about. Your boss and

boyfriend are the ones who should be ashamed." He picked up the pepperoni again, but this time he lowered his hand and let Frank get a whiff. Immediately, it was snatched from his fingers. "You're being good, Frank."

"Frankendog," she reminded him with an eye roll. "Oh, I named him after Mayor Frank," she said, imitating him in a low voice that cracked him up.

"What else could I call him?" he asked. "Look at that monster."

"Frankenstein wasn't the monster. He was the scientist."

"Trust me, I know. My younger brother, Braden, is a bookaholic and made sure I knew that. Anyway, he's just Frank now." He shot her a look. "Smooth change of subject, DC. But don't I get any details? I mean, your boss is kind of a big deal. Did their affair go public?"

"Not as far as I know, but I quit the day after I found out. I couldn't stay in that town, which, in some ways, is smaller than this one. No one on the staff has texted to say they've heard about it, so I guess they're keeping it on the DL."

"How'd you find out? If you don't mind me asking."

"I don't," she said, taking a sip of her soda. "I kind of suspected something weird between them for a few months before I confirmed it, but their jobs intersected, too. He's a lobbyist, and she's a congresswoman, and she had control over some bills that really affected his clients. We all had to be at some events together, and I just...got a vibe, you know? Then..." She looked away, her brows drawn in thought and what he suspected was one crappy memory. "I smelled her perfume in his car, if you can even believe something that cliché." She tried to laugh, but her voice caught.

"Oh, Sadie." He took her hand again, cursing the fact that he not only didn't get rid of that hurt, he brought on more. "I'm sorry to make you talk about it."

She shook her head and fought the tears, trying to smile. "I practically threw myself out of his car in the pouring rain. Then I had to walk to find a signal so I could call an Uber, and that's when I heard my little darling Demi crying for a new life. We both got one that night."

He squeezed her hand again. "Good for you for walking."

"Of course I walked. I walked right into my boss's office the next day and resigned."

"Man, your job and your boyfriend, both gone in one fell swoop. How long ago was this?"

"About a month. I packed up the next day, ignored his calls, and ran away to Bitter Bark to lick my wounds and figure out my next move."

"Oh. You *are* on the rebound."

"This is fake, remember?"

"Shhh. We sit in the shadow of Thad Bushrod himself." He nodded toward the founder's statue. "I have a confession, too," he said softly. "I did Google your boss after I saw your résumé."

"So you saw that she's gorgeous, looks ten years younger than her forty-two years, and she was blessed with a bone structure that's as stunning as her brain."

"Brain? She screws around with her staffer's boyfriend? Sounds pretty dumb to me."

"No, she is not dumb. And neither is he. Plus,

he's…" She tipped her head. "Very successful and her equal in the looks department. In all ways, they deserve each other."

He wasn't buying that. "A lobbyist sleeping with a congresswoman? That can't be legit."

"It's not illegal. Neither is married, but I agree it's not ethical."

"So why didn't you blow the whistle on them? At least put a dent in their careers, if not ruin them?"

She shook her head. "I don't want to ruin anyone's career. For one thing, I learned everything I know from having her as a mentor and I still believe that this country needs people like Jane in Congress. And the way Washington works? She'd have been the one scandalized, and Nathan would have gotten high fives and a promotion for his 'lobbying' prowess." She used air quotes and then let her hands thud to the table. "The fact is, I had nothing to gain from going public, and people I care about could have been hurt or lost their jobs, and let's face it, I'm the one who looks like the biggest fool of all."

"Could not disagree more," he said vehemently. "Plus, you picked up and moved on. They'll crash and burn eventually, if they haven't already."

"Losing both of them hurt," she admitted on a whisper. "I thought I loved Nathan, but oh my God, Jane was my *idol* from the moment I met her. I worked as an intern in her office in Austin when she was a first-year congresswoman, and I was in college. I had her on a pedestal higher than the one old Thad is standing on over there. And I…"

When she didn't finish, Connor gave her hand a squeeze to urge her on.

"I wanted to be exactly like her."

He knew that admission hurt, but he was still stuck on *I thought I loved Nathan*. A month ago? This woman wasn't ready for anything, but then…he wasn't really offering anything but a fake relationship.

She pushed back then, closing the pizza box. "Thank you for lunch and for listening, Connor. You got more out of me than I planned to share."

"Thanks for trusting me."

She gave him a rueful smile. "I'm not sure I'll ever really trust anyone again," she admitted. "But it is nice to try."

"See what I mean?" Nellie Shaker leaned back in her office chair and gestured toward the files and papers she'd spread on the desk and the legal pad Sadie had filled with pages of notes. "This isn't a job for a lightweight."

"No one said it is," Sadie agreed.

"Or a *dog*," Nellie added. "Cute as the idea, and the idea-haver, might be."

Sadie managed a smile, but nothing in her wanted to dive into a mudslinging session against Connor. "Frank isn't going to make decisions about traffic flow," she said. "Obviously, Connor is. But I do actually have experience with managing congestion after rapid growth. It was a problem in a small town in our congressional district, and we found solutions."

"But don't you dare suggest canceling events like Paws for a Cause or Bark in the Park," Nellie warned her. "I have to tell you I was in the room the day that

Chloe Somerset—now Kilcannon—presented that idea to the Tourism Advisory Committee."

Sadie leaned forward, touching the diamond ring—owned by that very woman—resting heavily on her left hand. "Was it well received?"

Nellie gave a soft hoot. "They darn near booed her out of the room, and Mitch was the loudest. But Shane Kilcannon came to that meeting instead of his father, and he liked it." She smiled. "And he liked Chloe."

Sadie glanced at the ring. "The dogs have been great for this town."

"Great enough that if you campaign against them, you'll alienate a lot of people. Although, how could you since you're engaged to Frank's owner?" She made a face Sadie couldn't quite interpret. Doubt? Amusement? Curiosity?

Sadie returned her attention to the notes before Nellie could start asking personal questions. "How about parking? Is it a problem like the traffic congestion?"

Nellie snorted. "Try to get a space. But we do have several Uber drivers now, so there is that."

"Traffic might be a matter of turning some of the streets around the square into one-way or adding a light where there's only a stop sign now."

"Well, if you do anything to Ambrose Avenue, please find the money for repairs. It's cracking in half." Nellie tapped the town council report. "The entire infrastructure of the town is under duress. I don't have enough books in the library, the sheriff's department is stretched to the limit during those events, the square is starting to look seedy, and all of our precious resources are being used up."

"I'm going to make sure the people of Bitter Bark

know I can address all of that," Sadie said as she flipped the pad closed, ready to get to work and bring the hour-long meeting to an end. "Thanks for the insight, Nellie. I may run some things by you before I go public with any ideas."

"Please do." She brightened, standing up. "You're exactly what we need, Sadie," she gushed softly. "No one respects history more than I do, but sometimes I feel like Bitter Bark is stuck in the fifties, when the town had its first boom."

"There is a certain charm to its quaintness, though," Sadie mused as she slipped her bag on her shoulder and tucked the files and pad under her arm. "The trick is to keep Bitter Bark precious, but still allow for natural growth that helps everyone."

"Yes." Nellie came around the desk, her gaze dropping over Sadie, top to bottom. "I can't believe how lucky we are to get someone from a big city here. You are just what the Bitter Bark doctor ordered."

"Oh, thanks," she said, a little self-conscious.

"Maybe you can drop in on a few of our local clothing boutiques and give them some pointers on current fashions, too. Except for La Parisienne—and her clothes are usually way too expensive for most people—our retailers think last decade's looks are just fine. You should stop in and see Yvette, the owner. It's right where the Downtown Dresses used to be, do you remember?"

"Downtown Dresses?" She laughed softly. "I used to shop there with my mom. Every year I'd get an Easter dress there."

Nellie smiled. "How is your mom, Sadie? Does she ever come to town to see her parents?"

Sadie adjusted her notes and files and gave a tight smile. "She lives out West and doesn't get back here much. And she's fine, thank you."

"Does she still paint? I remember doing a library display of her watercolors one year when I was the assistant librarian. She was quite talented."

"She does," Sadie said vaguely, only she wasn't quite sure if that was true. She lived with a painter, so maybe.

"Tell her I said hello. And thanks for coming to see me," Nellie said as they walked out and parted at the double glass doors.

Sadie stepped into the late afternoon sun, glancing down to navigate the cracks in three stone stairs to the street, making a mental note to check that maintenance budget.

"Watch your step."

She looked up at the man's voice and nearly did trip at the sight of Mitch Easterbrook coming out of the next building, shocking her a little so fresh on the heels of a conversation about her mother.

"Thanks for the tip," she said, glancing behind him to see he'd just left the offices of the *Bitter Bark Banner*.

He closed the space between them, coming within a foot of her. "You want another one?"

"Not particularly."

He gave her a dismissive, dirty look. "You won't win, Mercedes. And neither will your fake firefighter boyfriend."

"Oh, he's a real firefighter," she shot back, lifting her chin to meet his penetrating gaze.

"You can't come in here and steal this from me."

She sucked in a breath. "Steal this…oh, that's rich. Like you didn't steal my family from me."

He locked his jaw so tight, she could see a muscle throb. "Let's get one thing very clear, young lady. You have something on me, and I know it. But I suspect there's plenty from your colored past that we could find, too." He angled his head, making her wonder if he was tipping it toward the *Banner*. Had he been in there suggesting they dig into her life in Washington? Trying to prove the engagement was fake?

"Are you threatening me?" she asked.

"I'm informing you." He crossed his arms and glared down at her. "I have waited years for this. Years. I lived through the endless Frank Wilkins regime and watched in horror when his wife got the pity votes in an emergency election after Frank croaked."

"Croaked? Is that how you talk about the dead you bury?"

"Don't even think about mocking five generations of undertakers. My name is embedded in this town, and that mayor's office is mine. So pull your stunts and spread your rumors about me and your mother, but nothing is going to stop me from winning."

"And you don't care who you take down in the process." All he was doing was making her certain that running for mayor was the smartest decision she'd ever made, and if she had to fake an engagement to keep him out of the office, she would.

"No," he said flatly. "But coming from Washington, DC, I'm sure you know that's how politics works. It's dirty, it's tricky, and sometimes people lose."

"They sure do," she agreed. "So brace for that, Mitch." She sidestepped him to end the conversation, watching the cracks in the sidewalk so she didn't trip. But the truth was, the land mines in the local population could be far more treacherous.

Chapter Eleven

From his vantage point by Thad's statue, Connor caught sight of Sadie just when she came into the square, walking briskly toward town hall for their chance to talk to the media.

Before he headed off to meet her, he took a minute to appreciate today's outfit and the woman who wore it so well.

"Tight slacks and high heels," he said to Frank, who was more interested in sniffing the grass. "Definitely one of my favorite looks."

She also wore a pink jacket with black trim that made her look sharp and tailored, with some kind of soft knit top underneath that draped over her breasts in a way that somehow managed to be professional but extremely feminine.

"And that hair," he murmured, tugging the leash. "Come on, Frank. You gotta appreciate fine fur." Burnished like bronze, all thick and long, her hair cascaded everywhere, making it impossible for Connor not to want to get his hands in it.

Frank barked as he saw her. "You recognize her? Good boy." He patted his head and started walking toward her. "Gotta say, I like our fiancée, Frankendog."

And from the way her step slowed and her dimples deepened with a smile when she saw him, she liked him, too.

"Look at you," she teased with just enough flirt in her voice for him to know she was admiring him with the same level of concentration he'd used on her. "Dress clothes two days in a row."

"No tie for Frank or me, though. Not after a twelve-hour shift."

Her mouth opened into a little O of surprise. "You didn't sleep last night?"

"I did, because we only had one call all night," he told her, reaching for her hand because he just wanted to touch some skin, though he covered the move by lifting it to check for the ring. "Didn't drop it down the sink, I see."

She laughed. "I can babysit a diamond, believe me. Why aren't you lingering right outside Mayor Wilkins's office, ready to pounce on the media when they leave her briefing?"

"Without you? Why would I do that?"

"To get extra time? To deliver your key messages? To make them fall in love with this guy?" She reached for Frank, but he circled around to Connor's other side.

"Why would I want any time without you? I actually don't know what a key message is. And the only love on the agenda is ours, remember? We've got an engagement to sell." He dipped closer. "By the way, fiancée, you are very, very pretty today. Betrothal suits you."

She flushed a little at the compliment. "Thank you. And you really should have one key message other than, you know, dogs."

He threw Frank a look. "He'll bark it out for me."

"Connor," she said on a sigh. "I've been studying this town and the issues. I don't want to make you look like you're, you know, a lightweight."

He snorted and then broke into an actual laugh. "I'm going to pretend I didn't hear that."

"It's just that you should have more to talk about than the dogs. There's more to Bitter Bark than being dog-forward."

"Dog-forward? Can I use that? It's got a nice ring to it. And so does this." He lifted her hand. "So show it off. Word on the street is that people wonder if we're making this up."

"We *are* making this up."

He shot her a look. "You want Easterbrook to win on a forfeit?"

All humor evaporated from her expression. "God, no. I saw him coming out of the *Banner* yesterday."

"Yeah, they already ran a story. Didn't you see it?"

She shook her head slowly. "Dang, I'm off my game not reading the morning paper. I was studying my notes about congestion and parking."

"Rose Halliday wrote it," he said. "Smartest reporter they have. The story was straight-up news about your candidacy and our engagement, but the subtext of doubt was in every line."

She nodded. "Will she be here?"

"She's here," he said. "I asked Chloe to check the mayor's office sign-in for me."

"Helps to have friends in high places," she mused.

"Helps to read the local paper."

"Touché, Lieutenant."

They reached the perimeter of the square, and he nodded toward a half-dozen reporters, some with cameras, at the top of the stairs.

"They're out of the mayor's briefing," Connor said.

"Who are all these people?"

"In addition to Rose—she's the dark-haired lady in the red dress—it looks like someone from the local TV affiliate, a radio guy, and a couple of journalism undergrads from the Vestal Valley College newspaper. Not a Washington-level media mob."

"How do you know them all?"

"They come to our calls, especially if there's news."

"Oh, of course." She squared her shoulders and tightened her grip on his hand as they crossed the street. "Still, that's a lot of people to lie to."

As they reached the bottom of the town hall steps, he turned her toward him. "Think one thought, okay?"

"What's that?"

"Easterbrook *can't* win."

"Now *that* I know," she agreed. "And to that end, I'm ready to talk about town maintenance, the budget, a traffic proposal, and how we can upgrade the lights in Bushrod Square."

"You won't get to do any of that if you—or Frank—lose. And if they don't believe us, we could lose even if we win the vote."

"But I still have to talk about the issues, Connor. This is an election."

"I thought you knew so much about small-town government."

"I do, but—"

"People come before politics." He glanced over his shoulder. "And here comes the media." He dipped his head, put his lips on hers, and gave her a featherlight kiss, but held it for two, three, four long heartbeats until they were surrounded.

"Is this engagement a hoax?"

"Are you faking it to meet the election requirements?"

"If it's not real, you might have to forfeit a win. Do you realize that?"

"Are you so afraid of Mitch Easterbrook that you have to lie about your relationship in order to win?"

"Is she going to marry the dog, too?"

Connor broke the kiss, keeping one hand on Sadie's shoulder and the other gripped around the leash when Frank barked and then did his level best to get between Connor's legs. "One at a time, ladies and gentlemen. Journalists with treats do get preferential treatment."

He led Sadie up a few steps so they could be slightly higher than the reporters, earning a quick glance of surprise and appreciation.

Like maybe he wasn't exactly the lightweight she thought he was. That *everyone* thought he was.

"Rose Halliday with the *Bitter Bark Banner*," the reporter announced, taking the lead and directing her words to Sadie. "Is it true you are not a resident of Bitter Bark?"

Sadie smiled. "Hello, Rose. Nice to meet you. The fact is that I grew up here, lived here more than half my life, and have owned a home in Ambrose Acres since 2002."

More than half her life? Connor did some quick math and decided that was probably true...by one year.

"And I've known her since high school," he added. "Did you know that? We go back, what, seventeen years, Sadie?"

The reporter ignored him. "And do you know that the third candidate, Mitchell Easterbrook, has uncovered a law that says neither one of you is technically qualified to run?"

"Not true," Connor said.

"If you're *really* engaged," Rose shot back, her hard stare on Sadie. "And let's face it, your opponent here isn't exactly boyfriend material."

Sadie drew back and leveled the woman with the same hard stare. "He's not? He is kind, funny, courageous, and beloved by his entire family." She waited a beat, then added, "And will you look at that tail?"

She gestured to Frank with a masterful deflection of the question, but when the light laughter quieted, she added a smile to Rose. "If, however, you're talking about my fiancé? Well, Connor is a firefighter, an EMT, and a first responder who is coming off a twelve-hour shift." She turned to him and gave him a slow once-over. "And he still kind of takes your breath away, doesn't he?"

Connor returned her smile. "How could I not marry this woman?"

"Mitch Easterbrook is insisting that this relationship is fake." This came from a college student wearing a T-shirt emblazoned with the Vestal Valley Coyotes imprint. "I'm with the *Coyote Call*," he added.

"Mitch Easterbrook is a fake." Sadie and Connor said the words in perfect unison, cracking up the entire group.

"At least you're in agreement on that," another reporter said.

"We're in agreement on a lot of things," Connor said. "Like adding a few more dog parks."

"And parking lots," Sadie said. "And I don't mean Ambrose Avenue on the weekend."

"No kidding," another man said. "I'm with KVVC radio, the sound of Vestal Valley County. My family and I tried to come into town to shop last Saturday and literally spent twenty minutes in bumper-to-bumper traffic."

"Are you going to address those problems as a couple, then?" Rose prodded. "And should your engagement be exposed as a hoax, would you be willing to drop out of the race?"

"Why would we?" Sadie asked her. "It's always an advantage to have as many qualified candidates to choose from as possible."

"But are you *technically* engaged?" someone called out.

Sadie lifted her hand and let the diamond sparkle. "Anything technical includes…hardware."

The crowd laughed lightly, and she reached to try to draw Frank out. "Let's not forget my real opponent," she said. "Come on, boy. Do you have those treats, Connor?"

He dug into his pocket and found the bag, giving her a look of appreciation as genuine as the one he got from Frank.

While they gathered their wits, he smiled down at

148

her. "I underestimated you, Ear Girl," he said softly.

"What did you call her?" Rose asked.

"Oh, just a secret pet nickname." He patted her shoulder. "Because 'honey' is so ordinary for someone with such *extraordinary* ideas."

Sadie laughed easily as a reporter with a camera on his shoulder made his way to the front, while a small group of onlookers started to gather.

"Rolling," he said. "Can you tell us how you plan to balance your engagement with running against each other?"

"Love conquers all, right?" she said, giving Frank's head a tender stroke and Connor's heart an unexpected tug. "We both take deep pride in Bitter Bark, the history of this great town, and the happiness of its amazing people."

Damn, she was good. And Frank seemed to catch the fever, swishing his tail, making the crowd *ooh* and *aww* while the cameras whirred and clicked.

"How do you feel about running against a nonhuman?" a reporter asked her.

"And he doesn't mean Mitch Easterbrook," someone from the crowd yelled out, getting a smattering of laughter.

Sadie didn't laugh, though, but she kept her hand on Frank's head. "To be honest, I see the appeal of a ceremonial dog mayor for Bitter Bark. Dogs are our bread and butter in many ways. But I think they have changed the dynamics of the town, and I've talked to people who want to solve the new problems, like congestion and even crime. As mayor, I hope to do that."

"And you, Frank?" someone asked the dog.

Connor stepped forward. "What Frank—and I—don't want to do is lose the energy and vitality Bitter Bark has found in the last few years. His very presence will increase fundraising at our many events, and he spreads the joy."

Frank answered by standing on his hind legs and thrusting his paws at Connor, getting a reaction from the crowd.

"Obviously, we want to send the message that we're..." Connor eased him to the ground. "Dog-forward."

"Dog-forward?" A reporter chuckled, writing down the quote. "I like that."

"Sadie's idea," he added quickly, putting a hand on her shoulder.

"Wow, you two are a team," the camera-holding guy said, his lens moving from one to the other.

"We sure are," Connor said, catching sight of Rose's dubious expression, but he ignored it, pulling Sadie closer so they could be in the shots together.

"Give her a kiss!"

"One for the front page!"

"Show us it's real!"

The hecklers from the crowd were getting serious now, making Connor and Sadie share a long look. For a moment, he forgot everyone else was there as he took a trip into the depths of those golden-brown eyes. He didn't know what he'd expected today, but it hadn't been this.

Maybe he'd thought she'd try to one-up him with in-depth knowledge of town problems, or try to prove to the media that she was as invested in the town as he was. He wasn't quite prepared for a partner, real or fake, and right then, he realized how grateful he was to have her out here on these steps.

"Oh, it's real," Connor said softly.

"Oh, come on," Rose insisted, exasperation in her voice. "How come no one ever saw you together?"

"I saw them practically making out at Bushrod's a while back," someone in the crowd called out.

Connor felt his brow flick up, and Sadie almost smiled at that. So their little first-meet was going to help them after all.

"Sorry," Rose said under her breath, looking from one to the other. "I'm still not buying it."

"Buy it," Connor said to the reporter.

"Prove it," she shot back.

Just as before, Connor could practically read Sadie's thoughts. At least, he thought he could. Her eyelids fluttered. Her lips parted. Her chest rose and fell with a breath, and her whole body moved one fraction of an inch closer to him.

Prove it.

He could think of only one way, and Sadie sure looked like she was thinking the same thing.

Without another second's hesitation, he lifted both hands and cupped her delicate cheeks, giving her a chance to slip away if this wasn't what she wanted. She didn't, so he lowered his head and whispered, "One for the crowd, Ear Girl."

He felt her lips rise in a smile just as their mouths joined in a kiss. Behind him, the crowd reacted, and Frank gave a few noisy barks, trying to get between them, which absolutely delighted the audience.

But all of that disappeared in a blur as he kissed her, long, slow, sweet, and tender. When they broke contact, her eyes were still closed, and her color had deepened.

"You believe us now, Rose?" he asked without looking away as Sadie's eyes opened slowly.

"Anyone can kiss," the woman hissed.

"Not like that," Sadie whispered with a little shudder. Then she turned to Rose and smiled. "Do you have any other questions?"

Chapter Twelve

When it was all over, Connor and Sadie walked through the square, letting Frank set the pace, both of them quiet until they were certain no one had followed them, and they were completely alone.

That happened as they neared the massive bronze founder's statue and stately tree at the center of the square, all surrounded by shrubs.

"So, Thad, old boy," Connor said as he stopped in front of the man, who stood with one hand up in a classic orator's pose. "I have so many questions. Like, did you know all along that this was a hickory tree when you planted it, claimed it to be a bitter bark, and named the town after it? Or were you just dumb as the dirt you stuck the seed in?"

"It's a hickory tree?" Sadie asked, surprised.

"Folklore has it that there was already a Hickory, North Carolina, not far from here, and he liked the sound of Bitter Bark, so he told everyone this was a bitter bark tree."

"Thad!" Sadie said on a dramatic sigh. "You lied?

Then why all the articles and statutes about morality and stable relationships?"

She felt Connor's gaze on her as she looked at the statue.

"You really surprised me out there, Sadie," he said softly.

"Didn't think I could work with you instead of against you?"

"I guess I expected you to come out with guns blazing, talking about infrastructure and budget cuts."

"We'll get to that," she said. "But it took this to beat Easterbrook."

"You know what we did, don't you?"

She reached out one hand, turned it over, and tapped the palm. "Had them eating out of this?"

"Yes. Not only did they buy the engagement…they kind of *embraced* the engagement. It was brilliant. You were brilliant."

She stopped at a bench facing the statue and dropped down on it, eyeing him. "I might have been wrong about you, too," she admitted. "I thought you would just joke your way through that, but there's more serious stuff going on in your head than I gave you credit for."

"I can be serious," he said, joining her after he unclipped Frank's leash. "Run free, pupper." But, of course, he didn't go six inches from Connor. "You're just confusing being funny with not being serious. Also, what was it you said?" He leaned into her. "Take your breath away, do I?"

She fought a smile. "You have your moments."

"And you have yours. Actual full hours and probably long days." He dropped back on the bench and locked his hands behind his head, watching Frank, who didn't stray. "Since you were so honest with me yesterday, I want to tell you why I'm running for mayor."

"Frank's running," she reminded him with a little nudge.

He laughed. "Of course he is. And we're getting married in the summer."

An unexpected shot of something warm and fluttery went through her stomach. "Set a date, did we?"

"June?" he guessed. "Don't all girls want June weddings or am I just thinking about my little sister?"

"I never wanted any wedding," she said softly, getting a surprised look from him.

"I thought all little girls fantasized about their wedding day."

"After seeing a divorce, I've never longed to be married," she said, a little surprised at her honesty, but not completely. He had a way of getting her to open up. "Now why are you running for mayor?" she asked, not wanting to lose that thread of the conversation.

She felt his shoulders drop a bit next to her, as if he'd let out a very small sigh.

"To be taken seriously?" he said. "To be…the man I'm supposed to be?" He let out a dry laugh. "Wow, that sounds douchey."

"I don't think so."

"You wouldn't. Tell another firefighter, and I'm ruined, though."

She suddenly ached to slide her arm around his, but she didn't, no matter how natural it might have felt at that moment. "Well, you take things seriously in your own way, it seems."

"I do. And that's probably…no, it is why I'm running. And Frank's just my insurance for a win." He threw her a look. "Well, he was. Not entirely sure I can beat you."

He bent over and picked up a stick, holding it in front of Frank. "Listen to me, doggo. When I throw, you fetch. Remember seeing all those dogs at Waterford do it?"

Frank stared at him with endless love.

"Here we go. Ready?" He tossed the stick, and Frank looked at it, then back at Connor.

"He wants you to go with him," she said on a laugh.

"No, boy." He rubbed the dog's head. "You are the fetcher. I am the thrower."

"He's scared of you disappearing."

"Man, you have no idea. Separation anxiety like I've never seen before, along with fear of strangers, desire to eat nonfood items, and refusal to submit to a belly rub."

"But you're making progress with him," she said. "Go, get the stick, and bring it back to me. He'll do it if you do."

He threw her a look as he got up. "Yes, I definitely underestimated you."

"Because I'm willing to play with a dog? Wow, you must think I'm a stone-cold bitch who's going to beat the pants off you in the election."

Twenty feet away, he picked up the stick and held it in front of Frank's mouth. The dog snagged it, dropped to the ground, and started gnawing on it like he'd been given lunch.

"No, Frank. You don't eat it. You take it to the

person who threw it. Watch." Connor freed the stick from Frank's mouth and jogged back to her, dropping onto the bench. "Now, what were you saying about getting my pants off?"

She laughed and gave in to the urge to slide her arm through his. And she got rewarded with one of those toe-curling Connor Mahoney smiles she liked so much.

"I said 'beat the pants off you,' not take them off."

"Shame. We could give new meaning to celebrating with a bang."

The next laugh bubbled up, along with some very natural warmth, at the joke. Which might not be a joke, considering how frequently she found excuses to touch him.

They sat like that for a long time, her arm in his, Frank at their feet, Thaddeus Bushrod looking down at them. They talked about the press conference, the town, his family, some people they knew in common, and what each of them would do as mayor.

When it came time to part, Sadie did the only thing that felt right. She invited him to walk her home and meet Boomie and Nana.

"I'd love to," Connor said. "But you know I've met them already."

"Not as my fiancé."

He slowed his step. "You know what I remember about your grandfather's house the night I was there? His sizable rifle collection."

"Damn straight, Mahoney. Be nice, or he'll shoot you."

He grunted. "No more pants-off and banging jokes."

"Don't stop those," she said, tugging him closer. "You make me laugh."

"Do I?"

"Mmmm. And you sure can kiss."

"I'm available to practice anytime."

She looked up at him, considering one more, right here in the square, with no one looking. "We should probably leave the kissing for our adoring public only."

"Chicken."

She didn't bother to argue.

"Oh, well, look at what we have here." Margaret Winthrop opened the screen door of her brick ranch on Cypress with a huge smile that immediately reminded Connor of his own grandmother. "If it isn't my future grandson-in-law." That smile faded instantly, replaced with a scowl that deepened a few creases on her face. "Boomie darn near had a heart attack when we heard. Hello, Connor, I'm Margie. Nice to see you again."

"And you," he said as Frank pulled on the leash for a sniff.

"We have cats," Margie said. "They're inside, and we'll sit out here. You can let him go."

He unleashed Frank and looked behind her into the house. "I'm happy to check out Mr. Winthrop, if you like. I mean, if he really is having chest pains."

"Nonsense. He's in the den watching TV. Jimmy!" she called. "The newlyweds are here."

"Nana, stop," Sadie chided her grandmother. "You know it isn't real."

"That's what the woman from the *Banner* said when she called a few minutes ago."

Sadie and Connor shared a look. "What did you tell her?" Sadie asked.

"That she should call Finola Kilcannon and talk to the source."

Connor made a face. "I better warn my grandmother to be careful what she says."

"She certainly isn't going to say it's fake," Margie said on a chuckle. "She and Agnes are sure to count this ruse as a Dogmother win, and I think they've set their sights on John Santorini next."

Sadie laughed as she sat on a porch swing. "Those two are hilarious."

"Unless you're their target," he said dryly. "And I wouldn't be so sure about what Gramma Finnie would say. She wants real engagements, not a publicity stunt."

"Publicity stunt? Is that what it is?" The ragged voice came from behind Margie right before Jim Winthrop appeared, his thinning gray hair a little unkempt, his blue T-shirt hanging loose on a narrow frame. He stepped onto the porch and reached out a hand to Connor as Margie disappeared inside. "Hello, young man. Nice to see you here without a stretcher."

Connor shook the man's bony fingers. "Nice to be here. And thank you for letting me get engaged to your granddaughter, even if it isn't real."

"And this is the dog who saved that kid?" He went right to Frank, who was still sniffing the perimeter of the porch, and rubbed his head.

"He's our local hero," Connor said. "And the next Mayor Frank of Bitter Bark."

Mr. Winthrop pointed a finger. "Now that was a great mayor."

"And will be again," Connor assured him.

Sadie moaned. "Nana and Boomie aren't going to vote for anyone but me."

"I don't know," the old man teased as he got settled into a chair. "I like dogs."

"Boomie!"

"And you, missy. I like you."

Margaret came back out with tea and glasses on a tray, along with a small bowl of water and a piece of turkey for Frank.

"Something special for our hero," she crooned, giving it to the dog.

"Thanks," Connor said, taking his tea. "And sorry again for giving your pacemaker extra work," he said to the older man. "I'm sure Sadie explained everything to you and why we're doing this."

The minute he said it, he knew he shouldn't have. Margie looked down at the porch boards. Jim was suddenly fascinated by his tea. And Sadie slid him a silencing look.

"You're doing the right thing," Margaret finally said, her voice tight. "No one would like the...option of, uh, an unopposed candidate."

"You still got that rock on your finger?" Jim asked with a deft subject change. "You better not lose that, missy."

"I wish you'd take it back to Shane and Chloe," Sadie said to Connor, sliding the ring off and handing it to him. "I can get something else that will do the trick."

"Speaking of things that do the trick," Jim said with a nod to Connor, "that pacemaker sure works—"

Jim's words were cut off by a loud, high-pitched screech coming from the side of the house.

"That's Demi!" Sadie shot up, and Connor looked around for the dog, stunned that he wasn't in sight.

"Where did Frank go?" He stood, too, almost getting knocked over when Sadie bolted by him.

"I don't know, but that was my cat."

He followed her off the porch, darting around the house to a huge side yard with a half-dozen large raised garden beds, all surrounded by tall oak trees. At the back corner, he saw what looked like an oversize dollhouse, where Sadie was running and Frank stood barking.

An orange cat had leaped on a low branch of one of the oak trees, hissing hard at Frank, who stared up at her, not two feet away and close enough to lunge.

"Oh no. She's going to jump him." Sadie slowed as she got closer, and Connor caught up. "Unless he attacks first."

"Don't move," he whispered, putting a hand on her shoulder to hold her back. "He's not aggressive, but this is a first for us. Will she go after him?"

"She might. I told you, she hates dogs."

To underscore that, Demi hissed again, her mouth wide, teeth bared, hackles raised as if she wanted to leap on Frank and tear him up.

"C'mere, boy," Connor said, taking one very slow step closer. "Back away, Frank."

But he didn't move, didn't even turn his head to look at Connor. He kept his gaze locked on Demi, his thick chest heaving a little.

"Frank, come here, buddy."

Frank did exactly the opposite, though, taking a step closer to the tree and making Demi let out a long, loud cry that was more anger than fear.

"Whoa, boy." Connor kept his voice steady and low. "Don't scare the pretty kitty. She's more afraid of you than you are of her."

Frank barked at Demi, who scrambled up to the next branch with another mighty howl.

"Hey, come on, now." He reached for the dog, who lunged toward the tree with another bark.

Demi squealed and climbed higher, flight winning out on fight against this much bigger, louder animal.

Connor got a hold of Frank's collar and eased him back, getting a loud bark, and that scared Demi even more.

She cried out and kept going higher, making Sadie run closer.

"Demi!" She watched in horror as the cat scurried up and out of reach. "Don't go any higher!"

But Demi ignored the order, moving on instinct now, climbing the almost bare branches at an alarming rate.

"Damn it." Sadie put her hands on her hips and looked up. "Get down here." But Demi was a ball of orange fur, curled on a branch, looking down.

With a good grip on Frank's collar, Connor squinted up into the branches, too. "She do this often?"

"Never. But she does come and go freely through a pet door on the other side of my little house right there."

"Can she get down?"

"Can she, or will she? This is one stubborn animal you're looking at. Also scared spitless."

"I'll get her," he said easily. "Can I take Frank inside?" He nodded to her guesthouse. "She won't come down while she can see him."

"Of course." With one more glance at Demi, Sadie walked to the door to unlock it. "Really sorry if she upset Frank."

"It's his fault for scaring the crap out of her," he said, leading the dog in and glancing around a surprisingly cozy studio-style home. "Nice garden shed, Sadie."

He walked Frank into the main room, past a kitchenette, noticing that the hardwood floors were covered with braided rugs, and the two windows had been lovingly draped with ruffled curtains.

"When I was a little girl, this old garage was where Boomie stored all his garden tools. That's why we call it that," she explained. "Then they renovated it with a kitchen and bathroom for my great-grandfather and left it as a guesthouse when he passed away." She added a smile. "Not the glass contemporary one-bedroom I had in DC, that's for sure."

"Good enough for Frank to cool off while I go climb a tree and save a kitten." He pointed at Frank. "You do not move, mister."

The dog dropped his head and collapsed to the floor, heavy with shame and his hatred of being reprimanded.

"Aww," Sadie crooned.

"You said there's a dog door? I don't want him to get out."

"It's in the bathroom, but I don't think he'd fit through it. Also..." She gestured to the dog, flat and sad. "He's not going anywhere." She reached down to pet him. "I'm sure Demi taunted you. She can be an absolute horror."

"He shouldn't have scared her," Connor said. "Come on, let's save a kitten in a tree. It's my specialty."

Outside, they both headed back to the oaks and looked up to see…nothing.

"Where is she?" Sadie pressed her hand to her chest. "Demi!"

Connor circled the trees, studying where the branches all collided and connected at the top, planning a route and praying the cat hadn't run away completely.

"My grandfather has a ladder, Connor."

"Which would get me halfway to where she was and…" He looked hard. "Where the *hell* did she go?"

"I don't know." Sadie bit her lip and stared into the dark green and brown of the trees. "But I'm worried."

He put his arm around her shoulders. "We'll find her, I promise."

Just then, he heard a faint cry from behind the front window in the guesthouse. Was that…

"Did you hear that?" he asked.

"It's from inside."

"She got back in?" His eyes widened in surprise, then horror when they heard a loud bark.

"The dog door in the bathroom."

They both launched toward the front door, Connor going first with Sadie right behind him, both of them braced for whatever they'd find.

"I don't see her," Connor said.

But he saw Frank, flat on his stomach, his face on the ground, staring under the sofa.

"That's where she goes when she's upset," Sadie said, both of them walking slowly into the room.

From under the sofa, the cat let out a soft mew.

Frank barked once, not very loud, then pushed up and jumped onto the sofa.

"Frank, no."

He got down immediately, but he had a corner of the blanket in his mouth. Holding on to it, he draped it over the front of the sofa, creating a cocoon underneath.

"Oh my gosh," Sadie whispered. "He's tucking her in so she feels safe."

"Frankendog," Connor said on a sigh. "Very slick move, bud." He looked at Sadie and raised his brows. "I guess we've confirmed that he likes cats."

Frank let out a low moan, not really a growl, but not a bark.

Demi replied with a noisy meow.

"Are they…talking?" Sadie asked.

Connor shrugged, taking a tentative step closer to watch the exchange. Then Frank inched a little toward the space under the sofa, whimpered again, then rolled onto his back with all four paws splayed in the most submissive pose Connor had ever seen.

Two seconds later, Demi came slithering out from under the sofa, taking a slow step toward Frank, who didn't move. She stuck her nose in his armpit, and he swooshed his tail over the floor.

"Well, what do you know?" Connor watched in utter shock. "I think Frank has found his lovey."

Chapter Thirteen

"**A** dog and cat connection? Not that unusual." Shane turned from his fridge and put a glass of cold water on the kitchen counter for Connor. "Especially a stray dog. Who knows who he hung with in the woods?" Shane nodded at the water. "Would you rather have a beer after a twelve-hour Friday shift? Except, you are holding my most precious possession in your hands."

Connor eased the baby from one arm to the other, balancing Annabelle in the crook of his elbow. He was rewarded with a soft slap on the cheek from her sticky little hand and a gurgle of joy. "Are you his most precious possession, Anna-B?"

"Not at four in the morning, she wasn't." Chloe came into the kitchen with Ruby, their Staffy, right on her heels. Frank stayed under the counter, not making any effort to befriend the other dog. No, Connor's dog liked *cats*.

"Give the poor man a beer, Shane," Chloe said. "He won't drop her."

"I don't need a beer," he said. "I need sleep. I only came by to return the ring because I've had it for too many days, and it's making me nervous. And to see this sweet angel." He bopped Annabelle's nose, getting a big, wet, gummy smile. "Plus, I had to tell you about Frank and the cat. I honestly never saw anything like it."

"Oh, Frank," Chloe crooned as she passed the dog, "do you have a girlfriend? Ruby's crushed."

"And he's been kind of mopey since we saw them," Connor said. "Like he needs a fix of his girl."

Shane lifted a brow. "Or you do."

Connor just shot him a look. "It's fake, remember?"

"Funny, that's what Rose Halliday is saying in her column in today's *Banner*."

Chloe picked up the newspaper on the counter. "Oh, and the Vestal Valley *Coyote Call* published Sadie's first interview, and my, she knows an awful lot about the maintenance budget and apparently has a very creative suggestion for traffic flow around the square."

Connor closed his eyes. "Yeah, maybe I need that beer and some access to the town council minutes."

"Oh, and there's an editorial on BitterBark.com that debates whether the engagement is fake," Chloe said. "Did you see that?"

"Don't sweat that, Connor," Shane said. "Five people read that website."

"Six," Connor said, tapping Annabelle's nose again. "And one of them is your mother."

Annabelle grabbed his finger with her little fist and shoved it in her mouth.

"Eww." He yanked it free and held out a hand to Chloe who, true to form, had a clean paper towel close at hand.

"Even though you think she's on your side, don't underestimate Rose Halliday," Chloe said. "She's intrepid and relentless. She damn near got the town council to cancel the Bow Wow Beauty Contest last year because she dug up some local who said it objectified dogs."

Connor looked to the ceiling. "Good grief, I remember that little controversy."

"Which wasn't little, thanks to the *Banner*."

"We're in agreement on Rose," he said. "I respect and fear her. But I'm going to win because of Frank. Do you think if I had him make some appearances with the cat, it would be pushing the cute factor too hard, or really appeal to cat people? They are kind of left out of a lot around here."

"You can," Chloe said. "But Frank is the *ceremonial* candidate. People are voting—or not—for you, Connor, knowing that you'll be the one actually sitting in the chair. Yes, there's a lot of love for the idea of a dog mayor, especially from my department. Tourism will benefit with Frank the Mayor at every event."

"That's my plan. But...traffic? Budgets? Cost of living and retail space? Sadie knows it all cold."

"Do you care about that stuff, Connor?" Shane asked.

"I care about Bitter Bark, so yeah. How is it you don't know that?"

"Because you just joke about Frank all the time. Have you even done any real interviews?" Shane screwed up his face.

"Not really," he admitted. "I hate them. I'll do the job when I have it, but I can't stand sitting there answering inane questions. Although, with Sadie..." He looked down at Annabelle, who was extremely fascinated by his earlobe. "It's kinda fun," he whispered to her.

"Dude." Shane came around the counter as if magnetically drawn to his daughter. "No one is going to vote for you if they don't know where you stand on things."

He dipped away, not ready to relinquish the baby Shane wanted back. "Your daddy has no faith in me. Or Frank."

She used her little palm to push up his nose, giggling at his reaction.

"I can get you a lot of information that's public, but takes work to access," Chloe said. "I'll email you some things that will really give you some talking points for the debate."

He huffed out a breath. "Debate schmebate." He crossed his eyes for Annabelle, who rewarded that with a menacing little fat-fingered grip on his nose.

"You can't send Frank up there 'to talk,'" Chloe said, using air quotes.

"I know. Definitely send me the materials, Chloe. Thanks."

Annabelle dropped her head and started using Connor's shoulder as her personal teething ring, the slobber already soaking through his FD T-shirt. "And I will thank you, Annabelle, to gnaw on my other shoulder to even things out."

Chloe laughed, leaning on the counter and watching the two of them with a smile. "I'm glad to help," she said. "I was beginning to think you weren't taking the mayor's job seriously. So was my aunt, to be honest."

Damn this reputation hanging over his head. Who

would run for mayor if they weren't a *little* bit serious? "Is that why I don't have her endorsement?"

She shook her head. "My uncle Frank didn't believe in them. But he did believe in this town, Connor. He had the same passion you do, and if you can get that across, you can win."

"But what if your 'fiancée' wins?" Shane asked. "Then what?"

"Then…I lose. What do you mean?"

"She'll have to forfeit the election when you two don't get married afterward."

"Not if we have a nice, friendly post-election 'breakup.'" He shrugged into the pool of slobber on his sleeve. "No one can actually prove the engagement was fake unless they eavesdrop on our conversations. Or notice she doesn't have that ring on anymore."

Chloe snapped her fingers. "Oh, I totally forgot I have one of those lab diamonds for when we travel. It's not worthless, but it's not as valuable as this one. Hang on a sec, I'll get it."

The minute Chloe left the kitchen, Annabelle whipped around, stared at the doorway, then took a breath to howl in fury.

"Whoops. We've lost eye contact with the mothership." Shane reached for her again, but Connor shook his head.

"I got this, man. I can calm her down." He hushed and patted her tiny back as it rose to power up for the next wail.

Shane just smirked. "You got this, huh?"

"Shhh, Anna-B." He tried to sway a little, but that made her cry more. "She's coming back. Your mama's coming right back."

She choked a little on the next cry. "Is she okay?" Connor asked.

"She's not happy, but it happens a lot. You sure you don't want backup?"

A giant drop of baby drool hung from her quivering lower lip. "Come on, now, Annabelle," he whispered. "She'll be right back."

She took a shuddering breath, closed her eyes, and was silent for a second.

"What does that mean?" he asked Shane.

"She's gonna blow."

He shot his smartass cousin a look just as Annabelle leaned forward and let out a tiny stream of baby puke on his shoulder and chest.

"She blew," Connor said dryly.

Shane reached for her, easily taking the baby from Connor. "Don't say I didn't warn you. My girl is a little bit pukey."

As Connor plucked at his shirt, Chloe came sailing back in. "Oh no. Did she get ya? Sorry." She held a ring box out to him. "Here you go. Let me grab a wet cloth."

Annabelle dropped her head hard on Shane's shoulder, shoving her thumb in her mouth and staring at Connor with that smug look that said she got exactly what she wanted.

"That ring should help convince the locals." Chloe wet two small towels in the sink and squeezed out the excess water, handing one to Connor, the other to Shane in a silent choreographed exchange he imagined they'd done a hundred times in the last six months.

"But you might need to do more." Shane dabbed at Annabelle's mouth.

"Like be seen in public together?" Connor guessed,

flipping the box open and blinking at the sizable rock inside. "Whoa. This is fake?"

"Oh, there's a debate about that," Chloe told him. "It's grown in a lab, not the ground, but who can tell the difference? That one was half the cost of a comparable diamond, and it's not super fancy, so Sadie can wear it without quite as much worry."

"Thanks for the loan, Chloe. You can have it back as soon as we break up." He made a face as he pressed the towel to the spot on his shirt. "And that sounds as stinky as this baby vom."

"Does it, now?" Shane laughed softly. "Remember when Liam and Andi got married, and it wasn't supposed to be real?"

"That was your dad's idea to protect Christian from being taken into custody by his biological father's family," Connor said.

"But it sure got real," Shane said, his message coming through loud and clear. "Like now-they-have-Christian-*and*-Fiona real."

"Who knew they'd fall in love after that fake marriage?" Chloe crooned.

"My dad," Shane said, then whispered into Annabelle's ear, "That's why they call your grandpa the Dogfather."

"Speaking of the Dogfather," Connor said. "What we really need is for the Dog*mothers* to claim another victory. No reporter is going to question the authority of Finola Kilcannon."

Shane chuckled. "Not to mention the other one. I'd put Yiayia up against Rose Halliday any day."

"I don't know." Chloe shook her head. "Gramma Finnie isn't going to lie. It's just not in her DNA."

"She might for a good cause," Connor said.

"Like you as the next mayor of Bitter Bark?" Shane asked.

"Like me really engaged to Sadie," he said. "If she thinks by talking this thing up, that will make it somehow become real? Oh man. She'll be embroidering 'Connor and Sadie Forever' on pillows and handing them out in Bushrod Square."

Shane nodded, fighting a smile. "But what if it *is* real?" He got a little closer, handling Annabelle like she was a natural extension of his body. "What if this woman is the one that takes Connor Mahoney off the market?"

Connor snorted. "Then pigs would be airborne, and the devil would be ice skating. I'll get serious about this mayoral race when it comes to issues, but I have no plans of really getting serious with a woman." He leaned into to talk to Annabelle. "Even if she is a stunning smokefest with heavenly hair."

Annabelle just sucked her thumb and stared at him.

"No plans at all, Connor?" Chloe asked, nothing but innocence and interest in her question. "You're *never* getting serious? Why?"

"Because..." He looked from one to the other. Did he have to explain it? "I don't want to? Will that work for you? I like things just the way they are, nice and easy and uncomplicated."

"Says the man running for mayor with his dog and using a fake engagement to bypass the rules." Shane cracked up. "Super uncomplicated, man."

"You know what I mean. I like the status quo. I don't want a..." *Loss.* "Girlfriend," he finished lamely.

"Well, you should know that when Gramma and

Yiayia get involved, they aren't going to back down and accept an 'amicable breakup,'" Shane said.

"They'll have to, and I can handle a little pressure from the octogenarians to help the cause. But you know what I can't handle? Eastercrook as mayor."

"Amen to that," Chloe said. "So you manage those grannies, and I'll pull some fact sheets and minutes from the council meetings that can help you in the debate. It's all public record, but I can save you the time of digging through the files."

"Thanks," he said. "Oh, and I told Sadie I'd help her get those thirty signatures she needs."

Shane gave him a look. "Helping the competition?"

"A favor for my fiancée," he said. "But I'm on duty all day tomorrow."

"Bring her to Waterford on Sunday," Shane suggested. "You'll get twenty in one afternoon."

"Good call. I'll ask her." He lifted the ring box. "Maybe I can propose again in front of the whole family. Get some pictures of it to make it official?"

"That'll definitely break the hearts of a dozen or so single women in Bitter Bark," Chloe joked.

Shane held the baby, who reached out two grabby hands like she wanted to chew the crap out of the ring box. "Say goodbye to your second cousin once removed...from the dating scene." Shane, of course, chuckled at his own stupid joke.

"Gimme that girl." Connor lifted the baby from Shane's hands, and she immediately blew a raspberry that sprayed his face, making them all laugh as he handed her right back. "Man, your baby is messy."

"It's all messy." Chloe came around the counter to give him a hug goodbye. "Relationships, marriage, babies. And believe me, Connor, no one was more afraid of messes than I was."

"So be careful playing with fire, Lieutenant." Shane's smile was huge and maybe a little superior. "'Cause you just might get *fried*."

Connor snorted as he leashed Frank and headed to the kitchen door. "Don't worry. I'm an expert with women *and* fires. I'll be fine."

But he could hear Shane and Chloe laughing when he closed the door behind him.

Chapter Fourteen

Something clunked outside.

Instantly, Sadie sat up and blinked into the dimly lit guesthouse. Demi stirred, then lifted her head, ears perked.

"You heard that?" she whispered, picking up the furry body to hold her close, as if the cat could help her against an intruder.

Demi purred and meowed and squirmed out of Sadie's hands, walking across the bed, her paws crunching over the papers spread out on top of the comforter. With a side-eye of deep disgust, Demi stretched out on top of two legal pads covered with notes and ideas for the debate.

"I know, I fell asl—"

Another noise outside cut her off, a thump like something—or *someone*—had bumped one of the clay pots in Boomie's garden. Demi sat up, on full alert now.

"Raccoon?" She pushed the coverlet back and slipped her bare feet onto the rug, blinking into the soft light from the end table. "The midnight oil," she muttered, but it was long past midnight.

Grabbing her phone from the table, she did a double take to see it was a few minutes before five a.m. Jeez. She must have crashed around one or so. For a moment, she sat still on the hard, uncomfortable sofa-bed mattress, half asleep, half—

A flash outside, instant and bright white, made her gasp. Was that lightning…or a camera?

She walked toward the window, grateful she'd closed the blinds last night, but froze in mid-step when she heard the distinct sound of footsteps on the stone walkway between this shed and the garden, retreating into the night.

A cold chill crawled over her skin as she split the blinds to peek out into the predawn darkness, suddenly feeling open and vulnerable and very much alone.

There were no lights on in Nana and Boomie's house, so they hadn't heard anything, or Jim Winthrop would be out there with one of his many firearms. She momentarily considered calling them to make sure they were okay, but waking them at this hour would just make them both so tired they'd sleep in and miss church.

Then there was another flash, this time through the window facing the street.

A reporter? "Why now?" she whispered to Demi, getting a yawn in response. "Because they want to know if Connor's here, I bet. I mean, if we're engaged, wouldn't he be spending the night?"

A slow, low, sexy little butterfly flipped around in her stomach. Just how far would they have to go to prove this was real? Overnights?

Still holding her cell, she looked down at the blank

screen, knowing that she could have him on the phone with one touch of the number he'd entered for her.

He'd said he'd be working a long shift, but wasn't that over now? Soon? And had he meant five a.m. when he'd said, "Call anytime" to her? If he was still at the station, he might be busy. If he was home, he might be...she realized she hadn't even asked him where he lived.

For some reason, that thought made her tap the phone and hit his name in the contacts.

"Sadie?" he answered on the first ring, his voice as clear as if it were five in the afternoon, rather than morning. "What's up?"

"I'm not sure, but I think someone is or was outside my place. Maybe...taking pictures?"

He swore softly. "I'll be right over."

"Really? Aren't you working? Or..."

"I'm just finishing a twenty-four-hour shift. I can be there in a few minutes, even sooner if the next shift is clocked in. Call 911?"

"If I hear something again, I can."

"Okay. Don't move. Don't leave your house. I'll be right there."

Another chill tiptoed up her spine, a different kind this time. Not fear, but...anticipation. And relief. And since when did she need a man to come check on a noise for her?

Apparently, since now.

She hung up and let out a breath she hadn't realized she'd been holding. Yes, she had wanted him to respond like that, if she were being perfectly honest. After a moment, she walked to the bed and scooped up the mess of papers, earning a harsh meow from the little lady sleeping on the traffic management ideas.

"No use letting the competition see what we're working on," she said as she dumped the whole pile on the tiny kitchenette table.

Demi looked sideways as she settled right on the dent in Sadie's pillow.

"What? He *is* the competition."

The competition who was flying over in the middle of the night after a twenty-four-hour shift because she heard a bump outside.

"Yeah, yeah, I know. But he's a natural protector, that big firefighter. It makes him feel manly to run over, probably in full uniform and a helmet, waving his…hose."

And she was in a tank top and sleep pants, and she would not change or comb her hair or even look in the mirror. She glanced at Demi, who was seeing to her own grooming at the moment.

"Okay, I'll brush my teeth."

She did, but just as she spit out the toothpaste, her phone hummed with a call from Connor, making her wonder if maybe he couldn't come over after all.

"Hey," she said when she put the phone to her ear. "It's okay if you can't—"

"I'm outside your front door."

"Oh. That was fast," she said, walking that way.

"My replacement shift was ready to roll, so I left right away. Frank and I just walked your yard and garden and didn't see anyone. Can we come in?"

She opened the door to find him standing with Frank, a flashlight in his hand, beam down. No helmet or jacket, but that tight-fitting navy blue FD T-shirt and khakis, which was quickly becoming her new favorite outfit on him.

"You okay?" he asked, concern visible in his eyes even in the ambient light.

"Fine, yes. I just…I was sleeping."

"So's anyone who's sane." His mouth lifted in a half-smile, and he reached the hand not holding the flashlight to her mouth, dabbing the corner. "Brushed your teeth, though."

She felt her cheeks warm. "I figured I'm up, so—"

Behind her, she heard a familiar hiss, turning to see Demi leap to the back of the sofa, watching them with wary interest.

Frank barked once and nosed his way into the house, bolting past Sadie before Connor could snag his collar. "He's kind of anxious to see her, I guess. Hey, we're not invited in yet, bud." He looked sideways to Sadie. "Or are we?"

"Of course," she said, stepping back.

Frank went straight to Demi, who gazed up at the bookshelves with her *pretending I don't care, but could be talked into something* look. Frank lunged at the sofa, and she flew onto the armrest and then to the ground, where they danced around each other in a circle, Frank's tail moving so fast and hard it was practically making a breeze.

Connor and Sadie watched, laughing as they circled faster, chasing each other's tails, then collapsed and stared into one another's eyes.

"He's literally in love with her," Connor said.

Sadie laughed and closed the door behind him. "Thanks for coming over," she said. "I'm sure you're exhausted."

"No worries. What exactly did you hear?" he asked.

"A noise in the garden, some footsteps, and then I saw a bright flash there and there." She pointed to the two windows. "Like someone was taking pictures, and I was…"

"You were scared."

"Not scared. On alert. And I thought about waking my grandfather, but…"

He smiled and put a hand on her shoulder, his palm warm on her bare skin. "It's okay, Sadie. Calling me was the right thing to do. If you're being stalked by some lunatic media person, it's probably because they're looking to see if I'm here. Maybe old Mitch himself trying to prove we're lying."

"That's exactly what I thought."

"So now my truck's parked outside after a twenty-four-hour shift, because where else would I go for coffee and company?"

She smiled, but mostly to cover the butterflies that seemed to multiply at the sight of Connor Mahoney, swooping around in their Sadie's Got a Crush dance. "Did you get any sleep on this shift?"

"A little, but we did have three calls overnight."

"What kind of calls?" she asked, walking to the coffeemaker on the kitchenette counter. "Any fires?"

"Someone smelled smoke, but it was a broken heating unit in the garage. And two medical calls. A lady with pretty severe food poisoning, but we took her over to Vestal Valley General for an IV, and the usual call to Starling." As he talked, he walked around the space, glancing at the papers on her desk, then peeking out a window.

"What's Starling?" she asked.

"Oh, that's right, you haven't been here since that was built. It's an assisted living facility right outside of Bitter Bark. As you can imagine, we go there a lot." Satisfied with whatever he didn't see outside, he continued his tour, pausing at the tall bookshelf next to the TV. "Tonight, it was for chest pains in eighty-nine-year-old Miss Clara Dee."

"Really?" She poured water into the coffeemaker. "Is she okay?"

"She's fine. She has chest pains about once a month since her husband died. The only thing wrong with her heart is that it's broken."

"Oh, Connor. That's so…" She turned from the sink to look at him, finding him leaning to look at the top shelf, peering hard at the Susan B. Anthony bust she'd brought all the way from DC.

"That's so…what?" he asked. "Heroic? Kind? Attractive?" he prodded, reaching up to touch it. "Which this lady isn't. Is this a woman?"

"It's *the* woman," she said. "Aunt Sue."

He turned to her, a look of disbelief barely covering a laugh. "You have a bust of your Aunt Sue?" His expression shifted to horrified. "Her ashes?"

She cracked up. "It's Susan B. Anthony. Aunt Sue was what she was called by Elizabeth Cady Stanton. They were—"

"Suffragettes," he interjected, pointing a finger at her. "See? I learned something in civics class." He reached for the piece, gingerly lifting it. "I'm guessing this was not a professional sculpture."

"I made it in eighth grade, and my dad helped." She smiled at the memory, at the hours they'd spent laughing and learning in the basement, with Mom upstairs. When they were still…a unit. Before Mitch and Mom…

"It's…lovely," he joked.

"It's dear to me. And be sure to push it back to the corner because Demi loves that thing and frequently jumps on that shelf to drape her paws around Aunt Sue. I don't want her to knock it off."

"Gotchya." He tenderly moved it to the back of the shelf, showing respect for the admittedly ugly clay art project that made the very short list of things she packed when she left DC in such a hurry.

"So, tell me more about this Clara at Starling," she said. "I didn't know EMTs got personally involved with the lives of people they help."

"In this town? Everyone's family. And Clara Dee more than most because she reminds me of my very own grandmother."

"Grandmas are sweet," she agreed, turning back to the coffee because diving over there and hiding her notes seemed stupid.

"They're also nuts, at least in my case."

"Yours are…colorful," she agreed.

"Well, only the little Irish one is technically mine. The Greek is my…hang on now. Yiayia is my uncle's new wife's former mother-in-law."

She frowned and nodded as she followed the trail. "Katie's first husband's mother? Actually, my nana told me all about how your uncle Daniel fell in love again after being a widower."

His examination of her little home apparently over, he settled his long, strong body in one of the kitchen chairs and shifted his attention to her. "Did she tell you about Nick, the cousin we never knew we had?"

She blew out a soft whistle. "Yes. Wild. My family is so small and uncomplicated, it's kind of cool to hear all the stories about yours." Leaning against the counter while the coffee brewed, she studied him... studying her. "What?" she asked when he smiled and shook his head a little.

"You sleep hot, no surprise."

"Sleep...hot? Is that some firefighter term?"

"Yeah, a danger to ignite any male in viewing distance."

She rolled her eyes, but had to fight a smile.

"Must be all that..." He ruffled his fingers near his head. "Hair."

"Must be." She brushed a lock over her shoulder, weirdly grateful she hadn't brushed it into submission. "Well, thanks. I'm sure you sleep hot, too."

"If I don't get coffee soon, you'll find out."

"It's almost ready." She turned and grabbed two mugs, physically unable to wipe the damn smile from her face. *You sleep hot.* The compliment rang in her ears, along with the sexy look in his eyes when he said it. After pouring the coffee, she turned to ask how he took it, and the smile disappeared when she found him poring over her papers. "Hey. Privacy alert."

He looked up. "You really do have a plan for traffic management."

She just let her eyes shutter closed. "Cream and sugar?"

"Black as night." He tapped the page. "Make Ambrose Avenue one way? Please open with that at the debate. I can taste victory."

She put the cups down and headed back to the fridge for creamer. "Mind your own business."

"But…one way?"

"Yes, one way. And Bushrod Boulevard can go the opposite way, then traffic will move thanks to extra lanes." He looked at her like she was certifiable when she came back to pour the creamer in her coffee. "It's a simple change and smart."

"Not if you're leaving the fire station on the way to a burning house in North Bitter Bark, and you lose at least three minutes getting a pumper truck around the square to make your merry way over to Bushrod Boulevard. Not smart in the least for the poor people whose house is on fire."

Oh. Truth be told, she hadn't thought of the emergency vehicles. "We'll work out the kinks."

"You work out your kinks, DC." He sipped the coffee. "Just please be sure to mention that to all the people at the debate. In fact, make it your main campaign message." He gave a sly grin. "Then prepare your concession speech."

"So Frank can bark out his?" she lobbed back.

He raised his coffee mug. "So be it, hot sleeper."

She sighed and slid into the chair across from him, taking one of the pages of notes and flipping it to cover all the rest. "Let's not talk about it, okay? I'm barely awake, and I can't think about mayoral politics at the moment. Do you think someone was out there?"

"Maybe. And I don't like that." He took a drink, eyeing her over the rim. "I can stay until it's light. Longer."

"Thanks. You should try and get a little rest."

"Yeah, big day at Waterford Farm. I hear everyone is making an appearance, and I do mean everyone."

She sipped her coffee, thinking about the list of

names her grandmother had gone over yesterday and some of the things Connor had told her the other day in the square. "There are so many Mahoneys and Kilcannons and Santorinis."

"They all fall into place eventually." He leaned forward. "Brace yourself, I'm bringing a ring."

Her eyes widened. "Seriously? Who sacrificed their engagement ring this time?"

"Chloe again, but not the real one. She said it's one of those lab diamonds she uses as her substitute when they travel. Have you heard of them?"

She put down her cup with a *thunk*. "Heard of them? They've damn near consumed my life."

"How?"

She didn't answer right away, deciding how deep into the conversation she wanted to go at this hour. "My ex, the lobbyist?"

"He offered you one, and you recoiled in distaste?" he guessed.

She smiled. "No. He and his client contact in the NLDA talked about them constantly." At his perplexed look, she explained, "National Lab Diamond Association. It's one of the growers groups, and Nathan leads their lobbying efforts, which are massive. They spend millions and millions trying to convince various government agencies that lab-grown diamonds are real."

"Why would that matter?"

"It matters plenty to the industry that mines organic, natural diamonds and competes with the manmade rocks. And the lab-grown-diamond business? Oh my God, they *literally* grow money. Nathan would get dozens of the stones to take to political events in an endless effort to lobby lawmakers and prove that they are made of precisely the same materials as mined diamonds, but they're grown in weeks and are so much more ethically and environmentally desirable."

"What's the difference in cost?"

"They can be less than half the price of a comparable diamond. Nathan was part of a team that won a major coup to have the FTC change the definition of a diamond to 'a mineral consisting of pure crystallized carbon.' It was a crushing blow for the diamond miners and producers, who would do anything to keep those lab diamonds off the market."

"I guess I can see why," he said. "The one Chloe gave me was pretty damn real-looking. Flash it around town, and people will believe it's real."

"Us or the diamond?" she teased.

"Both."

"And yet, neither one is organic." She angled her head and smiled at the irony. "It's the perfect ring for our engagement. Not quite real, but it could fool the outside world."

"That's kind of…sad." He picked up his coffee and gave her a wistful smile.

She rested her chin on her palm to stare at him unabashedly, so comfortable with his big presence in her little home. "You know, you really have changed since I knew you in high school, Connor. It wasn't fair of me to say the things I did the night we met."

He shrugged. "At least I'm no longer a loudmouth showoff with a chip on my shoulder."

"I never called you that."

"You didn't have to. That's what I was."

"What put that chip there back then?" she asked, intrigued.

"Oh, you know. Bad cards life deals."

He tried to sound nonchalant. Tried too hard, actually, and immediately Sadie knew what he meant. During her long conversation with Nana, they'd talked about how the whole town had been affected by the death of Joe Mahoney, a well-liked local firefighter who'd been killed on duty twenty years ago.

She remembered there'd been a tribute assembly in high school, with all the Mahoneys and Kilcannons, Connor's mother's family, in attendance.

He covered his thoughts by finishing the coffee, and when he put down the cup, she reached over and placed her hand on his. "Bad cards like your dad's death?"

He took in a breath like he was about to dismiss the question, or maybe even push up to leave, but after a second, that breath came whooshing back out.

"Yeah," he said simply. "Not that I want to blame my douchey behavior on that, but..." He shifted in his seat, letting his gaze drop to her hand. "I was sixteen when he died and pretty damn..." He swallowed, but didn't finish. "I guess I compensated by not taking anything too seriously, except football, and then, after I graduated, being a firefighter. Because those two things mattered to him."

She eyed him for a moment, once again forced to drop a few preconceived notions about Connor Mahoney. "That's understandable," she said. "It's a terrible age to lose a parent."

"There's no good age to lose a parent," he replied, pulling his hand away. "None of us sailed through that time easily. But my dad was also my football coach, and he was..." He laughed lightly. "He basically thought he was the second coming of Vince Lombardi. So not only did I lose the man at the head of our dinner table, I lost the one who met me on the field every afternoon that he wasn't on duty at the station and who somehow, miraculously, knew how to...fix whatever was wrong. A bad throw, a crappy grade, a fight with Declan, or a missed opportunity with a girl. My dad had...answers."

Her heart shifted a little, giving her a chance to revisit her memory of the boy and his swagger and realize that there was only a shadow of that left, but it was all she'd been seeing. "I'm sorry."

"Hey, thanks, but not your fault. When you lose your father at sixteen, it affects everything. The way to win, which is all he cared about for me, is to not let it wreck you." He picked up his empty cup in a mock toast. "It hasn't."

"But you're still single."

He gave her a look. "What the hell does that have to do with my dad?"

She lifted her brows and shrugged. "You tell me."

"Nah. My older brother's still single, too, though I think we have different reasons."

"What are yours?" she asked, surprised at how much she wanted to know.

"Why does it matter?"

"Uh...because we're engaged?"

He gave an almost smile. "Fine." He shifted in his seat, thinking, then looked at her to say, "I feel like that whole...serious relationship and marriage and family thing...is a game that I'm not sure I want to play."

"Getting married is a game?"

"A gamble?" he suggested instead. "A risk I'm not sure I want to take? However you package it, I'm fine with things that last a few weeks or a month. But then..."

"You get bored."

He held her gaze for a few heartbeats, intensifying the quiet intimacy of the moment. "That's not it."

"What is it, then?"

His lips curled up. "Pretty deep for five in the morning after a twenty-four-hour shift, Ear Girl."

She leaned in a little. "How else can I find out your deepest secrets?"

His blue eyes flickered with surprise. "You want to know them? Why?"

"My old boss used to say, 'Information is power.'" She smiled. "Maybe I want a little power."

He inched closer, too, reaching over the little table to put his hand over hers. "You already have a lot of power. I spent twenty-two hours on a shift thinking about you."

Her heart flipped. "What about the other two?"

"Out on calls, when I don't think about anything but my job."

She couldn't look away. The pull of his attention was too strong, and the heat curling through her was absolutely delicious. "And what exactly did you think about for twenty-two hours? How to debate me?"

"If by 'debate' you mean 'kiss you until you can't breathe,' yeah."

She had to fight not to shiver in front of him. "God, you're good."

"I can be." He took a slow breath and stood up, his broad shoulders rising and falling, his gaze unwavering. He stepped around the little table and reached for her, drawing her to her feet. "You know what would be a horrible waste?"

She shook her head, vaguely aware of need rolling over her, powerful, dizzying, and real.

"All that toothpaste you used so I would kiss you."

"You think that's why I brushed my teeth."

"I know it." He lowered his head and let his tongue graze her lower lip. "Mmm. Minty fresh."

She wanted to smile, but she wanted to kiss more. "No one's watching us, Connor."

"I hope not."

"I mean…we don't have to."

"Yeah. We do." He pressed his lips against hers, pulling her in so she could feel every hard muscle and angle of his body. She tasted black coffee and tangy peppermint. And Connor. Hot tongue and sweet lips and warm, wet kisses.

Arching into the kiss, she wrapped her hands around his neck, drawing him closer as he splayed his fingers over her back and cradled her in his arms.

"C'mere," he said gruffly, guiding her toward the open sofa bed. "Just let me kiss you."

She didn't argue. How could she with her mouth attached to his, her fingers digging into his back, her body melting against him?

He eased her onto the bed, half sitting, then falling back, kissing her throat and jaw as his big hands stroked her back and dipped over the curve of her rear end.

"This is it," he murmured into the kisses.

"This is…" She felt her eyes widen as heat curled through her. "What?"

"My fantasy. All freaking day." He trailed his

tongue along the line of her jaw and headed back to her mouth. "Twenty-four hours."

"Twenty-two," she corrected into the kiss.

"I lied. Even on calls." He slid both his hands into her hair, finger-combing the messy, morning strands and moaning with pleasure. "I just wanted...this."

"Yeah." She couldn't lie. She'd been thinking an awful lot about it, too. "Yeah, nothing like...*oh*." She gasped as he pulled her on top of him, the ridge of a massive erection shocking her. And all she wanted to do was...press against him.

But Frank barked so loud it made them both freeze for a moment.

"Pay attention to your own girl, Franko." He coasted his hand from her hair to her shoulder, hovering over her breast as he held her gaze. "'Cause I'm really into mine."

But Frank barked again, more furiously, and Demi flew from wherever she was to the top of the kitchen cabinet, as she frequently did when someone was at the door.

"Is someone here?" Sadie asked in a hushed whisper, trying to quell the quivering in her body.

Very slowly, Connor sat up and inched her to the side, frowning in the dim light at Frank at the foot of the sofa bed, his ears pointed straight up, his green-gold eyes sharp and alert as he barked at them, but stared at the door.

Connor held up his hand for her to stay where she was and then pushed off the bed, walking to the door with Frank, who stayed nearly glued to Connor. He might bark like a guard dog, but the poor guy was still not thrilled with strangers.

Connor stood still at the door, cocking his head to listen. "I think I heard someone," he mouthed to her. "Can I go out?"

She nodded since there was no window on that side of the house, and no matter who was out there, they weren't going to stay when a six-foot firefighter and his dog warned them off.

He guided Frank in front of him, turning the deadbolt, then the knob, opening the door. Frank barked again, loud and a little bit frantic now, growling and pulling Connor forward.

Sadie sat stone-still, staring, waiting, shivering from the shock of heat that had gone ice-cold, but not able to hear anything except the dog's barking. Connor took him outside, letting him lead.

"No one's out here," he called between barks. "But damn, Frank smells something. What is it, bud?"

Sadie stood and ventured closer to the door, braced for anything as she took a slow, deep breath, inhaling the scent that Frank smelled.

Braced for anything but *that*.

"What do you smell, Frank?" Connor asked again.

"Shalimar," Sadie whispered. He smelled the sweet, sickly, spicy scent that would haunt Sadie for the rest of her life.

Why in God's name had Jane Sutherland been lurking outside Sadie's front door?

Chapter Fifteen

Frank pulled, barked, stopped to sniff, and pulled some more, leading Connor into the garden, then down the path toward the street.

"What is it, boy? What do you smell?"

He slowed his trot, growled, and stayed so close to Connor that they almost both tripped. Together, they marched toward the white fence that enclosed the property, with Frank sniffing as they went, barking only occasionally.

Pulling out his phone, Connor turned on the flashlight and aimed the beam at the street, right into a parked car that definitely hadn't been there when he pulled up a while ago. He'd have noticed a pricey white Beemer on the streets of Bitter Bark.

He hopped the fence, leaving Frank, who barked in a quick panic, and walked toward the car, flashing the light over the empty front and back seats.

"Is it parked illegally, Officer?"

He spun around at the woman's voice, barely audible over Frank's barks, shining the light right in her face.

"I can move the car," she added, using a hand to shield her eyes and face.

He hardly heard the words, so he held up one hand toward the dog. "Frank!" He shouted the name. "Quiet!"

Frank stopped barking and no doubt collapsed to the dirt in misery at that tone. But Connor had to concentrate on the woman in front of him. He lowered the light so he could still see her but not blind her.

"Is it?" she asked. "Illegally parked?" She shook back some blond hair to reveal the tapered features of an angular face, her eyes hard to see behind dark-rimmed glasses. His first impression was…harsh. Brittle. Sharp. Though some might call her beautiful.

"I'm not an officer," he replied. "But you're trespassing."

"On the street?" Even her voice, with a rasp and edge, sounded like it could cut things.

"You were in that yard."

She glanced past him. "I was looking for Sadie Hartman."

"At six in the morning?"

She didn't answer, but pushed her glasses up as though getting a better look, then she smiled, which did little to soften her features. "Oh, you're the other mayoral candidate. The one she's acting like she's engaged to." She nodded as if she were putting puzzle pieces together. "And that's the mayor dog."

Her oddly distinct voice had an air of condescension in it, and amusement, and vague familiarity. "Do I know you?"

She shook her head. "No. And you probably don't want to if you're friends with Sadie. But I wanted to talk to her."

"At six in the morning." he repeated, with emphasis.

"I had to leave DC late last night and I just got here."

DC...*oh*. He suddenly knew why she looked vaguely familiar, though he didn't think he'd ever seen a picture of the congresswoman wearing glasses. This was the boss who banged Sadie's boyfriend. He recognized the fine blond hair, the strong cheekbones, and well-defined jaw, and the voice he'd heard give a speech on YouTube the other day.

"What are you doing here?" he asked.

She gave a tight smile. "So she told you."

"We're engaged," he said, letting a little wryness into the words.

She rolled her eyes with a look to the sky. "I can't imagine that'll work, but Sadie is nothing if not creative. Leave it to her to think outside the box when there's a campaign roadblock."

He didn't bother to claim credit for the idea. Instead, he shifted to a wider stance, feeling as protective as Frank when it came to this woman...who was not getting one inch closer to Sadie.

"Can I help you with something?" he asked, making no effort to warm up to the lady he disliked on sight and on principle.

"I wanted to ask her a question." She glanced beyond him at the dog and the house. "But I guess she's still upset with me."

Still upset? He opened his mouth to reply, but the woman's whole expression suddenly changed into something warmer, softer, and slightly more real.

"There you are," she said with an almost maternal coo. "Sadie."

196

He turned to see Sadie had emerged, standing next to Frank, a hand on his head, a sweatshirt pulled on over the tank top. "How the hell did you find me, Jane?"

"Honey, your name's all over some silly story about running for mayor. A quick Google search would tell anyone in the free world how to find you." She took a few steps closer, but Connor blocked her.

"At this house?" Sadie asked.

"Listed as a second emergency contact in your employee file," Jane said with lightning speed, as though expecting the question.

"You're not welcome. Is that clear enough?"

Whoa. He'd heard Sadie when she was serious and seriously pissed, but he'd never been on the receiving end of that much ice.

Jane let out a noisy sigh and came closer, tucking shaky hands in her jacket pocket. "I get that, Sadie," she said. "I really do. If it's any consolation, everything is…over. And I'll do anything, absolutely anything, to make it up to you and have you come back."

Sadie sucked in a breath, then let it out with a laugh. "You think I'd trust you again?"

"No," the woman said simply. "But for the record, I acknowledge that I made a terrible mistake, and I'm asking for your forgiveness."

Sadie stared at her, silent.

"Okay, then." She took her hands out, wringing them as if she were trying to calm herself. "I hurt and betrayed you, Sadie. Can we talk about it? Can I come in?"

Sadie's gaze stayed locked on her former boss. "No," she said simply.

"Sadie, please, listen to me. I know how you feel, but I am so, so sorry. You really don't understand, though."

"Oh, I understand." Sadie's voice was sharp.

"The whole thing was…foolish and…and a mistake. Nathan's bereft that you're gone."

"Please, Jane," Sadie said softly. "Leave now."

Jane swallowed. "Okay. Well, good luck with your mayoral campaign. Believe it or not, I'd be proud to offer up my endorsement or campaign for you."

Sadie snorted. "Thanks, but I got this."

"I'm sure you do." She turned to Connor and let her gaze drag up and down him, a little too long and uncomfortable for him.

"Goodbye," he said pointedly.

She leaned in to whisper, "She's not over him yet, and I think they could still work this out someday. He still loves her, and God, Nathan Lawrence was her whole world, and she will never, ever love another man like she loved him."

"Why are you telling me this?"

"Because information is power, my friend."

Yes, he'd just heard that from Sadie. "What do I need power for?"

"So you win that campaign."

"Why would you be on my side?"

She raised her brows as if the answer were obvious. "Because if she loses, she'll come back to Washington, and I need her. I need her back on my staff because I'm…dying."

"Excuse me?"

"Without her," she added. "I'm dying without her." With that, she pivoted to her car, got in, started the engine, and drove away without glancing back at them.

He watched the taillights for a moment, frozen at the force of her presence, breathing in the lingering scent of perfume that reminded him of a schoolteacher he never liked. He turned slowly, almost afraid to know if Sadie had heard any of that last exchange.

But she was gone, already almost back inside, with Frank.

He followed, using the gate instead of jumping the fence, heading back to the front door that she'd left open for him.

"Well, that was weird," he said as he stepped inside.

She was on the bed, with Demi in her arms and Frank sitting at attention at her feet, panting at the cat. "Yeah."

"Are you okay?"

She shrugged and stroked the cat's head. "Frank came with me," she said. "Isn't that progress?"

Something in her voice sounded broken, and it smacked his heart.

"She wants you back," he said. "You heard that, right?"

"I didn't have to. I know she wants me back. I'm still friends with staffers, and I've heard the place is total chaos now."

"Would you reconsider?" he asked, a little surprised at how much he didn't want her to say yes.

"Did I sound like a person who would reconsider?" she asked. "I can't forgive her."

"Or him," he added.

When she didn't answer, he looked up and found

her staring at him with only a question in her golden-brown eyes. "What else did she say to you?" she asked softly.

Why lie? "That he's not over you. And you probably aren't over him."

She snorted.

"And that you'd never love anyone else like you loved him."

She continued stroking Demi's head, looking down. "Maybe she's transferring her own feelings to me. She doesn't like to lose people once she has them in her grasp."

"Did she have you?"

"In some ways, yes," she admitted. "Our relationship was complex. Mentor and student, boss and employee, even mother and daughter, though she's only about seven years older than I am. Seeing her out there was…hard."

He put a hand on her shoulder. "I could tell. Are you okay?"

"I was better before she showed up." She managed a wistful smile. "Sorry about the interruption."

"Sorry she showed up and wrecked you."

"She wrecked me a month ago." She blew out a breath, the first sign of tears in her eyes.

"Hey, Sadie. C'mere." He wrapped his arms around her and pulled her closer, once again only wanting to take that pain from her expression.

"Should I forgive her?" she asked on a whisper. "Is that the right thing to do?"

"My grandmother always says that hate hurts the vessel it's in, not the one it gets poured on." He gave a dry laugh. "Something like that. With a brogue."

He felt her smile against his chest, giving him a little kick of satisfaction.

"Maybe you can forgive her, Sadie. Forgive them both."

He felt her collapse a little in his arms. "No, I can't."

Nathan Lawrence was her whole world, and she will never, ever love another man like she loved him.

Sharp, edgy, wily Jane Sutherland had certainly given him information that he could use…but not to make sure he didn't lose an election. To make sure he didn't lose his heart to a woman who'd already given hers to someone else.

Chapter Sixteen

Sadie never thought she'd long to see the ubiquitous Hello, My Name Is... sticker on someone's chest, but that political-function staple would really help a lot on a Sunday afternoon at Waterford Farm. The big country kitchen teemed with strangers, and Sadie would be grateful to know a Kilcannon from a Mahoney from a Santorini.

"Don't worry, you'll get to know everyone soon enough." A spunky teenager she hadn't met yet sidled up to Sadie, cuddling a baby in her arms. "I'm Pru, daughter of Trace and Molly, who is Connor's cousin, and this is my baby brother, Danny. Welcome to Crazytown."

Sadie laughed. "Okay. Molly and Trace. Now, I did get a complete rundown on the way over here, so give me a second...the vet and the therapy dog trainer?"

"Very good. Did he tell you everything? Like how my dad showed up after fourteen years needing help for Meatball?"

Sadie nodded, remembering the remarkable and emotional story Connor had shared about Trace's time in prison, never knowing he'd fathered a child. "I'm happy your family is united."

"Same." She swayed the baby, who looked less than six months old, but had a decent amount of dark hair on a head lying contentedly on his sister's shoulder, one hand gripping a lock of her long hair.

On Sadie's other side, a gorgeous young woman with a pixie cut and wide eyes the color of espresso joined them. "Greetings, new girl. I'm Ella." She extended a hand as delicate as her fine features. "Your fake future sister-in-law, fourth child and only daughter on the Mahoney side. Mom likes me best, and no matter what my brother told you, I am, under no circumstances, to be called Smella."

Laughing at the introduction, Sadie shook her hand, admiring the twentysomething with the look of a young Audrey Hepburn about her. "He did, actually, mention that nickname. He told me I *had* to call you that."

She rolled those stunning brown eyes. "If I didn't love my big brothers so much, I'd hate them."

Pru snorted. "You worship them all, especially Connor."

Ella shrugged. "Sometimes he's my favorite, but other times, when he gets all protective, like when anyone with a Y chromosome comes within a two-mile radius of me? Then I want to kill him." She grinned at Sadie. "So thanks for the distraction, Sadie. Maybe I can scare up a date while he's running for mayor and following you around, tripping over his own tongue."

"Happy to help," Sadie said, doubting very much that the young woman had any trouble getting a date.

Ella lifted a tall Bloody Mary. "Did you get one of these? My cousin Darcy is in charge of the pitchers today, so they are strong."

"I have one." She tipped her head to the glass on the island counter next to her. "But I haven't met Darcy yet."

"I'm right here." Another woman cozied up to them, a sunny blonde with a blinding smile, a veritable ray of sunshine, and Sadie warmed to her instantly. "Maker of strong drinks, dog groomer, youngest Kilcannon, and…" She looked at the others. "What else does she need to know?"

"That you are attached at my hip," Ella said, then made a pouty face that somehow managed to make her prettier. "Or were until you got married last summer, and now that hip belongs to the great and powerful Josh Ranier."

"Oh, I met Josh," Sadie chimed in, happy to recognize a name. "He was the one with two little white dogs, right? Connor introduced me when we took Frank out to the pen."

"The two little white dogs are Kookie and Stella, but you are not expected to learn the dog's names, too," Darcy assured her.

"But you are expected to come and see the grannies," Pru said. "In fact, they sent me in here to escort you to them."

"Ohhh." Ella lifted a brow. "You've been summoned by the Dogmothers."

"Of course, I'd love to see them." Sadie picked up her glass. "I met them at my grandmother's knitting group. Where are they?"

"On the patio," Pru said. "Normally, they'd have

jumped you the minute you arrived, but…I think they're a little miffed about what happened."

Sadie drew back. "What happened?"

They all shared a look of amusement. "You do it," Darcy said to Ella. "You're better than I am."

Ella cleared her throat, angled her head, and adjusted the neckline of an imaginary sweater. "'The lass was supposed to be a campaign manager, not an opponent!'" She used a thick, spot-on brogue.

"Oh dear." Sadie made a face. "Have I angered the powers that be?"

"Honestly, you can't *anger* Gramma Finnie," Ella said. "She's the sweetest human on earth and loves nothing more than when I do her brogue. Now, the Greek grandmother?"

Just then, another beauty joined the small group, who Connor had introduced as Cassie, his sister-in-law and daughter of Katie. Good God, she needed a cheat sheet and a family tree. And maybe another drink of the strong Bloody Mary.

"Did someone call for a Greek?" Cassie shook a head full of thick black hair and trained an ebony gaze on Sadie. "I represent the Mediterranean side of the family, joined courtesy of the marriage of my mother to her father." She pointed to Darcy. "*And* I have the distinct advantage of being married to Connor's younger brother, Braden. So I can literally speak for *all* sides of the family—Mahoney, Santorini, and Kilcannon. What do you want to know?"

"Is the Greek grandmother mad at me?" Sadie asked, surprised that deep inside she cared very much what the two older women thought. They were responsible for this sprawling, loving, lively extended family, and Sadie respected that.

"I don't think she's *mad*, per se," Cassie said, obviously choosing her words carefully. "For one thing, Yiayia doesn't have quite the short temper she used to."

"Mellowed with age?" Sadie asked.

"You could put it that way," Cassie said.

"And she's heady from her matchmaking successes," Pru added. "The Dogmothers take their grandchildren's romances very seriously, and after you..." She pointed at Cassie. "And them..." She shifted her finger to a couple working side by side at the stove. Sadie remembered them as Grace and Alex. "They are not going to accept defeat with Connor."

Sadie just widened her eyes, and Ella put a hand on her arm. "They expect you to marry him."

"Like, for real." Pru lifted her brows.

She choked softly. "I mean, I could tell they were trying to, you know, nudge me in his direction for a date, but...seriously?"

"First of all, the Dogmothers don't nudge," Cassie said, holding up her left hand to show off a sparkling diamond. "The Greek one will shove you in the direction she wants you to go, and the Irish one will soften your resolve with clever proverbs and shots of Jameson's until you agree to anything."

They all laughed but Sadie. She just placed her fingers on her forehead and closed her eyes like it was all too much, making the others playfully clink glasses.

"She knows she's finished," Pru said.

"Might as well set a date," Ella joked. *Maybe* joked.

"You couldn't find a better family."

Sadie nodded at Cassie's comment. "Y'all are pretty darn dazzling."

"Dazzling!" They exclaimed in unison, toasting their drinks as Pru shifted the baby and gave Sadie a nudge. "Ready to see the grannies?"

Sadie took a deep breath and lifted her own glass. "Take me to your leaders." She swallowed a gulp of spicy tomato juice, got a kick of courage from the generous amount of vodka, and tapped little Danny's button nose. "Come with me, young man. It'll be fun, right?"

"Oh, the trouble with trouble, lassies, is that it always starts out as fun," Ella teased in her fake brogue.

Their laughter rang through the house as they all headed off to face the Dogmothers, with Pru practically pushing Sadie in the right direction.

Connor's grandmother put a gnarled, knotted hand over his and rubbed her age-smoothed palm across his knuckles. "Lad, I'd move heaven and earth for ye. But I won't lie."

"I'm not asking you to lie, Gramma." He shifted on the hassock in front of her, where he stopped to chat. "I just need you to help me by telling a lot of people how excited you are about this engagement. And take all the credit for it. I know you want to do that."

"Because what I say is *true*," she replied pointedly. "And this...isn't."

"Or is it?" Yiayia, sitting next to Gramma Finnie in

a matching rattan rocker, leaned forward to ask the question. "Because if it is…"

He lifted a brow, wishing he could at least assure them there was a chance this relationship was real—because that predawn kissing sure felt real, and if Jane hadn't shown up? He knew where it was going.

But the exchange with Jane Sutherland changed everything. Sadie was on the rebound at best and still in love with her ex at worst. And then, when he went home to shower and change, he did an internet search on Nathan Lawrence, and plenty of photos showed up with one gorgeous congressional staffer on his arm.

The guy didn't look bad, either. No firefighter, but no slouch in the physical department, with an air of wealth and success he wore like a designer suit. There were enough pictures of the couple smiling at each other, hand in hand or arm in arm, for Connor to realize it hadn't been a casual relationship, which only added to the possibility that Jane Sutherland had told him the truth.

If so, then he didn't want to pursue Sadie. Sure, maybe she downplayed the relationship, or maybe she was so wounded from Nathan's cheating that she didn't want to admit how deep her feelings for her ex really ran, but why would he take the chance?

He didn't play to lose.

"It's real…enough," he said softly, glancing at the door where he knew Sadie could show up any minute, since Gramma and Yiayia had sent Pru to fetch her. He wanted to use the moment alone with them to ask his favor—that they "spread the word" for him. Because he had to remember what mattered and not get caught up in this "engagement."

What mattered was this election, which took on only more significance now. Even if she won, who was to say she wouldn't run back to DC when Nathan Lawrence crooked his finger?

"What is that supposed to mean?" Yiayia asked. "Real enough for...what?"

"For us to qualify under Bitter Bark's stupid hundred-and-fifty-year-old rules."

Gramma Finnie gasped softly. "'Tis nothin' wrong with old Thaddeus Bushrod's rules. "'Twas a good man with good intentions."

"Come on, Gramma. You've been around awhile, but you didn't know Thad personally."

She lifted a white brow. "Seamus kept a copy of the *History of Bitter Bark*, written by Captain Bushrod, lad. I've never read it, but Seamus told me it was mostly rules for how a man should live his life. Good rules."

"Where is that book, Gramma?" Connor asked.

"I gave it to your mother many years ago, and if I'm not mistaken, she gave it to your father." She toyed with the top button of one of her zillion old-lady sweaters. "The legacy Thaddeus Bushrod left was that this town has been governed by good, stable men— and one woman, counting sweet Blanche Wilkins— who understood that family is what makes up the heart and soul of this town."

"Family and dogs," he interjected. "And I give you..." He put his hand on the dog lying at his feet. "Mayor Frank."

Gramma smiled down at the animal. "He's a dear one, no doubt about it. All of the dogs of Bitter Bark are, but dogs come with families, lad, and I'm with Captain Bushrod on this one," she said. "I think the mayor should be committed to one person and building a life on a solid foundation. Not…" She lifted a white brow. "Playing the field."

He looked at Yiayia, who shrugged. "I'd cover for you, son. I've no problem with a little bit of stretching of the truth for a good cause. At least, that's what I tell myself every time I get Botox."

He smiled at her easy, self-deprecating humor. "A perfect analogy, Yiayia."

"Maybe, but I doubt it will persuade your grandmother."

He looked at Gramma Finnie, whose entire wrinkled countenance said one thing: *I canna tell a lie, lad.* Also, she'd never used Botox.

"Okay, fine," he said on a sigh. "Side with Thad, then. You don't have to tell anyone it's real."

"Oh, I won't. I'll tell them the *truth.*" She picked up a thick glass with a few fingers of amber liquid he knew damn well wasn't the dregs of iced tea. "I'll tell them it's as fake as a female leprechaun."

"Gramma!"

"Finola!"

"What's with all the gasping?"

Connor turned to see his mother coming up the steps to the patio, Colleen Mahoney's sweet smile firmly in place as she eyed the three of them.

"Oh, nothing, Mom. Just that Gramma Finnie wants Mitch Easterbrook to be mayor of Bitter Bark."

His mother curled a lip. "He's disgusting on so many levels."

"And not exactly the paragon of family virtues you want so much to elect," he said, only partly under his breath.

Mom dropped onto the empty sofa, flipping back that long, dark blond ponytail she refused to cut. "He's a phony," she said, blunt as always. "He's heartless, and his wife is a fool."

"But he *has* a wife," Connor said. "And apparently, that's more important than having standards, ethics, or caring about the people of this town, according to Thad Bushrod. Do you have a copy of his *History of Bitter Bark*, by the way?"

His mother drew her brows, a distant look in her blue eyes. "I do," she finally said. "Joe loved reading it, and I put it with his stuff in the attic. Do you want me to find it?"

"Not if it's any trouble," he said quickly, never wanting to put his mother in a position to unpack her grief once again.

"It's me he wants to trouble," Gramma said.

"I just want your...support."

Gramma tsked and closed her eyes. "Lad, I'm not going to tell a lie. No, I'm no fan of the undertaker. But..." She glanced at Yiayia. "Lying at our age is dangerous business."

Connor frowned. "Why?"

"We're closer to our Maker than you are," Yiayia explained. "So the answer is simple." She crossed her arms and looked hard at him. "Make it real." Yiayia gave him a tight smile. "Get on your knee, slide that ring on her finger, ask her to marry you...and *mean* it."

He stared at her, silent as a million unfamiliar emotions went to war in his chest. "I barely know her," he finally whispered.

"Then start working on that," Yiayia said.

"Let's compromise, lad." Gramma Finnie leaned all the way forward and put both hands on his face this time, turning his head so he would look her in the eyes. "Make *me* believe it, then I'll be confident tellin' the whole town what you've found with her."

"How? When?"

Just then, he heard feminine laughter on the other side of the screen door.

"Now would be a good time," Gramma Finnie said. "And how is up to you, but I'm a big fan of the grand gesture."

The minute she said it, he knew what to do.

Sadie appeared in the doorway, surrounded by his sister, cousins, and sister-in-law. She fit right in with the gorgeous group, all of them holding drinks except Pru, who held little Danny. As they lingered on the other side of the open slider, laughing at something Ella had said, Connor glanced at his mother, whose blue eyes were sparkling as she returned his gaze.

"Don't go anywhere," he mouthed.

She flicked a brow upward in surprise, but nodded.

Sadie and the rest of the women stepped out to the patio, fanning out, chatting, greeting the grandmothers, and taking seats. But Connor stood and reached his hand to Sadie.

"Getting to know everyone?" he asked, guiding her to sit next to him on the wide hassock in the middle of it all, somehow instinctively knowing that's where this had to be done.

"It's only a little overwhelming," she said, perching next to him and turning her attention to Gramma Finnie and Yiayia. "But I know I'm in trouble with these two beautiful ladies, so I've come to make amends."

"No trouble, lass." Gramma pushed her bifocals up her nose, making her blue eyes look a little blurry but no less serious. "'Twas our mistake in thinkin' that ye would have listened to the suggestion."

"Ouch." Sadie bit her lip. "I'm sorry. Your hearts were totally in the right place and..." She added one of those heartbreaking dimpled smiles and a look at Connor. "Your taste is impeccable."

"So there's hope, then?" Yiayia asked.

"There's always hope." Sadie reached for each of their hands. "I'm honored that I got to be a Dogmother consideration. I hear you've got some pretty amazing success stories. You should start a matchmaking business in Bitter Bark."

"Look at her," Connor joked. "Helping out our Small Business Association already."

"Guess that's the mayor coming out in me." She gave him a saucy wink. "But seriously, you two are legendary."

"And you are butterin' us like a piece of burnt toast, lassie." Gramma Finnie's eyes twinkled at her, the old woman as charmed as Connor was.

As Connor watched Sadie work her magic, he became aware that the sprawling porch corner was filling up. Garrett and Shane had come over from the kennels, along with their wives and babies. Molly joined them, quietly taking Danny from Pru's arms and settling on a chaise next to Trace. Aidan, Beck, Braden, Declan, Uncle Daniel, and Katie were on their way across the grass to join everyone gathered on the patio.

With each new arrival, Frank seemed to inch a little closer, lifting his head to assess the newcomer, then dropping his chin back on Connor's foot to hold him in place.

He absently stroked the dog's head, weirdly comforted by his presence, too. Fake or real, funny or serious, whatever direction he chose for this moment, he somehow knew it mattered.

"I still think you'd have made a great campaign manager," Yiayia said. "And Connor still would have needed a fiancée."

"Don't second-guess, Agnes," Gramma Finnie said, smiling at Sadie. "I can see now that she has a yen to be a mayor, so…"

As they talked a little more, Connor did a quick headcount, just as Liam and Andi, with their young son, Christian, and toddler, Fiona, came outside from the house. Then came Alex and Grace, with Alex's twin, John.

That was it. Every family member who lived in Bitter Bark was present and accounted for.

Something Sadie said made everyone laugh, pulling his attention back to her.

"Oh, I like this lass," Gramma announced. "And she would have been perfect for our Connor."

That got a big laugh, loud enough that no one heard him whisper, "Would have been?" Except Sadie, who turned to him with a question—no, that was more of a playful challenge—in her eyes.

"She has every attribute for our next mayor," Connor said. "Except one."

"That Frank can beat her," Garrett said.

True, but Connor didn't answer. Instead, he reached into his pocket to close his hand over the tiny box with the fake diamond ring. As he did so, he slid one knee to the hard wooden planks of the patio, getting a very noisy gasp from damn near everyone gathered there.

Everyone except Sadie, who just stared at him when he lifted the box.

"Oh..." The sound escaped her lips like a soft whimper, somewhere between shock and...fear. "I thought you were going to just...hand it off to me."

"And miss this moment of..." He slid a side-eye to Gramma Finnie. "Impressing my grandmother with how real this is?"

"Real?" Sadie coughed softly. "It's not real, Connor."

"She means the diamond, Gramma," he said quickly. "It's lab grown."

"Whatever that is," Gramma Finnie said, lifting her glass for another deep drink. "But by all means, continue, lad."

"Please," Sadie said, trying to make light of the moment with an easy laugh. "Don't stop now that you've got the crowd, Connor."

He narrowed his eyes, trying to silently communicate his intent. "It's not a charade."

"It's not a..." She hesitated as if she didn't even want to finish, searching his face, looking for some kind of explanation. "It's not?"

"Not at all."

Her eyes flashed with what could be described only as fear. Because...

She will never, ever love another man like she loved...Nathan Lawrence.

With him on one knee and her sitting, they were eye-to-eye, and for a long stretch of too many heartbeats, neither said a word as he held her gaze. He heard someone's phone click with a photo, which he would definitely want to give to the *Bitter Bark Banner*.

He sensed his mother leaning closer to witness something she probably thought she'd never get to see. He was aware of Uncle Daniel standing in the door, looking down like the patriarch putting his very own blessing on the moment.

"Mercedes Hartman," Connor said softly.

"Oh, her full name," Gramma whispered, leaning over to Yiayia. "That's promising."

"Will you do me the honor of officially and honestly and really..." He slid a glance to Gramma, who had both hands pressed against her mouth, her eyes watery with tears.

He froze for a second. What it would feel like to really mean this? To look into the eyes of a woman he didn't want to ever lose, a woman who could be his partner, his lover for life, and the mother of children he didn't even think he wanted, but every time he held Annabelle, he realized what he was missing...

Was it Sadie giving him those insane thoughts? Or was it because of this classic, clichéd moment that unfolded due to a weird set of circumstances and needs?

As he got a little lost in the depths of her eyes, he had a shocking thought.

It *could* be Sadie. It *could* be real with her. Someday.

But he had to ask now because everyone was looking, she was waiting, and his knee was starting to hurt like hell.

"Will you marry me?" he finished, opening the box to another noisy round of gasps and reactions.

She gave a light, uncertain laugh. Like she might say no. Or maybe she was wondering the same things he was.

"Say yes, lass," Gramma Finnie whispered.

Sadie slid a teasing look at the older woman. "Is that an order, Gramma?"

"It's...a wish."

Sadie smiled and tapped the lid of the box, and then he could read her look. He knew what she was about to say. *That's not real. That's not organic. And neither is this.*

Which would ruin everything he was trying to do here.

Was it all an act for the grandmothers? Was it all just for the pictures and the signatures and the election?

In that one flash of a moment, he wasn't sure, and maybe neither was she.

"Of course I will," Sadie said, holding out her left hand.

A cheer rose up, with glasses clinking and cousins hooting and even a few dogs barking as he pulled the ring out and put it on her finger. Leaning close to her, he brushed her lips with a kiss, which made the crowd noise louder.

He gave her a hug, their mouths next to each other's ears.

"Nice fake, fiancé," she whispered.

"The ring or the proposal?"

"Both."

He opened his eyes and looked over her shoulder

217

to meet his grandmother's gaze. She looked utterly and completely joyous.

Job done. Proposal sold. That had to be why both their hearts were hammering out of their chests, and they were both trembling. That had to be it.

Chapter Seventeen

Sadie checked the mirror in the little bathroom one last time. She'd skipped the skirt and jacket, opting for a simple navy sheath dress with gold buttons and white epaulets on the shoulders that felt professional without being too formal.

She pulled her hair back into a clip, wearing minimal makeup and simple diamond-stud earrings. Mined diamonds…unlike the one on her hand, which she still hadn't quite gotten used to.

Glancing down, she twirled the solitaire and swallowed, remembering, as she did every time she looked at it, how dizzying that proposal had been. Yes, it was obviously for the grandmothers' benefit. She and Connor knew they needed those ladies to brag about another matchmaking success to get the town to believe them and ignore the work Mitch was doing in the background to undermine their plan.

But that didn't make the whole thing—everything with Connor, as a matter of fact—less thrilling. And damn, the thrills hadn't stopped all week long.

She'd spent the better part of the past week with Connor when he wasn't on duty at the fire station, visiting various businesses and meeting people. He generously introduced her to everyone he knew, which was pretty much the entire town. He was skilled in sliding the attention to Frank, but had backed off a lot on his dog jokes and spent plenty of time listening to people.

She shouldn't underestimate his ability to be mayor…which he could showcase at today's event.

As she grabbed her bag, she glanced around for Demi.

"Where are you, kitty?"

At the unexpected meow to her left, she turned, doing a double take to find her long orange body draped around the Susan B. Anthony bust on the shelf.

"Look at you, little suffragette." She stepped closer to scratch Demi's head and ease the clay sculpture back to a safe corner. "You cling to Aunt Sue and wish me luck, okay?"

She purred and pawed the slightly misshapen base that Sadie and her father had once worked so hard to create.

Then they both heard a loud bark outside, and Demi sat straight up, her ears turning like little radars.

"Is that your new boyfriend at the door?" Sadie asked.

Demi meowed and gave her a look as if to say, *Is that yours?*

She rubbed her thumb along the engagement ring as she walked to the door. "I guess the answer is yes. But what's he doing here? We were supposed to meet at town hall."

"Sadie?" Connor called. "Please tell me I didn't miss you."

She opened the door. "I don't know. Did you miss me?"

He inched back as if the impact of her was just too much. "Oh, hell yeah. Love the military look."

"Is everything okay?" She stepped to the side to let Frank in, since nothing was going to stop him from getting to Demi. "I thought we were meeting at the town hall before the debate."

"We need help," he admitted. "Frank's having a setback."

Frank headed straight to the bookshelf, and Demi jumped down to meet him. In less than two seconds, he rolled over, and she pawed at his belly, nuzzling her nose in his fur.

"Looks like he's *on* his back. And happy. What's wrong?"

"He will not go six inches from me. And if I even talk to someone or bring him near a group, he cowers in fear." He let out a sigh. "He's gonna tank today."

They both turned to watch their pets, with Frank looking like he'd died and gone to heaven, while Demi walked over him like he was her personal playground.

She bit her lip, because it was funny, and they were adorable, and she'd never, ever dreamed Demi could show such affection to a *dog*. "People are coming to hear you, Connor, not see Frank perform tricks like he's a trained seal."

"Tricks?" He snorted. "If he'd look a stranger in the eye, that'd be a good trick. He's supposed to be the guy who puts the fun in functions, remember? The whole dog-as-mayor thing can only work with a really friendly dog."

"He looks pretty friendly right now."

"Because the only creature he responds to is Demi."

"Especially if by 'responds' you mean 'turns into a quivering mess of submission and need,'" she said on a laugh.

"The right woman can do that, I guess."

The way he said it and the flirtatious look he added sent an unholy heat right through her. And just a hint of suspicion. "What are you buttering me up for, Connor?"

"Would you bring her?"

She choked softly. "Bring Demi? To the debate? In the town council meeting room? She's a cat! Besides being unpredictable and possibly draping herself on Mayor Wilkins's head for amusement, I can't leash her like you can a dog. And let's not forget that I would be giving a pretty major unfair advantage to the competition."

"And getting the votes of the cat people."

She crossed her arms, watching the antics as they started chasing each other's tails again. "It would provide comic relief."

"And she's not going to go far from him. If she does, someone will pick her up and give her to you."

"And Mitch would have a cow."

"Side bonus, but I think we'll have enough animals for one small-town mayoral debate." He tipped her chin up toward him. "Is that a yes?"

"You ask me that a lot, you know that?"

He held her gaze and drew a little circle on her chin with his thumb, sending chills right down to her toes. "When you say yes, I've won. And I love to win."

"Think you're going to win the debate today?"

"Against you? Probably not. But we have a mutual goal: defeat Mitch. We'll let the cat-vs.-dog people figure out who they want to vote for."

She smiled. "You're right. Then yes, we'll bring Demi."

He didn't say anything for a moment, but he didn't have to. She could feel the electricity arc between them as he moved a centimeter closer. And she had zero ability to step away. No, in fact, she tipped her face up and was as complicit as he in the kiss they shared.

It was light, a seal of the deal, but left her wanting more.

Frank barked, suddenly on his feet and trying to get between them. Demi mewed with fury that he'd left her. And Sadie just slid her arms around Connor's neck and parted her lips to taste more of him.

Another bark and mew.

"They don't like when we kiss," she murmured into his mouth.

"Tough. I do."

"We'll kiss when we beat Mitch today," she promised.

"Oh yeah." He drew her into him and ignored the dog and cat to kiss her again. "We'll do more than kiss."

She backed up, brows raised in question.

"We'll have dinner," he said quickly on a guilty laugh. "I've been trying to get you out on an official dinner date since we met."

"Deal. We beat Mitch, and we'll have dinner." And do more than kiss, she mentally added. "Color me... incented for victory."

He gave her a smoky look and reached down to scoop up Demi. "Here's your good-luck charm."

She put her nose against Demi's cold one. "Let's go get 'em, tiger."

A few minutes later, she was in Connor's truck, holding tight to Demi as they neared the town hall on a very crowded Ambrose Avenue.

"We definitely have to do something about the traffic in this place," Connor mused.

But Sadie was focused on the crowd that spilled into the square. "This many people care about the mayoral debate?"

"More than I expected, too." He glanced at her. "Do you want to walk through that crowd and shake hands? Because to be perfectly honest, I'm not sure Frank's quite ready for that."

"Can we park in the back and still get in?"

"Yes. There's an entrance only town employees can use that leads into the basement. It's where the sheriff's office used to be. And you can see my dad."

"Excuse me?"

He whipped onto a side street. "There's a gallery of first responders who died in the line of duty since the town was incorporated. There's a picture of Joe Mahoney I love to salute when I walk by."

She reached for his hand and smiled. "I'd like that."

He parked in an alley she hadn't known was there, took her through a side door of the town hall and through double doors into a long hallway. On both walls were portraits and paintings of about twenty men from the 1800s to…today. At the second-to-last picture, he stopped, closed his eyes, and then touched his forehead.

Sadie stood back, her gaze locked on Connor, her heart tripping at the quick, quiet, classic gesture. As if he understood just how somber the moment was, Frank sat right down and stared at the picture.

After a second, Sadie stepped closer to look at the photo of Captain Joseph John Mahoney.

She stroked Demi's head in her arms while she studied the man who didn't look that much older than Connor right now. His eyes were as blue but the resemblance wasn't that strong. Still...

She inched closer, a tingling sensation pirouetting up and down her back. "Wait a second." She held her breath for a moment, letting her mind go back to a rainy day and a helpful stranger...and an umbrella she wished she still had. "I met him!"

"You did?"

"Sadie! Connor! What on earth are you doing down here?"

They turned toward Mayor Wilkins, rushing down the hall, her navy pumps clicking on the linoleum. "I thought I was the only one who used this secret entrance." She shook her head, smiling as she greeted them. "I'm always finding you two in the strangest places." Mayor Wilkins looked past Sadie at the picture, then nodded, understanding. "A truly great man," she said with a sad smile. "I'm sure he'll bring you luck today, Connor. Sadie, why do you have a cat?"

They exchanged a look, and Sadie laughed. "She's for *my* luck, Mayor."

The other woman rolled her eyes as if she just didn't get these two. Then she gave a nudge. "Hurry up. We start in a few minutes."

With one more glance over her shoulder at the photo of a man she'd never forget, Sadie suddenly had a completely different insight into Connor. He'd claimed his father made him some kind of tunnel-visioned winner. But based on one thirty-second conversation, she now saw the man next to her in a very different light.

"When did you meet him?" Connor whispered.

"I'll tell you later," she promised.

Traffic. Budgets. School playgrounds. Bushrod Square decorations and teachers' salaries.

The panelists' questions were asked and answered, but the audience spent most of the time laughing over the unexpected guests on the small stage where members of the town council normally sat, with Mayor Wilkins in the middle.

Bringing Demi had been a stroke of genius. Frank was out of his shell. In fact, the son of a gun was showing off for his girl, occasionally walking the stage—mostly to get another treat from Connor—and then settling right between Connor and Sadie, with Demi poking out from under his tail while they both napped.

Mitch tried to ignore the animals and made only a few snide remarks, but had the wherewithal to know that more than that would just lose him what little of this crowd he had.

Overall, Connor felt like his own performance was solid, Mitch's was overconfident, and Sadie sailed through like the master of politics she was. She had a shockingly deep understanding of the issues that faced the town and some innovative ideas on how to fix them, easily showcasing her national-level experience. She also deftly managed two questions about her seventeen-year absence with a story about her childhood and a picnic in Bushrod Square that the crowd ate up.

And there wasn't a single question about their engagement, even from Rose Halliday, who was one of the moderators. But then, he and Sadie had been out and about in town for a week now, and they'd done a pretty convincing job of being a couple.

Hell, he thought as he glanced over and checked her out as she made her final point, *he* was convinced they were a couple.

"And that concludes the round of moderator questions," Nellie Shaker announced from her seat at the center table. "The floor is now open to townspeople if you'll please use the mic stand at the center of the room. State your name and ask your question. Form a line, if necessary."

At least five people hopped out of their seats and headed toward the mic, as if they'd been waiting to pounce on the chance.

With one more look at Sadie, Connor gave her a wink as the first woman reached the podium. Sadie smiled, then winked right back.

"Aww, that's sweet," said a fifty-something woman he didn't recognize standing at the audience mic. She'd obviously caught the silent exchange. "I have a question about this romance."

Both of them looked at her, and Connor sensed Sadie stiffen a little at the woman's warning. *Okay, here we go. Is it real? Prove it!* How would she—

"Where did you two meet? And how long until you knew you were in love?"

He froze for a moment and heard Sadie suck in a soft breath.

"Oh, sorry!" the lady said. "I'm Mary Jo Norton and…" She gave a lighthearted laugh. "Inquiring minds want to know about the mayoral romance as much as we want to know about the town budget."

Laughter rolled through the crowd, a little nervous and maybe as surprised as Connor and Sadie were.

"It's all we want to know!" another woman in the audience called out, increasing the laughter and getting Connor and Sadie to share one more look, this one surprised.

"Who do you want to answer that question?" Connor asked, buying time. Of course, they didn't want to lie, so—

"I'll take that one," Sadie said. "We met in high school, but barely knew each other. More officially, we met at Bushrod's like, well… How many other people in this audience met their match at Bushrod's?" A whole bunch of hands went up, along with clapping and laughter. "In fact," she added, "one of my first acts as mayor might be to convince Billy to change the name back to Bushrod's from Bitter Bark Bar, if only for all the people who met their spouses there."

That got a friendly round of applause, which Connor added to, shaking his head because she never failed to amaze and amuse him.

"You don't agree with the name change, Connor?" she asked him.

"I don't know," he quipped, leaning on his podium

to look at her. "If Billy hadn't changed the name, you might not have been lost looking for it, and I might not have talked to you. And then…" He turned back to the crowd to finish, but Mitch leaned into his mic.

"You'd still be chasing everything in a skirt, Mahoney," Mitch grumbled his pathetic attempt at a joke.

As if that bastard had room to talk. Irritation shot through Connor, but the low-grade boo that hummed in the meeting room easily tempered his response. Mitch was digging his own grave. *Pun intended.*

"Not anymore." Sadie practically sang the words into her mic, and every head turned like a tennis ball had just bounced over the net to the other side of the court. She held up her left hand, making that lab-grown diamond sparkle like her eyes were at that moment. "Connor Mahoney is officially off the market."

"Woo hoo!" That was a firefighter, Connor thought. Probably Ray.

"What was the second part of your question, Mary Jo?" Sadie asked, easing into a relaxed smile.

"How long before you knew you were in love?"

Sadie sighed like the very thought of it was almost too personal to share. "Not long. Right, Connor?"

"Well, love can be…a whirlwind." He swallowed, suddenly more comfortable with the topic of teachers' salaries than love. "And strong. And it doesn't take long if…" *If you're faking the whole thing to win an election.*

"I know the minute, the time, and the day," Sadie said, smooth as silk. "It was the day we got back to my house, and that little girl right there"—she pointed to Demi, curled next to Frank—"climbed a tree. Connor didn't even hesitate, despite being in dress clothes. He was ready to go to the top branch to save my cat."

Another resounding *awww* from the females in the audience. Okay, the firefighters were doubled over in laughter, and the gang that took up his two friends-and-family rows were sharing looks of humor and disbelief.

"Next question," Nellie called out.

Another woman walked up to the mic, younger than Mary Jo and very familiar. Connor drew in a silent breath as he recognized Emily Cullen, an attractive nurse at Vestal Valley General Hospital he'd dated briefly a year or so ago. She'd wanted to get serious, and he'd told her honestly and from the beginning that he wasn't looking for a wife.

He braced for a demand to know why she hadn't been the one, and Sadie had. He glanced at Mitch, suddenly wondering if maybe this were a setup. He wouldn't put it past him.

"I'm Nurse Cullen," she said when she reached the mic, then gave a quick smile to Connor. "But you know that."

"Of course. How are you, Emily?"

She took a slow inhale, and he felt his whole body tense in anticipation. This could be bad. This could be just awful. This could be—

"Engaged, as well." She held up her hand. "I'm marrying Dr. Ron Kipfer next month."

"Awesome." He broke into a wide smile as relief rocked him. "That's just great, Emily. Congratulations."

"Thank you. And to you."

She was a class act, he remembered. A pretty woman who loved her job...but really wanted to settle down and have kids.

"Do you have a question, ma'am?" Mitch interjected. "Or is this just a nice friendly reunion for you two ex-lovers?"

Emily shot Mitch a dismissive look and turned back to Connor, then Sadie. "I'm curious how Connor proposed."

"Excuse me," Mitch said in a strained, put-upon voice. "This is a political debate."

"Personal questions are allowed," Nellie answered. "Audience members are encouraged to get to know all of the candidates to understand how they might handle important issues."

Mitch looked skyward and started to respond, but Sadie cut him off.

"We got engaged in front of Connor's entire family," she said. "It was the sweetest thing. He got down on one knee and..." She blushed a little, shaking her head at the memory. There was no way she was faking that...right? "Gave this woman the proposal of her dreams."

"Hogwash!" Mitch shouted, silencing the response from the crowd. "I know for a fact she's lying, and so does everyone on the Election Committee." He practically spat the words, he was so certain he was right. "They found out about the Bushrod charter that requires a candidate to be married, widowed, or betrothed, and left the room, then came back five minutes later with this whole engagement story concocted to make us all look like fools!"

In his pocket, Connor's cell phone vibrated, but

he ignored it as he formulated an answer, glancing into the crowd to think. As he did, he happened to catch Shane's eye, and he lifted his cell phone surreptitiously with a silent demand that he look at his.

Sliding it out of his pocket, he instantly saw the picture Shane had just texted.

"So if you think this town is dumb enough to fall for this—"

"Excuse me, Mitch," Connor said, holding up his hand. "Nellie, may I post another image to the screen?"

"Absolutely, Connor."

"We don't need any more pie charts about dogs and tourism," Mitch groused.

"That's not the topic." Connor tapped the screen of his phone and linked the photo to the council room projection screen the A/V guys had set up when they started. "Here we go. The moment I popped the question, in full view of what looks like at least twenty of my brothers, sisters, aunts, uncles, mother, and the two greatest grandmothers in the world."

He heard Gramma Finnie and Yiayia hoot and caught them doing a high five as he turned to look at the screen, seeing the wall-sized image of him on one knee, holding the black box, his entire family gathered with various expressions of joy, surprise, and maybe a little shock.

But it wasn't his family he studied as the photo left Mitch speechless and the crowd oohing and clapping.

It was the look on Sadie's face that he couldn't believe. He'd been so focused on making his point with his grandmother, he hadn't taken a mental picture of Sadie, because he knew it wasn't real. How could he have missed the way she gazed at him at that moment?

No one in this room could think that gaze was fake…not even him.

He turned to her, half expecting that sly smile when she teased him or shot back with her sarcastic wit. But, no. She was a mirror image of the woman on the wall right then, her dark eyes warm, her smile wide. Suddenly, his heart felt like it shifted around in his chest, stirring something deep inside him. Something…that had never stirred before.

"As I was saying." Sadie spoke softly into the mic, finally shifting her gaze from him to the audience. "The proposal was memorable and crowded, but that's life with a man from a family like his."

The rows of Mahoneys and Kilcannons and Santorinis cheered that statement.

"Next question, please," Nellie called out, making an effort to quiet the crowd and move the event forward.

"Not sure I can handle any more," Connor joked.

"I sure as hell can't," Mitch mumbled.

Another woman hurried to the microphone, someone he recognized but couldn't remember from where.

"Bernice Maynard," she said, turning to give a little wave to Gramma Finnie, who sat at the end of the row, literally holding hands with Yiayia.

Oh yes. A church choir friend. He'd gone to her house once at Gramma's urging to check all her smoke alarms. Her husband had died a few years earlier, and she hadn't changed the batteries since then.

"Hi, Connor," she said.

"Bernice. Change those smoke alarm batteries lately?"

She flushed. "My grandson visited and did it just last week."

"Good girl."

Mitch let out a sigh so noisy and frustrated, it vibrated his mic, making Sadie, and most of the crowd, chuckle.

"I'd like to know if you have nicknames for each other," Bernice said.

"I'm sorry," Mitch said. "I'm registering a formal complaint. This is all sweet and cute and lovely, but how the hell do nicknames help this town pick the best mayor?"

Bernice leveled him with a look. "I'll tell you how, Mitchell Eastercrook. My husband, Elmer, who you may remember because you charged me an exorbitant amount to bury him and then overcharged me for the headstone, called me Buttons. And when we were in the middle of a big fight, he would look at me with those sweet hazel eyes and say, 'How can I fix this, Buttons?' And then I just melted right down to my bones. I think it says a lot about a man who has a nickname for his woman, so you can just take your formal complaint and stick it where...it belongs."

Applause erupted, along with some boos aimed at Mitch, and a whole lot of laughter as the debate essentially disintegrated into something more like *The Dating Game*.

Nellie Shaker reached over and borrowed Mayor Wilkins's gavel, pounding them all to order. "Can you answer Bernice's question?" she asked Connor.

He wasn't about to tell them he called Sadie DC half the time and Ear Girl the rest. Those names weren't exactly *Buttons*.

At his moment's hesitation, Sadie leaned in. "I'll answer," she said. "I love a good nickname, too. I like to call Connor by his title, Lieutenant, because let's face it, who doesn't love a man in uniform?"

"Amen, sister," Bernice quipped. "And him for you?"

"Well…" Sadie laughed nervously.

"If it's too intimate, then—"

"Oh, no, it's not that kind of nickname. It goes all the way back to the very first time we met, seventeen years ago. Remember I told you that we knew each other in high school?" At the crowd's reaction, she nodded, drawing them in with that magic she seemed to have sprinkled all over her. "You may know this, but back then we stood on another stage and debated. We ran against each other for class president, and I lost, but probably because my campaign slogan involved an ear."

A smattering of laughter came from the crowd.

"I wanted my fellow students to know what I want you to know. That I was—and am—experienced, approachable, and responsible. I used the acronym EAR and blew up images of an ear for my posters." She rolled her eyes with a self-deprecating laugh. "I know. It's embarrassing, but true. Back then, when Connor of course was the perfect gentleman and kindly offered his condolences on my campaign loss, he shook my hand and called me…Ear Girl. I never forgot it."

She sure didn't. But now you'd think it was the

greatest thing anyone had ever called her, but really, she—

"And sometimes he calls me that today," she finished.

"Awww."

"So sweet."

"Ear Girl for mayor!"

"I do still call her that," he admitted softly into the mic, unable, like the rest of the crowd, to take his eyes off her. "But now it means...enchanting, adorable, and r-r-r-really hot."

The last word tumbled out from a brain that was fried from an hour of debate and a woman who'd somehow crawled under his skin and taken up permanent residence there. But his pathetic r-word didn't seem to matter to this crowd. He damn near got a standing ovation, with thunderous applause and a look from Sadie that could be described only as perfection.

"We have time for one more question," Mayor Wilkins announced. "And I'll ask it. I'd like each of you to please tell a personal story that voters might not know about you. Lieutenant Mahoney, why don't you start?"

A personal story? He went blank for a moment, then remembered a fallback he'd prepared. He tapped his phone again to call up another picture. "I'll tell you Frank's story," he said easily, while a picture of a grinning three-year-old with both arms wrapped around Frank's neck flashed on the screen. "This is Dylan O'Keefe, who would not be alive today if not for this dog, who is courageous, loving, and obviously has a soft spot for creatures of all kind."

"Awww!" The natural reaction to the heartwarming sight rolled through the crowd.

"Seriously, I've been part of a lot of rescues, and I've never known a dog to pull a boy from rushing water."

"Which would never have happened if that child's father had been paying attention." Mitch's comment brought the crowd to stunned silence. As every eye turned toward him, he shrugged. "Just keeping it real, ladies and gentlemen, which as you know…" He pointed to the other two podiums. "These two are not. And I had hoped we'd get some actual questions from our townspeople on the subject of how they are circumventing the rules that our forefathers laid out for this town."

"Give it a break, Mitch," a female voice called out.

"We love the mayor couple," someone else chimed in.

"How about your personal story, Mr. Easterbrook?" Nellie said quickly to quell any further outbursts.

Mitch nodded and leaned into his podium. "Thank you, Nellie. Of course I have many, considering my family has been in Bitter Bark for five generations and in all that time has been the one and only organization that every grieving family can count on in the darkest times of their lives. So my best personal memories are helping them, the good citizens of Bitter Bark, when they need it most."

The crowd was silent, and that, Connor suspected, was because the locals were being polite.

"Ms. Hartman?"

Sadie nodded, gathering her thoughts for a moment. Connor watched as she lifted her chin to speak, ready for something that would be smooth and political, something that would show her caring for the community or her recognition of the issues and troubles they faced.

"Once, when I was about to turn fifteen, I went through a very sad time in my life." She inched closer to the mic, looking past Connor to shoot a quick, almost imperceptible glance at Mitch, who averted his gaze to stare down at his podium.

Holy hell, Connor thought, remembering exactly what happened to her when she was about that age. She would share that here? Hadn't she said her family had kept that secret? Would she use her mother's story as a sure way to destroy Mitch Easterbrook? His whole body tensed as he looked to his side to watch her, ready to catch her, defend her, support her, whatever she needed.

"It got so bad one day that I packed a small suitcase and headed down Bushrod Boulevard toward the bus station at Vestal Valley College. I wanted to run away." She waited a beat as the crowd completely silenced. "I picked a very rainy, wretched morning to run away," she added with a sad smile. "It was a torrential downpour, and I got soaked. On the way there, I stopped under an awning, right outside of the bookstore. A man walked out and started to open his umbrella. As he did, he looked at me and must have been able to tell my face was wet with tears rather than just raindrops."

The slightest catch in her voice made her pause, and someone in the crowd sighed noisily.

"The man looked down at me and said something I'll never forget. 'It's okay to cry,' he said, kind of looking at the packed bag at my feet. 'Just don't unpack and live in the middle of your misery.'"

The words twisted Connor's gut and took his breath away. He could hear the rest of the sentence, even though she didn't say it. *Move on, find purpose, walk past defeat, because you're on your way to a win.*

Joe Mahoney's words never really left his heart.

And, he thought with a smile, they hadn't left Sadie's, either.

He heard a soft murmur from that row of people he loved, looking out to catch the exchange of surprised glances between his mother and Declan. Both had surely heard that speech a time or two in their lives.

"I've never forgotten those words," Sadie said. "Or the fact that the stranger gave me his umbrella and told me to be safe. I never got his name or saw him again, but now I know that's never going to happen. Not long after that encounter, Captain Joseph Mahoney died in the line of firefighting duty."

A soft gasp and audible reaction rolled through the crowd, but Connor didn't really hear it because of the blood thumping from his pounding heart.

Sadie looked at him with a sad smile. "Because of that man, I stayed dry, I stayed safe, I stayed in Bitter Bark, and I never unpacked and lived in the middle of misery, no matter what life threw my way."

"And now you're engaged to his son!" someone yelled out.

"It's fate!"

"It's perfect."

The comments came, along with another noisy round of applause as Connor stepped away from his podium at the same time Sadie did. They both reached out and slid into the most natural embrace. He turned his head just to make sure no one could see the emotion on his face, while Mayor Wilkins used the gavel and formally ended the debate.

Mitch was grousing into the mic and finally gave up, marching off the stage. As he realized Connor had left the podium, Frank stood to trot over to them, and Demi followed, letting Sadie scoop her up.

"Damn, Ear Girl." He ran his thumb along the side of her cheek, lost in the not-quite-shed tears that dampened her eyes. "You came to win."

To win the debate, to win the day, and whether he liked it or not, to win his heart. Because he'd never been more ready to give it away.

Chapter Eighteen

For the entire time Sadie had lived in Bitter Bark, Ricardo's had been the pinnacle of dining in town. Maybe it wasn't the hippest eatery she'd ever been to, but it was authentic and unique with red leather booths and a menu that might look ordinary at first glance, but was full of surprises and delights.

Across the table sat a man who was just as authentic and unique, and definitely full of surprises and delights. The post-debate celebration dinner had been everything Connor promised for their first official date, at least as far as conversation that kept them both laughing and the constant hum of electricity that zinged between them.

Sadie hadn't expected the date to include a dozen locals stopping by their table to congratulate them on their engagement, show them the home page of the town website—featuring Frank and Demi, dubbed Fremi—and ask to take pictures, even though Frank wasn't there.

Despite all the interruptions—maybe because of them—Sadie was thinking about how much she didn't want the evening to end when the server brought them tiramisu and cappuccinos to end their meal.

"So, I think my mom's voting for you after that story you told about my dad," Connor said as they took their first bites of the shared dessert.

Sadie laughed. "She told me that after the debate. But I'm pretty sure you're getting the Mahoney-Kilcannon-Santorini vote, which alone might be enough to win."

"*Frank* is getting the vote," he corrected. "I kinda miss him tonight. I hope those two are okay alone at your place."

"Well, you can't bring a cat to a restaurant, even in Bitter Bark, and Frank wasn't about to leave her when you came to pick me up." She held her fork midbite, looking over the little mound of creamy sweetness. "It wasn't a 'story,' you know. I didn't…make that up."

"Oh, I know that. Anyone who ever met Joe Mahoney knew he was the king of the motivational quote, and they'd be surprised he only gave you an umbrella. Most of the time, it was the shirt off his back and whatever money was in his pocket."

"It's just that you haven't mentioned it tonight, and I wondered if you thought it was, like, a political gimmick."

"Come on, Sadie. I know you better than that."

She smiled, glad that he did. "I was so stunned when I saw his picture," she said. "It was on my mind from the minute we started the debate, the unbelievable coincidence that it was him that day. Your father coming out of a bookstore."

"He loved to read and passed that on to Braden," he told her.

"With it on my mind, I couldn't resist sharing when Blanche asked me to tell a personal story…"

She reached past the dessert to touch his hand. "What a kind and wonderful man he must have been, Connor."

He nodded. "Very...motivational."

"You think he's the reason you hate to lose?"

"Oh, he is. Losing was weakness. So was negativity and fear. He despised weakness of any kind, at least in Declan and me. He mellowed out with Braden. And with Smella?" He snorted. "He was just mush with that little girl."

She stared at him for a long time. "Obviously, you know him better than I do, since I met him for thirty seconds. But think of the lasting impact he had on me."

"Amazing," he agreed.

"I don't think he just instilled in you a fear of losing." She squeezed his hand. "I think he also made you a man who cares a lot—deeply, in fact. You crack jokes, and you have this outward appearance that everything is easy and fun and not serious, but inside? You are truly one of the most caring people I've ever met. And I would give a lot of credit to Joe Mahoney for the molding of that man."

He stared at her for a long time, his expression softening. "No one has ever accused me of being..." He swallowed. "Thanks, Sadie. Thanks for taking the time to see that in me." He turned his hand over and threaded their fingers. "No wonder everyone in this town is crazy about you." He winked. "And I do mean *everyone*."

She smiled at the compliment. "I think they're crazy about *us*. Bitter Bark seems a little enchanted by the mayoral engagement."

He laughed. "We're good together."

"There's our next mayor." The booming voice of Ricardo's owner made them both turn to see the handsome Italian chef coming to their table.

"Which one of us?" Connor joked.

"After today? I'm thinking you should just run as a team. No one is talking about anything else tonight."

"Well, at least they're not talking about Mitch Easterbrook," Connor said, keeping his voice low.

"Mitch *who*?" Ricardo joked. "You buried him today, if I can make that really bad joke."

They both laughed, sharing a look.

"We feel good about the debate," Sadie said. "And are loving celebrating here."

"Good, because the meal's on me." He put his hands lightly on the table and leaned over to whisper, "I have to say, I didn't quite buy what you were selling at the Election Committee meeting that day you announced this, but after watching you two today? All I can say is congratulations to the future Mr. and Mrs. Mahoney, Bitter Bark's first power couple. This entire town is cheering for you two and will be dancing in Bushrod Square on your wedding day. More tiramisu?"

Sadie and Connor both just stared at him, then she managed to shake her head. "No, thank you. We're good. And thank you for dinner."

"My pleasure!" He moved on to another table, leaving them in stunned silence.

"I think I underestimated how much people like a good romance," Connor mused.

"They sure do," Sadie agreed, trying not to think about how all those people would react if they knew the truth.

When they finished, Connor pulled out his wallet and laid down a few twenties as a tip, then guided Sadie through the restaurant and out into the chilly March night, automatically getting closer as they walked and talked.

Ambrose Avenue was nearly empty, but the lights glimmered on the many trees in the square, where a few people strolled along with some dogs.

"So I guess we fooled the town, Ear Girl. They believe us."

"They believe *in* us," she said. "And that's a little scarier."

"Scary because only one of us can win the election?"

"Scary because...amicable breakup, remember?"

"Oh, that. I don't like to think about it," he said, tugging her even closer. "All that rioting in Bushrod Square instead of dancing."

"I didn't think we were building up such... expectations," she said. "It was just supposed to be a way to stay in the race. And now..."

"Now..." He stopped in front of the tall statue. "There will be dancing in Bushrod Square, according to Ricardo."

She tipped her head back as he slid his arms around her and pulled her closer, circling once in an easy dance move, making her laugh.

"It's almost as if they think we really like each other," he whispered into her ear.

"Can you imagine that?"

"Uh, I do. Frequently."

"Connor." She sighed his name. "It makes things so complicated."

"How so? You like me. I like you. The town likes us. Sounds pretty uncomplicated to me."

"Until it isn't."

"You know what your favorite football coach and umbrella donator would say?"

"Complications make you strong, and defeat is for the weak?" she guessed.

He guided her to the bench that had become one of their favorite spots. "He'd say the guy who doesn't go for what he wants is the one sitting on the sideline watching the guy who got it."

She studied him for a moment, a flashing memory of his father in her mind's eye, but then it was gone, and all she could see was a handsome, kind, funny, wonderful firefighter who liked her a lot. "What is it you want to go for?" she asked.

"You." He breathed the word and placed his free hand on her cheek, gliding it back to thread his fingers in her hair. "Like I said, we're good together. And I want to be together."

"That's a big step for you, isn't it?"

"Not with you."

The simple, honest admission rolled through her, warming her more than any wine or coffee. He closed the space between them completely, raising her face to kiss him. His lips were so tender and gentle, but still melted her. She could taste vanilla and nutmeg, and a man who knew exactly what he was doing with a kiss.

Heat ribboned through her, tightening everything and making her reach up to wrap her arms around his neck and pull him closer. He moaned softly, the sound making his chest vibrate against her as he deepened the kiss.

She felt her back bow, the need to get her whole body closer to him taking over all her thoughts and leaving her with one: more.

Parting her lips, she let their tongues touch, that sweet sensation stealing her breath and making her heart knock hard against her ribs.

"Steady there, Ear Girl," he murmured into the kiss. "We could ignite."

"Mmm." She let her fingers coast up and down his strong neck and the corded muscles of his shoulders, aching a little to have no sweater or shirt or anything else blocking her from the feel of him. "Good thing I know a firefighter."

He chuckled into the kiss, then took a breath and intensified everything, pulling her so close she was practically on his lap, his hands slowly traveling over her throat and skimming her shoulders, heating everything with need.

Some voices floated their way, coming from behind, forcing them to separate.

"Let's get home," he murmured. "Before a picture of this bumps Fremi from the home page."

They stayed arm in arm in the shadows, stopping once, then twice, then a third time to kiss again, both of them silently surrendering to the fight. They laughed a little, kissed some more, and by the time they neared Jessamine Court, Sadie knew Connor wasn't leaving her tonight.

Suddenly, he stopped walking two houses from Nana and Boomie's yard. "Do you hear that?"

She closed her eyes to listen. "Dog barking?"

"That's Frank."

"Are you sure?"

247

He didn't answer, but let go of her shoulder to take her hand and hustle them both closer to the house, and the barking definitely got louder.

"Let's go around the side," she said. "There's a faster way to the house through the trees." She tugged him in that direction, a sharp worry growing with each frantic bark she heard. What was wrong with him?

"Maybe we shouldn't have left them—"

"Shhh." He stilled her in the shadow of a huge oak tree. "Look."

Following his gaze, she spotted a tiny light in the garden. No, not a light. A phone screen, carried by a man.

"Damn it," she murmured. "Why do people think they can walk right up to my house and take pictures?"

"That's why Frank's barking. Stay here, I'll—"

The light flashed and illuminated the man's silhouette, making her blink like she might be seeing things. She saw shoulders, a head tilted in a familiar way, short, dark hair, and glasses. Was that...

No. It couldn't be. It *couldn't*.

The light dimmed again as the man lowered his phone and walked toward the street, away from them. As she watched that far too familiar gait, Sadie tightened her grip on Connor's arm for no reason except...she had to hold on to something.

What is he doing here?

"I'm going to go put a stop to this."

"No, wait." She clung to him.

"It's media, Sadie. Or someone Mitch sent. Doesn't matter, but it's late, and you deserve some measure of privacy."

Just then, a sedan pulled up and slowed down, but

the lights made Frank bark again. And then the car beams shined right on the face and body of a man she knew all too well.

"Let him go, Connor."

"Why? We can't let people think that's okay."

The man opened the back door of the car and climbed in with the familiarity of someone who'd gotten into a thousand taxis and Ubers. "Just let him go."

"Sadie." He tried to shake her off so he could go after the car before it left. "Some guy is lurking outside your house at eleven o'clock at night. I'm not going to—"

"He's not…some guy."

He turned and looked at her, a question in his eyes. A question she had to answer.

"That was Nathan Lawrence."

Chapter Nineteen

What the hell? As far as Connor was concerned, her ex skulking around in the dark wasn't just a good reason to go after the guy, it actually warranted a call to his buddy at the sheriff's office to go stop one of the few Ubers they had in Bitter Bark.

But Sadie didn't agree, and Connor wasn't at all sure how he felt about that.

"So it's perfectly okay for him to stalk you?" he asked after they got Frank calmed down.

"No, it's not okay."

"Then what's he doing here?"

"I don't know. He didn't call or text to warn me, so I really don't know. Or care. He probably wants to apologize. We never even had another conversation after I found out, so he never really had a chance to say he was sorry, but he doesn't need to be pulled over by the police like a common criminal."

"Then he should call and say, 'I'm sorry.' And hey, trespassing on private property is a common crime, so he qualifies."

She blew out a breath, curling Demi against her

chest and stroking the cat's head in her go-to stress-relieving move. "Nathan is a lot of things, not all of them nice, but he would never, ever hurt me."

Connor stared at her, not sure she actually heard her own words.

"Physically," she added. "He obviously did plenty of emotional damage."

"I'm going to take Frank out," he said, grabbing the leash he'd left on the table. "While I'm out there, I'll be walking the perimeter to make sure it's clear."

"Okay, thanks." She turned to look out the window, her shoulders sagging a little as her strokes on the cat's head increased in speed.

"Hey." He walked to her, sliding his arms around her waist. "Sorry for going full-on bodyguard."

"It's fine. It's who you are." She turned to him, a storm of hurt in her eyes. "I just thought I was done with him."

"Then let me have my friend Deputy Carter pull the Uber over and be done with him. Scare the crap out of him and maybe mention that your new boyfriend is an overprotective firefighter."

She blinked at him. "My new boyfriend?"

He lifted her left hand. "Sadie. How you forget."

"Connor. It's not real."

"The engagement, maybe. The way I feel? Totally real."

She looked up at him, that storm in her eyes kicking up to a Cat 5. Demi crawled out of her arms and leaped to the ground, but Sadie didn't shift her gaze from its lock on Connor's. "Totally real," she repeated on a whisper.

"For me. How about you?"

Taking a deep breath, she wrapped her arms around his waist and dropped her head on his chest. "Don't leave tonight."

He pressed a kiss on her head. "I have a twelve-hour shift that starts at five a.m. And I intend to spend every minute until then right next to you, and if anyone who doesn't have four paws and fur thinks they can come near you, they'll be sorry."

He felt her surrender in his arms, giving him a nice surge of satisfaction.

"Lock the door while I'm out there," he said as he left to take Frank all around the property.

Out there, her grandparents' house was totally dark. While Frank sniffed around, Connor scanned the yard, the garden, and the quiet street where Nathan Lawrence had just disappeared.

What the hell had he been doing here? Other than the obvious—he wanted to win her back. Just like Jane, the boss. The two of them, cheaters both, who obviously couldn't live without Sadie.

But could she live without them? Was it possible she could rebound to her old boyfriend...her old job and her old life? If she lost the election, she might leave.

He didn't want that, he realized. If he had to fight for her, he would.

It was a risk, but he had to take it. Yes, he could lose, and lose hard, by falling for a woman who was fresh out of a relationship that hadn't had closure. But she was worth that risk.

He made one more slow walk around the yard, then knocked, and she let him in. He blinked as he stepped into the dim light, surprised to see the sofa bed open and made neatly, with two pillows. And one orange cat stretched out over one of those pillows. Demi rose and arched her back, meowed noisily and possessively, then slithered to the other pillow, somehow managing to drape her body over two at once.

Sadie had changed into a T-shirt and sleep pants, her thick mane up in some kind of a loose knot that left a few strands of hair falling next to her cheeks.

"I had to get out of that dress."

"I could have gotten you out of that dress," he said, unclipping Frank's leash. "Where are my pj's for the sleepover?"

She laughed. "I thought firefighters slept in their clothes."

"Or not." He took a few steps closer, wrapping her in his arms. "No one is out there, but I'm not going to lie, I hate that he was here."

"I do, too," she admitted.

He held her tighter, knowing he had to ask because she'd never lie. He wanted to know before…before they fell into that bed together. Because sex with her wasn't going to be casual or meaningless or forgettable.

"Sadie, do you still have feelings for him?"

"Feelings like anger? Hatred? Resentment? Yeah, lots of feelings. But not what you're worried about."

"I'm not worried, but I'm treading very unfamiliar waters," he admitted, turning as Frank jumped on the bed. "So's Frank. He sleeps with me. Like, right next to me. Sometimes under the covers."

"Lucky Frank."

He laughed. "I'll move him."

"And Demi? Because she sleeps with me."

"Wow, we have spoiled pets."

Frank took a few steps across the mattress, making the little sofa bed squeak under his weight. Demi didn't move, but kept her gaze locked on him. Then she let out a long, high-pitched, delicate meow, and Frank barked, the two of them absolutely unable to take their eyes off each other.

"He is completely in her territory," Sadie whispered as they watched the silent exchange.

"Let me get him."

Just before he reached for the dog, Frank took another step, and Demi moved off one of the pillows. She swished her tail, and in under a second, they'd curled into a perfect circle with Demi tucked into Frank's big chest, his paw hanging possessively over her body.

"And…they win the bed," Sadie said.

"No way. We'll…share." He sat on the edge and nudged Frank. "Come on, bud. Humans rule."

The dog adjusted his position, gave a sigh, and planted his chin on Demi's head the way he did on Connor's shoe.

"So this is how you two thank us for saving you from lives of scavenging for the next meal?" Connor asked.

Sadie came closer, then sat on Connor's lap, locking her hands around his neck. "Look, here's a little corner. Right here. We can sleep very, very close together. Just like our spoiled pets."

"I like the way you think, Sadie Hartman."

She looked down at him, holding his gaze. "You know what I like about you, Connor? Everything."

"Is that so?" He settled her more comfortably on his lap, the dog and cat forgotten. "Tell me more."

She stroked his cheek and tunneled her fingers into his hair. "I like the way you see life and handle situations and make me laugh and love your dog and treat your family and protect your girl."

"You're my girl?"

"Is that all you heard?"

He nuzzled under her chin and planted a kiss on her throat. "Pretty much. Something about situations and dogs." He lightly nibbled the same spot. "But that was the best part."

"Mmm." She let her head fall backward so he could have more access. "Yes," she whispered.

"Wait. Did I hear that right?" He inched back and looked at her, coasting two hands up her waist and thumbing her breasts along the way. "Was that a *yes*, Sadie Hartman?"

She laughed and sighed and rocked her hips against him. "Why, yes, it was."

"Yes to…" He slowly laid her down on their sliver of bed and pressed more kisses all the way down her breastbone, slipping his hand up her T-shirt to caress her bare skin and feel the nipple harden in his palm. "Everything?"

"Everything," she murmured, already unbuttoning his shirt.

"Including this?" He dragged the T-shirt up to reveal her body, admiring the slopes of her curves in the dim light, then lowering his mouth to taste her.

"Oh yes, definitely that."

He got the T-shirt over her head, and on the way it pulled the clip from her hair, which tumbled down like handfuls of heaven he could inhale and burrow his fingers into. She finished his buttons and pushed off his shirt, dragging it over his arms while she kissed every inch of skin on his shoulders and neck.

"How about yes to this?" Leaning up, he put his hands on the button of his khakis, flipping it open.

"Yes, indeed." She helped him with quivering fingers he found hot and endearing. She unzipped while he slipped his hands into the elastic of her sleep pants and dipped over her skin to realize she had nothing at all on underneath.

"And even this?"

She moaned in response, biting her lip as his fingers explored. "Especially that."

Her eyes shuttered as she drew in an uneven breath, and nothing could stop him from kissing her. She parted her lips and invited more, a little whimper in her throat as their tongues touched, her body arching into his.

Frank made a gruntlike sound, not quite a bark, making them freeze for a moment.

But before they could even laugh about the awkwardness of their four-legged audience, the dog rose and jumped off the bed, then Demi followed.

"Oh, we won the bed battle," Sadie said.

Connor lifted his head to see what Frank would do, considering if he needed to go outside, but the dog ambled far away to the other side of the room, with Demi, both of them curling up in a dark corner, the back of the sofa blocking their view.

"He's protecting Demi from something she's never seen before."

"Neither has Frank," he said.

"Yeah, right."

"Sadie, I've only had him, what, a month? Same as you and Demi."

"And you've been alone all that time?"

He drew back, searching her face. "A month? Yeah, Sadie. Trust me, I don't always live up to my reputation as Bitter Bark's most-active bachelor."

"I want to trust you," she said softly, grazing his cheek with her fingers. "I want to forget that people I've loved have let me down over and over again."

He nodded. Her mother. Her boss. Her boyfriend. "I'm not any of them," he said, brushing hair off her face. "And if Frank trusts me, you can, too."

She gave in to a smile that was so pretty he had to kiss her lips. And kiss them some more. And guide her into the center of the little bed.

"Frank's a smart guy," she agreed, lifting her hips so he could slide her sleep pants all the way off.

He dropped his gaze over her, taking in her whole body, every delicious curve and angle, every secret place and precious point.

"Connor," she whispered, tipping his chin up to end his perusal and look into his eyes. "This is most definitely a *yes*. Yes, please."

She didn't have to say it again.

Sadie wasn't sure what she'd expected from Connor as a lover, but it wasn't this much tenderness. Finesse, of course. Capable hands, swoon-worthy kisses, and a physique that could bring a woman to tears—check, check, and holy hell, *check*.

But it was the delicate way he handled her body, with the featherlight kisses everywhere and a gentle cradling in his arms as he turned her over, that made her want to hold tight to this experience and savor every sizzling second.

He made her feel extraordinary and priceless…and then he made her feel weak and knotted and ready for more.

"We have to be quiet," he whispered, pulling them deep into the sheets. "One noise, and Frank could pounce."

She bit back a groan and pressed her mouth against his hot skin. "I won't say a word…" She traveled over some very nice shoulder muscles as he dipped even lower to kiss her breasts. "Except, oh my God, that feels good."

He kissed his way down her chest, suckling her and stroking her skin, while all she could do was grip his broad, strong shoulders and guide his mouth to new places while his hand found somewhere else to pleasure.

Then, as she dragged her fingertips over his abs and closed her hand around the length of him, all her pleasure was momentarily forgotten. She wanted to watch *him* respond to her touch, and listen to *his* strangled breaths and sweet words, and drown in the sexy way he said her name over and over again, like she was all he ever wanted.

Heat built to a steamy crescendo, but he paused to find a condom in the pocket of his khakis, currently on the floor with the rest of his clothes. Once he had it, he gathered Sadie under him, straddling her to put it on.

Kneeling, he peeked over the sofa back, then gave her a look that said, *All is well over there.*

"Who'da thunk it?" he whispered as his expansive

chest rose and fell with shallow breaths. She splayed her fingers over his stomach, caressing and exploring each spectacular muscle, watching his torso tighten and rock into her touch.

"Fremi?" she asked.

"Pretty unlikely pair."

She snorted quietly.

"Almost as unlikely as…" He slid down to line up their bodies. "The loser in the back of civics class and the teacher's pet up front."

"You were not a loser."

His expression grew serious as he looked into her eyes and used his knees to gently spread her legs. "I could lose this one," he admitted in a gruff voice.

"Uh…pretty sure you're about an inch from victory at the finish line," she teased, rocking her hips to close that inch to nothing.

"Not…that." He glanced down to their connected bodies. "That's not the sure thing I'm worried about."

She touched his face, aware of how hot and damp his skin was and how the rest of him throbbed against her whole body. "You don't have to worry."

"No? You might not…rebound?"

She huffed out a breath. "Trust me on this, Connor, you're the only person in this bed thinking about that unwanted visitor tonight." She arched under him. "So stop and think about me."

"You're all I think about." He started to enter her. "You're under my skin."

"Good. Now get in mine." She added some pressure to his back to get him deeper.

With every inch more, she could feel everything fade away as Sadie's whole world focused on the place where they were joined, where pleasure coalesced and fire started to burn.

He filled her slowly, taking his crazy time, each second and inch making her want to scream for more of him. The whole time, he held her gaze or kissed her lips, then he closed his eyes and let go, adding pressure and speed and intensity.

She clung to his shoulders and took the ride, closing her eyes to concentrate on each flame of delight as it licked through her body and each curl of need as he took her to the edge and every single delicious sensation that twisted and turned and tortured her with an ache for release.

As he murmured her name and threw his head back with surrender, she gave in to what her body had wanted from the moment she'd turned around on the street and looked up into those unbelievably blue eyes.

This was what she wanted. This was all she wanted. Heady, insane, mind-blowing pleasure. Hers and his and theirs together.

When he finally fell softly against her and buried his face in her hair, Sadie listened to their ragged breaths and pounding hearts while the truth echoed softly in her head.

This wasn't all she wanted. Not even close.

She wanted everything with Connor Mahoney. *Everything.*

Chapter Twenty

Connor marched through the bay, hung up his gear, and huffed out a breath.

"Right?" Ray Merritt practically growled next to him. "Four calls in one morning. I'm gonna die if I don't eat."

"And sleep," Connor said, because he'd gotten precious little of that last night. Or the night before, or the night before…basically every night for the past ten he'd spent in Sadie's bed. When he wasn't there overnight, it was because he was here, at the station, and then she slept with Frank.

He was only a little jealous of his dog.

"Yeah, you seem a little out of it today." Cal Norton slipped out of his jacket as he notched his square jaw in Connor's direction. "Too much campaigning?"

Connor grinned and pointed at him as he walked by. "Hey, you have a string hanging off your T-shirt. Oh, wait. That's your arm." He cracked up and headed toward the back of the station, trying to decide which he wanted first, food or sleep.

Both. But first he wanted to call Sadie and wish her

luck on the interview she had with the *Bitter Bark Banner* that afternoon. She was taking Frank with her, too, so he'd get equal time.

And he'd kissed her for a solid five minutes after she told him that.

"Hey, Connor, you got a minute?" Declan walked out of the front lobby, holding a cell phone and slanting his head toward his small captain's office near the back bay.

"One," Connor said, following him. "Unless you have food. Then you can have two minutes while I chew."

"Well, I have something…" Declan gave him a meaningful look and closed the door as they walked into the glass-walled office that faced the inside of the station and the always-busy back bay, where a couple of firefighters were cleaning down a pumper.

"What's up?" Connor dropped into the guest chair.

"I just got a call from a buddy of mine who's the fire marshal in Dare County. We went to school together. He's a good guy."

"And?"

Declan sat behind his desk, leveling his gaze with a bit of a challenge in his Mahoney-blue eyes. "They're looking for a captain in Kill Devil Hills. He asked if I had a good man who's ready for the job."

Connor's gut tightened as he met his older brother's gaze and knew exactly where this was going. "You think I'd leave Bitter Bark?"

"I think you're ready for more of a professional challenge, and I think you'd make a damn fine captain."

"I'm running for mayor."

Declan lifted one dark brow. "First of all, Frank's running for mayor."

"That's ceremonial, and you know it. It's my winning strategy. What's second of all?"

"You might not win, you know. This town is in love with Sadie Hartman."

"Well, that makes"—*two of us*—"them very smart. And to be honest, I think the town is more enamored of the couple running against each other than any particular half of that couple. We'll see who wins." He frowned and leaned forward. "You think she's going to beat me?"

"I think you should have a backup plan for your life."

A minor kick of irritation threatened, but he just closed his eyes. Declan meant well. His older brother assumed the de facto leadership position in the family the day Dad died, and over the years, Connor had stopped fighting the hierarchy. "My plan is to be mayor. And maybe, if you, Stan, or Bowen get promoted to chief, I'll be in this office for one-third of the shifts. In the meantime, I'm good."

"It's Kill Devil Hills, Connor. On the beach. You'd love it over there."

"You *want* me to leave?" Connor choked softly.

"I want you to get what you deserve, and I know I'm standing in the way of that." Declan folded his arms over a broad chest, one that Connor knew contained a very kind heart.

"You and two other captains, big brother."

"Neither of them are going anywhere, Connor."

He nodded. "I know that. And if I win the election, I'll have my hands full and wouldn't even want to be captain. If I don't…" Then he'd have his hands full of Sadie Hartman.

"You don't seem very concerned about losing," Declan noted. "And that's incredibly out of character for you."

"So is…" He fought a smile. "Other stuff."

"Other stuff…like a certain mayoral opponent?"

He laughed. "Well, yeah, but it isn't Mitch Easterbrook stealing my precious sleep."

"Really." Declan shook his head as if the idea that Connor was serious about Sadie didn't have a place in his brain. "But that's only supposed to be until…" He didn't finish, studying Connor's face. "It got real?"

"Look, it's only been a couple of weeks, but…" He blew out a breath and decided to say it out loud. "I'm all in."

Declan's jaw loosened. "Damn. I mean, I can see why you're attracted to her, but how is she so different from every other woman you've dated and ditched?"

He flinched at the expression. "I don't ditch women, Dec. I bow out gracefully because I…" *Don't want to get kicked in the emotional nuts.* "I just do."

"But with Sadie, you won't?" He couldn't hide his skepticism.

"I…" He shifted in his seat, not sure how to explain why this was different. But it was. At least, every night and every morning and every other minute they were together, he was starting to believe it was different. "She gets me, and she gets *to* me," he said, knowing it sounded a little lame. "She makes me laugh more and think harder and want to be…better."

It was like she met that need that his father always filled, the motivator, the inspiration, the reason he wanted to, well, win. And she did it all without one pithy Lombardi quote.

His brother lifted his brows. "Sorry if I'm a little, uh, dubious, Connor. It's just...tigers and stripes and leopards and spots."

"Which is your completely pathetic way of saying you don't think I can change my ways?" Connor shot him a look, a little ticked at that. "Well, time will tell, won't it?"

Declan tapped his phone, staring at the screen, but suddenly seeming like his head went a million miles away.

"So, you gonna call your buddy and tell him I'm not interested?" Connor asked.

"I'm going to call him, but..." He gnawed on his lower lip, the way he did when he was thinking hard about the right thing to do. "Maybe I should take it."

"You? Why the hell would you do that?" Connor leaned forward. "Just so I'd make captain? That would be just like you, Dec. Please don't. Please. I'm old enough for my big brother to stop paving the way for me in life."

He finally looked up. "I stopped that a long time ago, Connor. I was just thinking that the Outer Banks are nice. Great place to live. Might...be better for me. I have friends out there, and in...Raleigh, though that's a haul."

Raleigh? His only friend in Raleigh was Evie Hewitt, a veterinary neurologist and Declan's lifelong close friend, if Connor recalled correctly. And from that look on Declan's face...he was definitely recalling correctly. Was his younger brother's newfound romance making Declan think about the veterinary neurologist the whole family thought he loved?

But before he could press the point, a high-pitched alert cut off the conversation. "Engine One, Ladder One, medical unit for two-car collision with injuries…"

Declan jutted his chin, a little relief in his eyes. "That's you, Connor."

Connor took one precious second to look hard at his brother. "Saved by the bell, huh?"

Declan just pointed to the door. "Collision with injuries. Get moving, LT."

March was getting downright lamblike, Sadie thought as she and Frank made their way down Ambrose Avenue, the sweet hint of spring in the North Carolina air adding to her already fantastic mood.

She paused at a store window, longingly gazing at a pale blue linen dress that suddenly made her want to be at a garden party, sipping a mimosa, toasting to the onset of summer. She stared at it for a few minutes, imagining how she'd look in it…and how much Connor would like it.

Sometime in the past few weeks, his opinion started to matter.

"*Bienvenue!*" a woman called from the open front door. "Dogs are welcome," she added in a thick French accent. "It is Bitter Bark, *n'est-ce pas? La ville des chien!*"

Of course, this was La Parisienne, the boutique Nellie had mentioned to her. Checking her watch and not surprised to see she was a few minutes early,

Sadie tightened Frank's leash and stepped inside the sunny shop.

"*Bonjour!*" A woman stepped out from behind a large table overflowing with spring-colored tops. "*Je suis Yvette!*" She clapped her hands. "*Ah, mais oui*! It is our mayor-to-be."

"One of us will be," Sadie said. "This is Frank, my noble opponent, and I'm Sadie Hartman."

The woman shook her hand and gushed over Frank, who didn't completely cower into the rack of dresses, but nearly. "Easy, boy," Sadie said, bringing him closer.

"It is so romantic," Yvette cooed in a French accent that she could have lost a long time ago, but it no doubt helped sell clothes. "You and the handsome firefighter and the dog with the fabulous tail. Oh, and the kitten! It's all my customers talk about."

"I hope they talk a little bit about the issues, too." Although traffic, congestion, rental costs, and teachers' pay seemed to have taken a back seat to their engagement.

Yvette arched a beautifully drawn brow that caused a few delicate lines on her fifty-something face. "Not as interesting, I'm afraid. But oh, I am dying to ask you the most personal question. May I?"

Is it a real relationship? she guessed. Although people had stopped asking the question publicly, especially since Connor and Sadie were always laughing, kissing, holding hands, or sitting close at local restaurants.

"What's that?" Sadie asked, ready for any of the standard questions they frequently got about how they met and when they planned to set a date.

Yvette came around the dress rack just as Sadie spotted the baby-blue dress. "Is he simply *enchanting* in bed?"

Sadie blinked at her, choking a soft laugh. "Um..." She cracked up. "Pretty much, yeah." She felt heat color her cheeks, but Yvette was the one who fanned her face.

"Then you must come to my back room and see my secret stash of French lingerie. I save the camisoles and bustiers for the customers who will wear them by candlelight and with champagne, *non*?"

"I'd love to see the lingerie," she said, already smiling inside at what Connor could do with a camisole or bustier. "But I have an appointment in a few minutes. Maybe on my way back?"

Yvette nodded and pointed a long, bright pink nail at Sadie. "You must. I'll create a selection just for you and your lover to appreciate. It will be *magnifique*!"

Sadie laughed at the way the woman kissed her fingers like she was a French chef and not a retailer. "We are thinking about a weekend away after the election..."

"*Oh là là*, I will help you make that weekend unforgettable!"

"I'll stop by later," she promised. "Bye!"

"*Très bien! Au revoir*!" She blew a kiss and sent Sadie off with even more of a spring in her step. Had she ever felt this way with Nathan?

She hated comparing the two men, and rarely did, mostly because it was like comparing summer to winter. Yes, they were both seasons. And that's where the similarities ended.

Connor brought out a side of Sadie she hadn't even

known she had. He made her feel joyous and hopeful and sensual and steady. He made her forget that a few people in her life had destroyed her, and insisted there was no direction to look but to the future.

And that future, she thought as she pulled open the large glass door to the *Bitter Bark Banner* offices, could very easily include each other. Waiting for the receptionist, who was on a phone call, Sadie looked around the tiny lobby, letting her gaze slide over some of the *Banner*'s biggest headline days in the past forty years. Yes, they screamed *small town*, but they also were part of her own childhood, and the fabric of this town was woven into her heart.

Did that sound like a campaign line? She didn't care. It was truth.

"Hello, Ms. Hartman," the young woman said as she hung up the phone. "They're all waiting for you in the main conference room."

Sadie frowned as the girl stood to escort her into the back office. All? Wasn't this a one-on-one with Rose Halliday? Before she could ask, she was whisked around a corner, and the receptionist tapped on the door, inching it open a tiny bit so Sadie couldn't actually see who was in the conference room. Whoever was talking stopped immediately.

The first tendril of worry made its way up her spine.

Rose appeared in the doorway, opening it just enough to slip out, which wasn't much for the petite woman. "Hello, Sadie." Her color was high and her eyes bright, the way she looked when she thought she'd asked a particularly brilliant and insightful question.

"Are you tied up in another meeting?" Sadie asked, already thinking she could make much better use of a delay by visiting Yvette's back room.

"Oh, no. I want you to come in here." She gave a dismissive nod to the receptionist, who hurried away. "But I want to be sure we're clear so nothing comes back to bite…us."

"Clear?" Sadie looked past her to the closed door. "Who's in there?"

"My editor, Ned, for one. We're recording, okay? Video and audio. You signed a waiver about that before, but I want to make sure you also give a verbal."

"Okay," she said.

"And nothing is off the record."

Sadie lifted her brows. "I reserve the right to speak off the record, Rose, but I thought this interview would be about my traffic plan. I've made some adjustments to it." Thanks to Connor, who had a more manageable idea and let her use it in her proposal, because he was wonderful like that. "But I still won't agree that nothing is off the record."

Rose tipped her head, giving in on the concession. "All right, then, here we go." She put her hand on the doorknob and beamed up at Sadie. "It's a big day for the *Banner*," she whispered.

A big day? That tendril tightened to an actual band around her chest. "How so?"

"Well, it's not every day we get someone of this caliber in our offices."

She knew Rose wasn't talking about her. Then Rose pushed open the door and swept her arm with a flourish toward the head of the conference room table. "I believe no introduction is necessary for you two."

Jane Sutherland stood and offered her warmest smile. "Hello, Sadie."

"What are you doing here?" Sadie barely whispered the words.

"I came to do what I always do with the media." She walked toward Sadie, arms extended for a hug. "Tell the whole truth. I think it's time this town knows everything about you, Sadie. And who better to tell them than me?"

Sadie let her arms dangle as Jane wrapped her in a Shalimar-laden embrace.

Chapter Twenty-One

Connor's day didn't stop until a little after five, when he got back from the tenth—eleventh?—call and dragged his sorry ass out of the station after a fast but burning-hot shower. He didn't want to spend one extra minute at work or away from Sadie, who wasn't answering his texts.

But she had his dog, so he hopped in his truck and drove to her guesthouse, already planning on how they should have dinner in and spend the night exactly as they had the one before.

Kill Devil Hills. Was Declan crazy?

Frank didn't bark when he approached the guesthouse, and after knocking, he realized Sadie wasn't there.

"She took the dog for a walk to the square."

He turned at the sound of a man's voice, spying Sadie's grandfather walking through the garden beds toward him. Connor's eyes popped at the sight of a rifle in his hand. "Mr. Winthrop." He felt his heart drop and knew he'd seen the old man's bedroom light go on when he left Sadie's at four forty-five this morning. "Everything okay, sir?"

He braced for a dressing down, but Jim just shook his head slowly. "I've had just about enough of it."

"Enough of…what?" His granddaughter's constant overnight guest? Yes, she was in her thirties and a grown woman, but…his gaze dropped to the .22.

"Trespassers. Lookie-loos and neb-noses." He jerked the barrel of the gun toward the guesthouse. "Caught some son of a bitch looking in her window today."

Fury, indignation, and the low-grade desire to use that rifle on whoever it had been rocked him. "What?"

"Just standin' right there." He pointed with the rifle again. "Cupped hands on the glass, like some kind of damn Peeping Tom."

"Was she home?" he asked, horrified.

"No, no. She had a meeting that had her good and upset, and she stopped by and had one of her latte things with Margie, then took Frank to the square."

"Did you tell her about the clown looking in her window?"

He sighed. "I did, and she…" He shook his head. "I think she could take only so much in one day, and somethin' happened at the *Banner*, though she wouldn't say what."

"I'm going to go find her." He started to walk away, but paused. "Did you report this guy to the sheriff? Get his name?"

"I didn't report him. He ran at the sight of this, though." He gave the gun a shake. "Not sure how he did in those fancy shoes and million-dollar suit."

"Doesn't sound like any reporter I know. Sounds like…" Connor's heart dropped. "Could you describe him, Mr. Winthrop?"

He waved a hand. "Oh, tall, dark, kind of full of himself. I'm sure he works for Mitch and is looking for dirt on either one of you two. He had the unmistakable air of an undertaker about him."

Or a...*lobbyist*. "I'll talk to the sheriff's office," he said. "And I'll get her protection for when I'm on duty. You can rest easy knowing I'll be with her every minute otherwise."

His brows flicked as if to say, *Oh, I know you're with her every minute*.

"How long ago did she leave?" Connor asked as he headed toward the picket fence.

"A while. Oh! Wait." Jim reached out his other hand, and Connor immediately recognized the pink-gold tone of Sadie's phone. "Took off in such a funk she forgot this on the kitchen table."

"I'll give it to her," he said.

"Good. The thing's been buzzing like crazy."

"That's me trying to reach her," he admitted, taking the phone and dropping it in his pocket. But then Jim put his free hand on Connor's arm, looking hard at him.

"You know what she's been through."

He nodded, but didn't say anything, since she had told him she hadn't shared her breakup details with her grandparents, only her father.

"The girl's been hurt," he said, lowering his voice. "Her mama...she wasn't the best, and that's hard to admit, since she was my own daughter."

Was. How sad to have to use past tense. Connor nodded again, not sure where Jim was headed with this.

"My granddaughter could benefit from a man like

you," he said. "Strong, steady, and with a good family."

"Thanks," he said. "Just so happens I could, uh, benefit from a woman like her," he added with a smile. "But that didn't come out right. What I mean to say is she's awesome, and I want you to know I know that."

Jim's smile was slow. "And you aren't sayin' that 'cause I'm holdin' this stick, are you?"

"No, sir, I'm not."

His aging eyes danced. "Well, count me and Margie in with the rest of the town rootin' for this thing to work out."

"Me, too," he admitted. "Now I better find her."

Connor headed to the square, grateful for the last of the daylight, although it was dim enough for a few of the lights in the trees to come on, but not all.

As he crossed the street, he made a mental note that the new mayor should fix them so they all came on at once, but he forgot that note as her phone buzzed in his pocket. He ignored it.

It vibrated again when he entered Bushrod Square. As he headed north toward Frank's favorite spot near the playground, it vibrated two, no, three more times.

Who the hell wanted Sadie that bad?

But deep in his gut, he suspected who it was. The same person who lurked in her yard and looked in her window. The same person who broke her heart and stole her trust. The same person...

With the next vibration, he yanked out the phone and stared at the screen, all his suspicions confirmed.

Nathan.

Frank stood suddenly and barked, pulling Sadie out of her misery as she sat in the shadow of the founder's statue. She turned and followed the dog's gaze, her heart tripping at the sight of Connor in his navy T-shirt and khakis, walking toward her with purpose.

"I feel ya, Frankie," she said to the dog as she lifted a hand in greeting. "The man is a balm on a heavy heart." As he came closer, Frank took off toward him, and she followed, just about as happy to see him as the dog. If she'd had a tail, she'd have wagged it from side to side, too.

"Hey." She slid into his arms and let her head fall on his chest. "Man, have I had a sucky day."

"That makes two of us," he said, his voice a little tight as he inched back and held up her phone. "You're being paged. Aggressively."

She closed her eyes and didn't take it. "I won't even look at it. I've had enough of her for one day."

"Her?" He turned the phone as it vibrated yet again, letting her see a string of many, many missed texts and calls. "It's Nathan."

All the blood drained from her head so suddenly, she felt dizzy. Tightening her hold on Connor, she stared at the phone. "What does he want now? I've already been steamrolled by her."

She let out a sigh of pure disgust and exhaustion, trying to pull him toward their favorite bench, but failing because Frank was jumping on him hard and fast.

He appeased the dog with a head rub and kiss, but kept his eyes on Sadie. "What happened?" he asked.

"She showed up at the *Banner* interview," she told him as they walked.

"Jane?" he guessed, sounding as stunned as she'd been. "She crashed your interview? Why?"

As Sadie dropped onto the bench, the many answers to that question floated through her head. "She said she wanted the townspeople to know that she fully endorsed me and that I was all things amazing in politics and government, and..." She made a face, remembering all the quotable quotes that Rose had inhaled like a plate of Ricardo's lasagna. "That I have 'the heart of a small-town mayor and the brains of a congressional chief of staff.'"

He stared at her. "She came all the way from DC to give her opinion on you to the *Bitter Bark Banner*? She couldn't have done that with a phone call?"

The phone vibrated again, and she gave it a vile look. "Can I throw it for Frank to fetch?"

"If you want him to eat it."

She managed a smile. "Only for my love of him am I resisting the urge. Oh, Connor. Why are they doing this? Why won't they leave me alone?"

"They want you back," he said simply.

"She does." Sadie closed her eyes and remembered Jane's speech after the interview from hell ended, and they walked out together. "She offered me the chief of staff position, two pay grades up, and a sickening bag of perks that should be illegal to offer a congressional staffer, but you know, Jane pulls strings."

"Would you go back to DC?"

She turned and looked at him, touched by the note of dread in his question. "Of course not."

"Because of..." He nodded to the phone next to her on the bench.

"She claims they're finished," she said. "It was all

'a big mistake' that happened 'in the heat of the moment,' and he desperately wants *closure*." And a second chance, but she didn't add that, because she didn't even want to plant that ugly seed in Connor's handsome head. He looked tired and unhappy enough.

"Do you think that's why he's coming to your house and looking in your windows?"

She gasped. "You think that was him today? Boomie thought it was one of Mitch's lackeys."

He shrugged.

"Oh Lord." She dropped her head on his shoulder. "It was like a nightmare today. She fawned all over me, and the editor promised to endorse me tomorrow, and they took pictures and video for the website." She grunted and tried to let go of how horrible it had been to have to smile at Jane and thank her. "Then she practically followed me home, insisting she come to my house and meet my grandparents and…" She shook her head. "I finally got rid of her. And now…" She tapped the screen. "I'm going to get rid of him."

She felt Connor's gaze on her as she read a few of the messages, which sounded so much like what Jane had been saying. *Sorry…miss you…can't function without you…not finished with this chapter…please can I come and see you…come and see you…come and see you…*

They all blurred together. "No." She put the phone down. "You can't come and see me."

"You know, sometimes getting closure is a good thing," Connor said softly. "You might need it, too."

She shut her eyes as his words settled on her heart.

"It could help you." He put his hand over hers, making circles on her knuckles with his thumb.

"Because until you've completely let go...you might not be ready...again."

"You really think I haven't let go?"

"I think that when you can't say goodbye to someone, it haunts you."

"I said goodbye. Also a few other choice words. Then I..." She stroked Frank's head when he dropped his chin between them on the bench, his big eyes looking from one to the other. "Then I found Frank's incredibly unlikely girlfriend and left that town ASAP."

"And I found mine." Connor picked up her hand and pressed it to his lips. "And I'm afraid she's going to leave this town ASAP."

"Not a chance," she promised. "If only I had skipped the meeting and let Yvette sell me expensive French lingerie today."

He added a squeeze to the hand still near his mouth. "I don't know what you're talking about, but you have my full support."

She laughed and turned toward him. "Do you really think I have to close things with Nathan?"

"I think...I want your heart completely free and trusting. As long as he's lurking, with good intentions or bad, we're distracted from what really matters. Us."

Her heart folded in half at that. "I thought what mattered was a mayoral election and beating Mitch."

He searched her face, then held her gaze. "We'll beat Mitch with our eyes closed. Probably you now, with your big-time endorsements, but that's okay, because Frank will still put the fun in functions, and I will get to help make all the decisions because...I want to be right next to you when you make them."

"Connor." She whispered his name as he leaned in to kiss her, a sense of utter joy rising up.

"Now, answer his texts. Meet him somewhere public and safe. Close that book, and then I'll take you to my house for the night, just in case one of them decides to stalk you again. We'll bring Frank and Demi and hole up until my next shift starts, and you can tell me all about that French lingerie and how I can buy it for you. How does that sound?"

"Like heaven."

Chapter Twenty-Two

Bushrod's was packed with the early dinner crowd, but Sadie spotted Nathan almost immediately at a two-top near the front. He stood out without trying to. Yes, he was tall and handsome, but there was an arrogance to the way he held his head, which she used to think was confidence. He sat stiff and still, as if touching the table at Bushrod's was beneath him, but there had been a time when Sadie would have thought that was just his bone-deep elegance.

And yes, his face was chiseled in a way that always turned heads, but there was nothing inherently hot about him. He didn't have natural swagger that came from knowing that if he had to walk into a burning building to save a life, he not only would, but he probably did just that the day before. He didn't have a sense of humor that could make a woman laugh and want to kiss him, too. He didn't have hands that could be tender and searing at the same time, or a body that moved with purpose and grace, or a heart that cared for animals as much as people.

In other words, he wasn't Connor Mahoney and never would be.

She walked toward him, comfortable in the knowledge that Connor was sitting at the bar, where he could "keep an eye on things" while she talked to her ex.

There might have been a time in her life when that would feel overbearing and the polar opposite of the kind of "liberation" a fan of Susan B. Anthony would want. But protection didn't diminish her freedom; it enhanced her confidence to take the chair across from Nathan, look him in the eyes, and tell him to get the hell out of her life.

She got as far as looking him in the eyes when he reached for both her hands, squeezed tight, and then stared at the left one in horror. "Is that real, Sadie?"

"You would say it is." She managed to free her hands. "It's lab grown."

Most of the color drained from his face. "Where did you get it?"

She couldn't lie—it was kind of fun to throw him off his high horse by showing him just how fast she'd bounced back. "I think the proper question is who gave it to me. His name is Connor Mahoney, and if you—"

"Oh, the mayor thing." He seemed moderately relieved. "But..." He took her hand and studied the ring very closely. "HPHT? It looks like it."

"I don't know, Nathan." She couldn't even remember what manufacturing technique the acronym stood for, because the days when she cared about that industry were so long ago. She covered the ring with her other hand and looked at him. "And we didn't come here to talk about rings."

"Well…maybe we did," he murmured, running his hand over the condensation on his drink.

"What does that mean?" Was he going to get mad that she'd met someone? Because that would be rich.

"It means…" He swallowed, taking a minute to plan what he'd say, something he frequently did. "Look, Sadie, I made a mistake. A big one. A regrettable one. I got…swayed by status and power. It happens in Washington. But…" He held up his hand, not giving her a chance to interrupt. "But now I know what really matters. And I would like to try again. Please move back home."

She tried not to laugh. She really did, but she had to drop her head back and chuckle heartily. "Um… no."

"It's over with Jane," he said quickly, as if she were waiting for him to say that before she'd throw her arms around him and take him back. "I don't even talk to her. I assigned someone else to deal with lobbying her and am staying clear of her office."

"Too much of a temptation?"

"A reminder," he said softly. "Of what I gave up." He inched closer to look her in the eyes and reached across the table to touch her face. "You."

She eased back and took a steadying breath, happy that not one cell in her whole body had any reaction to his touch. Except for the need to recoil. And *close up shop*. After all, that's why she was here.

"Nathan, you can take comfort from the knowledge that I forgive you." There. It hadn't even been that hard to say. She did forgive him, because she didn't care about him, not one tiny bit. And that was *true* liberation.

"Do you really?" He seemed just a little desperate, and she almost believed him, until his eyes shifted down for just a flash of a second as he checked the phone on his lap.

"Yes," she said on a sigh. "It's too much weight to carry around not to forgive you. And I'll forgive Jane, too, since she made such a deal of things today."

"Oh. What happened today?"

Shouldn't he have been just a little more shocked that Sadie had seen Jane that very day? "She showed up at the local paper to sing my praises and try to help me get elected. Then she offered me the COS job, which might surprise the chief of staff she already has."

His brows flicked with interest. There was a time when he would have stared in surprise and shock and then congratulated her, knowing how much she wanted that promotion. How much she *used* to want it.

When he looked down at his phone again, she stole a glance to her left and caught Connor's eye at the bar, where he sipped beer and talked to Billy, the owner. He lifted the bottle in a secret toast, but she couldn't respond, because Nathan grabbed her left hand again, the phone in his other hand.

"Can I take a picture of it?"

She frowned. "Why?"

"You know the NLDA likes to see the product in the wild. It's part of helping people understand that they're as real as mined diamonds."

She felt her face squish up. "Is that really all you care about? Don't you even want to know about the man who gave this to me?"

His eyes tapered to dark slits as he leaned a little closer. "Sadie, listen to me. That man doesn't matter. He can't matter to you, because you loved me. And I believe in my heart of hearts, you still do."

"Do you even have a heart of hearts, Nathan?"

He held the phone up to snap a picture.

"Don't!" Fury shot through her, making her flip her hand and knock the phone hard enough to send it flying across the table. It landed on the floor next to her chair with a *clunk*.

At the bar, Connor sat up straighter, watching the exchange.

"Why would you do that?" she asked.

"Because I have to be...sure it's lab grown. I can send that picture to the association and—"

She cut him off with a swipe of her hand and leaned down to grab the phone off the floor just as it lit up with an incoming text.

Jane: No go. Try again tomorrow. Don't worry.

The words didn't make sense, but the heart emoji did.

Oh God. What the hell was their game? All the forgiveness she'd so magnanimously offered disappeared. In its place was anger, disgust, distrust, and every other bad thing she could heap on this man and the woman she once looked up to as much as her own mother.

No, honestly, more than her own mother. And neither Jane nor her mother deserved it any more than this poor excuse for a man. Liars, the lot of them.

"Here." She handed him the phone. "You missed a text. Goodbye, Nathan. You want closure? Watch, and you'll get it."

With that, she stood, pushed her chair in, and walked through the tables straight to the bar. With each step, Connor sat up a little straighter and looked more interested and curious.

When she reached his seat, she wrapped her arms around his neck and kissed him long, hard, and with tongue. His hands came around her back as he pulled her closer, giving every bit as well as he was getting in this kiss.

As they finally broke contact, all of Bushrod's exploded into applause, and next to Connor, Frank barked noisily.

When she turned to acknowledge the crowd's reaction, she caught sight of Nathan's back as he slithered out the door.

"Nice closure, Ear Girl."

Yes, it was. She smiled up at him. "Take me home, Lieutenant. And don't expect to get any sleep."

The whole scene at Bushrod's had been like some magical foreplay that had Connor and Sadie making out like teenagers in the truck until Frank literally pawed them apart. They kissed in his driveway, undressed in his living room, and left a trail of underwear on the way to his bedroom.

"I gotta admit, Sadie," Connor murmured against her throat as he worked his way down for a taste of her world-class breasts. "You had me a little nervous at the bar."

Holding his head, she lifted it to look into his eyes. "Nervous? About Nathan?"

"I saw you cover the ring and throw your head back with laughter, and then he touched your face, which I consider an invasion of my personal property."

She laughed, biting her lip. "I am not your..." Her voice trailed off as his hand dipped between her legs. "Okay, I am." She let out a whimper of delight. "But you had nothing to be nervous about. Please, Connor, don't talk about him. Not here. Not now. Just keep...yes. Do that. And more of...oh my *God*, do that again."

He smiled into the next kiss, which he planted on her nipple, getting a kick of pleasure as the tip grew hard under his tongue.

But he had to lift his head again, making her let out a little squeak of disappointment.

"But I really liked when you walked across Bushrod's like you owned the place and then kissed me like..."

"Like I owned you."

"Which, shit, you kinda do."

Laughter bubbled up. "So we're even. Owners of each other... Please stop talking and remembering that bar. I only want this. You. Now."

He followed orders happily, stroking her heavenly skin, rolling on top, then on bottom, then side by side to find new ways to intertwine and connect. Every time, every touch, every single sensation with Sadie was a little different from the one before. She made love like she lived, with unexpected joy and confidence and independence.

With that thought, he had to stop and eye her again.

"What?" she said with a laugh of feigned

impatience. "Don't look like that. I know you have condoms in the drawer right there. I watched you put them there last time we were here."

"No, it's not…" He shook his head, unable to get the phrase out. "We don't *own* each other, Sadie. You know that."

Her smile wavered. "Of course not. Why?" She stroked his face, the lust clearing from her eyes as she looked at him. "What's wrong?"

"This is big," he said, the words slipping out without any mental preparation or editing. He wasn't trying to charm or amuse or impress her. He just wanted to tell her what was in his heart.

"What's big…other than the obvious?"

He smiled, but shook his head. "No jokes. This is…big." Why couldn't he think of a better word? Real? Amazing? Permanent? They all sounded like something they'd say on the campaign trail. But this change in his life was huge.

She sat up a little, still holding him, but looking into his eyes with a question in hers. "What is it, Connor? What are you trying to tell me?"

"I guess that…I couldn't stand to lose you." He held her a little closer, pressing her against him. "Not just lose, which yes, I'd hate. But to lose *you*. It's not a game or a contest or an election or…or…casual dating. Not this. Not anymore."

She blinked at him, nodding slowly. "I feel that, too."

But did she feel it as deeply? As wholly? As…forever-ly as he did? He didn't know how to ask her without sounding pathetic or desperate or like he was pushing this relationship too far, too fast.

But he wanted to. He wanted to push it as far and as fast as it could go and never look back.

"It's not casual," she agreed in a whisper. "Nothing about this is casual."

Maybe she did get it. "You really feel that way?"

"Connor. You shouldn't have to ask." Kissing him, she rolled over so she was on top, moving like magic over his body, taking...yeah, taking ownership. And God, he wanted her to have it.

He closed his eyes and went along for the ride, inhaling her sweet scent, clutching handfuls of her incredible hair, lost in the sound of his name on her lips, and building to something much more complicated and mind-blowing than a simple release.

As he pulled her along to the same exquisite place, Connor felt tears sting his eyes and sweat trail down his temples. His skin was on fire, his body was helpless, and his whole heart and soul felt like they'd finally found their way home.

Chapter Twenty-Three

S adie opened her eyes when the mattress dipped at the ungodly hour of four thirty.

"Do firefighters' wives ever get used to this?" The words slipped out in a sleepy, half-conscious state, but the minute they were out, her eyes popped wide open.

Firefighters' *wives*? What was she thinking?

"Yes, and so do some firefighters' *husbands*," Connor answered, obviously not rattled by her insinuation. "Such sexism from a Susan B. fan."

"It's early for us suffragettes."

He sat on the bed and kissed her hair, stealing a slow ride up and down her bare body with his hands. "And those spouses and partners are grateful for the twelve-hour shift that beats the hell out of the twenty-four. I will see you…" He found her mouth. "At five fifteen tonight rather than five fifteen tomorrow morning. Good, right?"

"That's good," she moaned as his big, callused hand skated over her way-too-stimulated-for-this-hour body.

"What are you doing today?" he asked.

"I think I'll go lingerie shopping," she murmured, arching and practically begging for more. "For that French stuff."

"French stuff?" He leaned over and circled her nipple with his tongue. "That sounds hot."

"That is…" She clasped his head and added some pressure. "Hot."

"I have to go, but how are you going to get home?"

"It's not a long walk," she said, rising up on her elbows. "A mile to town? I can take Frank. He adores me, you know."

"Who doesn't?" He brushed some hair off her face. "You're going to walk from here to town in the heels you had on yesterday?"

"I have sneakers and jeans over on that chair. I changed into slacks and dress shoes before we went campaigning a few days ago, remember? I just need a top. Don't you have something I can wear?"

"Yeah." He got off the bed and went to the dresser. "Here's a Bitter Bark FD T-shirt. Walk of shame, baby."

"Are you kidding? Walk of *pride*." She grabbed the T-shirt he tossed at her and squished the navy blue cotton over her face, inhaling the scent of his detergent. "I love you in this shirt."

Oh crap. Did she really just say that? As if saying *wives* hadn't been bad enough?

"It ought to get you some votes," he joked casually. Maybe he missed the *love* part? "See you tonight, Ear Girl."

"Bye." She wiggled her fingers and stuffed the shirt under her cheek, turning over to catch a few more hours of sleep.

She woke when another tongue was on her cheek, this one way too large and frantic to be Connor's.

"Frankendog," she murmured, grabbing his head for some love and peeking out the blinds to see the sun was well up. "You need to hit the grass, big guy. And we better get home and check on our girl, Demi."

He barked as if the name meant something—and maybe it did. A few minutes later, she was headed toward town with Frank on his leash, walking with that same spring in her step she couldn't seem to hide lately.

"Nice shirt, Sadie," a stranger called as she walked past town hall toward the square.

"Thank you! And thank you for your vote," she called over her shoulder.

A few more people commented, and two stopped to pet Frank, and one actually asked about the traffic problem, but Sadie eventually made it around the square and back home.

She almost stopped in the main house to hit up her grandmother for a latte, but then she remembered it was choir practice morning for Nana, and gardening club at the local hardware store for Boomie, so she headed straight to the guesthouse to feed Demi.

As they neared the door, Frank barked, pulling on the leash excitedly.

"You really like her, don't you?" she teased. "You do realize that you are actually not the same species, right? Like, you can't be together in that very special way. Of course, you're both fixed, so I guess cuddling does the trick for you two."

He just yanked harder as she fished the house key from her bag.

"You know she's not going to be quite that excited to see you, don't you? She'll pretend to be bored. She'll let you chase her tail. Then she will…" She finally found the key as Frank put his head down, his tail between his legs, and let out a growl that literally rose the hairs on Sadie's neck. "What's the matter—"

He launched at the door the way he did whenever he saw Connor, slamming his front paws at the wood and knocking it wide open.

It wasn't locked?

She rushed after him and froze at the sight of a man, his back to her as he yanked kitchen cabinets open, pushing dishes around.

"Party's over, Sadie. Where the *goddamn hell is it*?"

"Nathan?" She stared at him as her purse slid off her shoulder and hit the floor with a thud. What was he doing here?

When he turned around, her first thought was that he'd never looked that way before. Crazed. Furious. Completely out of control.

Her second thought was…*run*.

But he lunged at her, close enough to grab her arm. "I mean it!" he shouted in her face. "I've tried for too long to get into this place, and there was always a guy or a dog or an old man with a gun. You have got to tell me where the hell it is."

She tried to free her arm, but he had a good grip, tight enough to leave a mark. The reality of that sent a shot of adrenaline through her body so strong she could taste it in the back of her throat.

"What are you talking about?" she ground out.

Next to her, Frank growled, still cowering in front of a stranger when she so needed him to attack.

"Give it to me," he ordered.

"What?"

"Give it to me, or I...I..." He squeezed his eyes shut. "I don't want to hurt you, Sadie."

"You already are." She wrested her arm free and shook it, managing to take a half step back. "What the hell is going on?"

"I need that bust, Sadie. You have to give me the bust."

What? "The Susan B. Anthony bust?" As she said it, she was vaguely aware that Frank had circled the sofa, still growling. Then he let out a loud bark. She stole a glance at him, praying he was about to protect her, but he was looking right up at that corner bookshelf...where the bust was.

Why in God's name would Nathan want it? She had no idea, but if Frank was looking up there, it was because Demi was next to it, hiding from the intruder in her new favorite place.

"Why do you want it?" Sadie asked. She didn't plan to tell him where it was since he obviously hadn't seen it.

"None of your business."

"Um, Nathan." She crossed her arms and stared him down. "You've broken into my house and admitted that you came here several times to do that. And now you're demanding to know where something I own is. I'd call it very much my business."

"Why I want it isn't your business." He looked around again, still not seeing the bust as he scanned her kitchen and table and all the papers she'd spread out to prepare speeches and plans for being mayor.

"Yes, it is."

He took a step closer, all his handsome, commanding, powerful presence suddenly becoming menacing, forcing her back. "Sadie. Just give it to me and call it a day. We'll leave you alone."

We. "Is Jane in on this?"

He didn't answer for a second. Then, he nodded. "Look we tried all kinds of ways to get in here and find it. When I went to your apartment and it was gone, I—"

"What difference does it make?" she demanded, furious that he'd gone to her apartment after she left. Of course, he had a key, but *why*? "It's mine. I made it as a kid with my father. Why would you and Jane try 'all kinds of ways' to get it?"

"Because..." He looked around again, a little frantic. "Where the hell is it?"

She swayed backward, *none* of it making sense and all of it so incredibly...wrong. But in her peripheral vision, she saw Frank jump in the air, making them turn. A soft hiss came from the shelf, the sound of a confused and scared cat who had to ward off trouble.

Nathan didn't hear it, though. He wasn't tuned to the cry of a hidden cat he didn't even know she owned.

He looked away as if the dog was nothing but a bother, still not seeing the bust tucked in the corner of the shelf. "I thought he was some kind of guard dog."

"Or you would have broken in sooner," Sadie said. "To get a piece of my life that has no value to you. What is going on, Nathan?"

This time, Frank's bark and jump were serious and furious, aimed at the shelf where Demi was. The bookshelf wobbled and scared the cat. As she leaped out of her hiding place, her tail knocked over a book, and that shook the shelf again. Frank launched one more time, maybe at Demi, maybe at the shelf, but it was enough to topple the clay bust.

Sadie sucked in a breath, watching Aunt Sue sway with instability on her uneven base, then crash to the floor with the hollow shattering sound of hard clay.

"Oh my God!" She lunged toward it, but Nathan grabbed her arm with frightening force.

"I'll get it!" Nathan insisted, pushing her away. "It's mine, Sadie. They're mine."

"It's bro—" She froze in shock as she looked at the six or seven large chunks of clay on the ground, but there was something more. Very small and shimmery somethings. A dozen, maybe two, teeny tiny pieces of glass...

Oh no. They weren't *glass*.

"Nathan," she whispered as everything suddenly made some kind of sense. "You hid diamonds in there?"

Before he could answer, Frank dived for them. He grabbed a mouthful and then another as Nathan practically sprang to get to him.

"No!"

Frank gobbled some more, turning to Nathan with wild eyes like he might just take a bite out of his face.

"No, Frank!" Sadie flew at the dog. "Don't eat those!"

"Stop it!" Nathan tried to grab him, but Frank managed one more lick and cleaned up what was left, bolting away to a corner to cower and...

"He swallowed!" Nathan shrieked. "He ate my goddamn diamonds!"

Sadie stood in frozen shock, her hands on her cheeks, her mind whirring with what Connor had told her. Might not be fatal…might need an X-ray…sharp edges cause internal bleeding.

Oh God. She had to get Frank to a vet. *Now*.

Nathan grabbed both her arms and whipped her around with more force than she thought he had. "I'm taking him. And you can't stop me."

Like hell she couldn't. On instinct, she jammed her knee up, narrowly missing his crotch as he managed to avoid it. His eyes got as wild as Frank's as he yanked her across the room.

"Frank, help me!"

But the dog, chastised, had flattened in shame.

"In there!" Nathan shoved her toward the bathroom and pushed her inside, pulling the door to slam it shut.

Was he an idiot? It didn't lock from the outside. Then she heard a chair scrape across the wood floor, and she vaulted at the doorknob. She twisted, but it was too late.

Son of a bitch! He'd jammed the door closed with the back of a kitchen chair.

"Nathan!" she screamed, but the only response was Frank's desperate bark.

"Shut up, you stupid beast!"

He did, of course, no doubt falling to the floor again in abject self-pity.

Her heart cracked like that damn clay sculpture as she thought about poor Frank out there with that maniac. She grabbed the knob and shook it again, trying to break it off, cursing herself for dropping her purse with her phone in it when she walked in the door.

"Open your mouth!" Nathan demanded. "Ouch! Don't bite me!"

Yes, Frank. Bite him. Take a finger or two from that slimy thief.

"Out we go, monster. I can lift you."

He could...no! He couldn't take Frank! Panic rolled over her in waves, paralyzing her as she imagined what he might do to that sweet dog. Not race him to a vet like she would.

Would Nathan hurt a dog? She had no idea. She certainly hadn't thought he was capable of...this. But obviously she didn't really know him—or Jane—at all.

The front door slammed. No. No. *No!*

She spun in a circle, trying to be calm and think. There wasn't a window in here, but... Her gaze dropped to the two-foot-square plastic-covered dog door. Could she squeeze through there?

She dropped to her knees and stuck her head through, then pushed farther, the metal edges digging into her shoulders. She might make it. Or she might get stuck there until someone found her.

And by then, what would have happened to Frank?

Tash opted for no siren, at least while they were in town, but she still drove the ambulance like a life depended on it, flying down a surprisingly empty Ambrose Avenue for that time of the morning.

"Second time this month," Tasheema muttered as she passed a car on the left. "One of these times, Miss Clara Dee really is going to be having a heart attack."

"I hope not," Connor replied with a smile. "I really kind of like when she takes my hands and says, 'But it is broken, young man. It broke when Henry died.'"

His EMT partner shot him a look. "Listen to you, Mahoney. All romantic and shit. What a difference love makes. Goin' all soft on me now."

"I'm not soft." Nothing on him had been that morning when he left Sadie, that was for sure.

"But you *are* in love."

He picked up the radio, trying to concentrate on dispatch.

"Connor?" She dragged out his name on a laugh. "Are you in love?"

"I'm in something," he admitted. "At the moment, it's an ambulance on the way to a call, so can it, Tash."

"Why? Everyone knows it. If you can't see for yourself, let me tell you what's what, m'dear. You are in love."

"Who knows what love is?" But if it felt like his happiness, well-being, and possibly next breath depended on knowing he'd be with Sadie far into the future and maybe beyond...then yes. That's what he felt.

The doubts from the night before were long gone. He'd made the decision when he walked out this morning to kick his worries about her rebounding to the curb. She was done with that guy, that life, and that city.

"You know who knows what love is?" Tash pulled him from his thoughts. "Miss Clara Dee. You can ask her how it felt when she met Henry. Nothin' she likes to talk about more."

He smiled, knowing it was true. How did someone know when they had something like Clara and Henry? Or…his mind skimmed over all the weddings and engagements there'd been in his family over the past few years. Was this…

"Oh, I see some traffic up there," Tash said. "Hang on, takin' the back route."

Tash whipped around the bend, and Connor smiled, knowing this would take them right past Sadie's grandparents' house and, of course, the guesthouse. Would she have made the walk of shame yet?

He liked thinking of her traipsing through town with his dog, wearing his shirt and that satisfied smile from all they'd shared the night before.

As they came up to the corner where the house was, he noticed a black Buick SUV right outside the gate. Was someone visiting? If that—

Just then, he saw Sadie tearing ass from the back of the guesthouse, running like a crazed woman toward the fence. She screamed something, but he couldn't hear it with the windows up. Had Frank gotten out? Demi?

He almost asked Tash to stop, but knew he couldn't possibly do that, not on their way to a call. As they got closer, he cracked his window, his heart kicking up as he saw her hair flying as she ran like a life depended on it.

He opened his mouth just as he heard her scream, "Nathan! Nathan!"

The SUV started up at the very minute she reached the fence, which she vaulted like a track star. She lunged at the passenger door. "You are not leaving without me! Don't do this!"

She banged on the window so hard he could hear her fist hit the glass.

"You're right, I need you! Please come back! Please, please don't do this. I need to go with you. Please, Nathan, I'm begging you to take me with you!"

Connor's blood turned to ice with every word, and bile rose in his throat. With each strangled breath, he stared at the whole thing, getting one last glimpse as Tash sped the ambulance past the scene. He had just enough time to see Sadie yank the passenger door open and throw herself into the SUV as it took off, leaving him to stare at the Washington, DC, license plate.

"Whoa," Tash whispered. "What the hell was that all about?"

"I have no idea."

Except he did have an idea. And it meant...he'd lost.

Chapter Twenty-Four

Sadie wasn't the least bit surprised to see Jane at the wheel. She was, however, stunned to see that Frank had bitten Nathan, who was swearing up a storm while Frank rolled into a ball as far away as he could get from everyone.

The poor baby had to be completely freaked out. All the work, all the training, all the progress… undone in a morning by this idiot.

"I'm coming back there," Sadie announced, not waiting for permission to crawl over the console to the back seat. Frank was pushed into the corner behind the passenger seat, his head down, but his eyes were filled with nothing but sorrow. And maybe pain, though he didn't whimper.

"Oh, sweet boy." She wrapped her arms around his neck. "I'm going to help you."

"You better help *us*." Nathan practically spat the words at her. "Because this stupid mutt just ate about two hundred thousand dollars' worth of lab-grown diamonds."

"All of them?" Jane choked from the driver's seat.

"I snagged a few he missed," Nathan said. "But what the hell kind of dog eats rocks?"

Sadie whipped around to him. "What the hell kind of person steals from his client and hides the booty in an innocent person's apartment?"

Her words bounced around the lush interior of the luxury SUV, and the silence that followed was like an echo.

"I'm right?" she asked with a mirthless laugh. "That's what you're doing? Stealing manmade diamonds from the association that trusts you to represent them?" Disgust roiled through her.

Jane and Nathan exchanged a look in the rearview mirror, silent.

"They track those things when you take them out to show lawmakers how real they are, you know," she reminded him. He couldn't be that stupid. He had to know that. "You can't simply help yourself to whatever you want."

He closed his eyes. "How many times have you heard me say they grow money, Sadie? Trust me when I say that they don't care about a few stones they grow for PR. No one is going to miss them if they're taken in small amounts."

She drew back, her jaw unhinged. Had she known he was this greedy? How did she miss that?

"Then what about you?" She leaned forward to direct the question to Jane. "Miss Ethics Above All?" She slathered the question with all the repugnance that ricocheted through her body in that moment. "You would risk your reputation and job and, God, jail time to split a few hundred grand with Nathan? What is *wrong* with you?"

Again, they exchanged a look that spoke volumes Sadie didn't understand, with Jane's right hand on the wheel tapping with that nervous twitch. Of course she was nervous. She was a *criminal*.

"I thought you two broke up. You both…wanted me back so bad." The words tasted bitter because they had been such a lie.

"We wanted in your house," Jane said. "We tried every tack we could think of, and if you thought we were still together, we knew we'd never get anywhere. We peered in every window and couldn't see the damn thing. Nathan tried to get in while I did that interview, and I went there while you had a drink, but there was always a dog, a boyfriend, or a man with a gun."

"Thank God for all of them."

"But we're out of time now." Her hand trembled so hard she dropped it on her lap, giving Sadie a measure of satisfaction knowing that this hurt Jane, too.

No wonder Nathan had been horrified when he'd seen Sadie's ring. He wasn't jealous; he probably thought she'd found the diamonds and made herself a ring. As if.

Sadie just shook her head and turned her attention back to Frank, who seemed remarkably fine, considering he'd just eaten a handful of crystallized carbon.

"How do you feel, Franko?" She stroked his head and coaxed his mouth open, looking for any signs of blood. Or diamonds. She lifted his lips to see his gums were pink. That was good. If they weren't, she'd be terrified he was bleeding internally.

He nuzzled into her hand, clearly grateful for the familiar face and affection.

"The closest vet is in town," Sadie said. "Or we could go to Waterford Farm, which would mean taking the next right."

Silent, Jane turned left.

"You are taking him to a vet?" Sadie didn't mean it to come out as a question, because there was no choice in the matter.

"He can go to a vet after he...gets rid of them." Jane made a face. "It'll be unpleasant, but we'll deal."

They'd *deal*? "Why?"

Nathan waved his hand to quiet her.

"No," Sadie shot back. "I have every right to ask a million questions. Like, forget why you're doing this, you're both obviously blind with greed, and I'm blind for not seeing it. Plus you hid your contraband on *my* property."

"It was the safest place I could think of," Nathan said. "I stuffed them in that plugged hole in the bottom and cushioned them with cotton, and I didn't think that thing would ever break. Of course, I never dreamed you'd run off and take it."

She choked a dry laugh. "You're both sick, you know that?"

"Just one of us," Jane whispered, the words so soft, Sadie wasn't sure she'd heard right. Then she hit the accelerator and headed north, flying past a sign that said Sweetgum Springs.

"Where are we going?" Sadie demanded.

"Somewhere to wait out the dog's...business," Jane said. "Is there some way to, uh, encourage that?"

Was there something she could say or do to get out of this car with Frank? She rubbed his belly, thinking of options. "Dog food." If they stopped at a convenience store, she could run, find a phone, and get help for Frank.

Nathan thumbed his phone. "This site says just let 'em poop regular and not feed them."

"He did that this morning already," she said.

"Meaning this could take hours," Jane said.

"Wait. Wait." Sadie shook her head hard. "Are we seriously having this discussion? I'm talking with the two of you about a dog pooping diamonds like it's normal? Nothing is normal about this. What the hell is wrong with you two?"

Jane's twitch intensified, and now her whole arm sort of vibrated. Sadie had seen that happen only once before, the day she stood in Jane's office and accused her of sleeping with Nathan.

"You want me to drive?" Nathan asked, his voice suddenly lower and more gentle.

"No, no, I'm fine."

"You're not fine, Jane." He reached to the front seat and put his hand on her shaking shoulder. "Your eyes okay? I can drive."

Sadie looked from one to the other, taking in the exchange, missing a piece of...something. Nathan wasn't generally a nurturer, and Jane would sooner cut off that quivering arm than give up control in a situation like this and...

"Tell her." The command came from Jane, simple and clear.

"I don't think—"

"Tell her, Nathan. She needs to know I'm not a common, greedy criminal, and neither are you."

"Uh, *she's* right here." Sadie leaned forward, scrutinizing Jane. "Tell me yourself."

She swallowed. "I can't. I can't say the words."

Nathan dropped back with a noisy huff. "She has ALS."

"What?"

"ALS. Lou Gehrig's—"

"I know what it is." The news washed over her, easily drowning out the hate and resentment that had built up toward Jane. "Oh my God, Jane. That's…" A death sentence. "Terrifying."

Nathan tipped his head. "The thing is, it doesn't have to be…the end. And that's why we're in this car talking about pooping diamonds."

She waited for more, completely confused.

"We're doing this because…" Jane lifted that shaky hand, hitting the steering wheel with a hard tap as if demanding her body obey. "Nathan's firm is handling a client in the pharmaceutical industry who is putting a drug up for FDA consideration that is showing some extremely positive signs in early testing. It could be the cure everyone is hoping for."

"Oh. That's wonderful."

"It will cost five hundred thousand dollars a dose."

Ouch. "So you're fighting for legislation to lower the cost," Sadie assumed, well aware of all of Jane's hard work in the health care sector. The cost of prescription meds was one of her most intense fights in Congress.

"She can't get the cost lowered," Nathan said. "It's a very, very expensive drug to manufacture."

"But I can be first in line to buy a dose, which is an arduous and time-consuming process to make, the minute one becomes available…if I make it that long." Jane let her eyes close for a moment. "And if I have half a million dollars. And as you know, the diamond labs literally grow money."

"That you stole," Sadie said, looking at Nathan.

He met her gaze. "Look, I'm not going to lie. I love her, and I'll do anything for her. Save her life? It's a no-brainer."

Sadie waited for the impact of that, but there certainly wasn't any jealousy. Nathan loved Jane. She hadn't seen it coming, but now it made such perfect sense. They were so right for each other, so much alike, that it was no wonder Sadie had thought she loved both of them. Their drive and focus and ability to mow down every obstacle had been so attractive to her.

In some weird way, they belonged together.

"I wish you had told me sooner," she said softly. "I would have bowed out gracefully and let you be a couple."

"I tried to fight it," Jane admitted. "Nathan did, too. We both care so much about you, Sadie. But I had just found out about my…condition, and I happened to be at an event with Nathan that night and…" Her voice cracked. "He's been there for me the whole time."

Sadie sighed. "Well, I guess I understand why you're doing this, but it's still illegal."

"You're not going to help us?" Nathan asked.

"I…" Was she? "I don't know what I'm going to do, but…" She tightened her grip around Frank, who was pressed against her like a second skin. "But I won't leave this dog. Not for one minute. Please take him to a vet for an X-ray. After that? I don't know."

"You have to help us, Sadie." Nathan put his hand on her leg. "You care about Jane. And you did care about me. What's a few dozen lab diamonds to you? You're faking your engagement to some firefighter so you can become mayor. You don't really have a leg to stand on in the ethics department."

She stared at him, letting the words sink in as Jane accelerated onto a highway, taking a bend in the road a little too fast.

"You're going to help us, Sadie," she said with that same cool that she had when delivering an order to the staff.

"I'm going to help Frank," Sadie replied. "Beyond that..."

"You're going to cover for us," she ground out. "And you can stick your ethics up your ass. I've bent over backward for the lab-grown-diamond industry and passed laws that helped them make hundreds of millions of dollars. They can pay for my goddamn medicine!" She flattened the accelerator and whipped around another corner.

"Hey, Jane, settle." Nathan leaned forward suddenly, the move making Frank bark. "Don't lose it now."

"Lose it?" Sadie asked on a whisper.

"It's part of the disease," he said. "She can be... erratic."

She swerved and worked to right the vehicle, making Sadie gasp. "Then she should pull over and let the rest of us live."

"We're going to hide in the woods with that dog," Jane announced, turning the wheel sharply to take a side street that turned into a steep hill. "We're going to wait to get our diamonds and convince you, Sadie Hartman, how important this is. It's my *life*. I'll do what I have to."

The words and threatening delivery sent a thousand chills up Sadie's arms and a black ball of fear into the pit of her stomach. Jane wasn't stable. She wasn't healthy. And she was—

She veered out of their lane suddenly, nearly plowing into an oncoming truck.

"Jane!" Nathan yelled. "Pull over. Pull over, now!"

They were almost at the crest of the hill, not able to see the other side, when Jane gunned it, as if to prove she could do anything she wanted.

Blood thrummed in Sadie's head as she held Frank and realized with a shock that she hadn't buckled her seat belt.

"Slow down!" she screamed at Jane, fumbling for the belt behind her just as they topped the hill at such a high speed the whole SUV literally left the ground for two sickening seconds, landing hard.

She swerved again, but then started careening downhill, as if she had her foot on the gas, not the brakes. Sadie screamed, and Nathan unsnapped his belt, diving between the front seats to get to Jane. The move made her whip the wheel, sending the SUV spinning around, airborne again, until it landed on the steep embankment with a jolt. The front of the car cruised into the muddy swale, the impact not enough to explode airbags.

"Oh my God," Jane whispered into the sudden silence.

"What the hell?" Nathan moaned.

Sadie landed on the floor with Frank on top of her. She pushed him up and managed to do a total body check, but nothing hurt.

"Are you both okay?" she asked.

"Fine, just…stunned," Nathan added. "Jane?"

Her only response was a soft sob of defeat.

"Let me open this door." Sadie unlatched the door and pushed it open, and immediately, Frank scrambled out. "Wait, Frank, wait."

He barked once, landed on the ground, and started to run.

"No!" Sadie launched herself up and out, sliding in some mud on the hill. "Frank, stop! Stay!"

But he ignored the order, tearing off toward the thick woods.

She'd never find him in there! With one glance back to the car to see Nathan helping Jane upright, she made a sudden decision. She couldn't lose Frank. She couldn't, especially if he was hurt. The idea of him curling up in the dark woods and bleeding to death shot through her like a gallon of adrenaline, sending her running as fast as possible after the dog.

"Frank, stop!"

Her pleas didn't slow him down, but the forest did a little. She was able to keep him in sight as he seemed to find a path between the trees, dodging rocks and branches, sliding through bushes, and running like he knew exactly where he was going.

Her heart hammered as they ran deeper into the woods, the sun nearly blocked by the trees, even though they didn't all have thick leaves yet. They tore through the branches, her feet pounding and occasionally stumbling, but she wouldn't stop. Frank had to give out before she did. She had to get him, had to save him.

Suddenly, after passing through a thicket of trees, he ran to the top of a steep hill and disappeared over the other side.

"Frank!" She was so out of breath, his name barely came out, but she forced her legs to keep going, each step burning as she hiked to the top. "Frank, it's me. Don't leave me!"

She crested the hill, looked down the slope on the other side, and…he was gone.

"Frankendog!" Frustration and fear rocked her so hard, she almost fell, which would have sent her down to the creek rushing about forty feet down the embankment.

Where did he go?

She looked left and right, and neither direction looked safe for the dog to have gone down. She turned, peered into the woods, and examined the hill again.

Then she heard him bark. Faintly, fairly far away, but that was him, barking over and over again.

She followed the sound, gingerly making her way over rocks and dirt that slid out from under her every few steps. She scraped her hands when she slipped, but swallowed the pain because losing Frank would be so much worse.

"Frank!"

He barked in reply, urging her on, but still out of sight. If she could hear him, she could find him. She stopped every few seconds to listen for him, definitely getting closer.

Come on, boy. Show your face. Show me where you are.

Just before she reached the bottom, a ledge jutted out and curved around the hill, and his barking got louder. She lurched around the side and almost screamed for joy when she found him at the very edge of the ledge, leaning over, barking at something near the bottom.

"Oh, Frank." She fell to her knees next to him, overcome with relief.

He never turned, but leaned out even more, barking like he did when he saw Demi and couldn't get to her.

"What is it? What's wrong?" Still on her knees, she crawled to the edge and peered down. About fifteen feet below was the creek, rushing noisily over rocks and around trees.

"You can't go down there, boy." She tried to pull him back. "We have to get back to the road, and I sure hope you know the way."

But he was having none of it. He kept barking and staring intently. Not at the creek, but at something… She squinted down to see roots and branches sticking out of the brush about six feet away. "What is it?"

His bark grew a little more furious as he stared.

There was nothing there…except…what was that? Something small, navy, like a tiny beanie cap or a glove, just dangling from a root, with some twigs and dirt stuck to it.

"That's what you want? Sorry. We got bigger fish to fry, Franko." She managed to stand, but her legs were shaking hard from the run.

He dropped to the ground and somehow made himself heavier, his ears down, his tail still, but that incessant barking at a lost glove, or whatever it was, wouldn't stop.

"Frank!" She pulled at him, but he didn't budge. "We have to go. You could be sick. I don't have a phone. Why are you not understanding how dire this is?"

He stared at the navy thing and barked like it was all that ever mattered to him.

"Oh, for God's sake. Okay. I'll get it." It wouldn't be easy, but she could possibly get partway over the ledge. Then maybe grab it with the tip of her foot and bring it to one hand? If it would get him to move, it might be worth a try.

"Really? You really want me to do this for you?"

He just barked.

"Fine. Because I love you. And the man who owns you. There, I said it. I love him. Are you happy?" She crawled to the very edge, turned around, and started to slowly drop her legs over.

Thank God, the barking stopped while he watched, rapt.

"You're surprised I love him?" She ground out the words as she clung to the ledge for balance. "Well, imagine how I felt when I realized it. Which was...I don't know, a few minutes ago when I was running after you like..." She grunted and stretched her leg toward what she could see now was a child's mitten dangling from the branch. "Like a crazy woman because I know that Connor would be..." She huffed out a curse when she got her toe under it and lifted, but it didn't move.

Frank barked.

"Not helping, but okay. One more try." She twisted her body, extended her leg, and caught the mitten thumb on the edge of her sneaker. "There we go," she whispered.

As if he sensed the need for quiet so she could finish the operation, Frank stopped barking, leaning closer to her.

"Now if I can just get it…" She lifted her leg and let go of the ledge with her right hand, holding on with her left. "Right like this…" She plucked the disgustingly dirty mitten from her foot and slapped it on the ledge with a smack of victory.

Frank pounced on it and slammed his paw on her left hand, making her scream and instinctively yank free, sending her right off the ledge. She opened her mouth to scream again as she tumbled down the cliff.

She felt the scream tear at her throat as she flailed, somehow managing to grab on to the same root that had held the mitten. But now her feet dangled about six feet above a rushing, spring-fueled creek.

Above her, Frank leaned over the edge and stared at her, his treasure held firmly between his teeth.

"Help me," she cried softly, trying to get some kind of footing to climb back up. "Frank, please."

He backed away and started around the ledge the way they'd come.

"Don't leave, Frank. Please, please!"

But all she heard was the sound of his paws on dirt as he left her hanging several feet from ice-cold, rushing water and rocks.

She bit her lip, fought tears, and clung to the root with the strength she had left.

Chapter Twenty-five

"**A**re you sure my blood pressure is normal? And that heart rate?" Miss Clara Dee actually looked devastated.

"Right where you should be," Connor assured her, on one knee next to her rocker.

"But I'm not where I should be," the old lady murmured. "I should be with Henry."

"When the time is right." He patted her arm gently, not wanting to leave another purpura on her aging skin. "He'll be there when you get to him."

She didn't answer, but her old eyes grew wide with surprise as his comm device crackled and beeped.

"Engine One, Rescue Two, vehicle lost control, currently stranded on Sweetgum Springs Road. Call came from passing driver who was waved off."

He clicked the button to silence the call, since they wanted the other EMT and Miss Clara Dee looked so sad. "I know you miss your husband," he said softly. "Maybe there's a nice man right here in Starling for you."

She chuckled and patted his cheek. "If he looks like you, maybe."

"Hey, Connor." Tasheema signaled him.

"Almost done, Tash." He wrapped up the blood pressure monitor and smiled at the old woman. "But it was nice to see you again, Miss Clara Dee."

"I think you want to hear this." Tash came closer, lifting her comm device. "That stranded vehicle? Black Buick Enclave with DC tags."

He stared at her for a moment.

"I asked dispatch, who said there are two passengers, male and female, and they apparently turned down help from the truck driver who pulled over, but the vehicle's in a ditch."

He searched her face, thinking. Could Sadie be hurt? What was she doing out in Sweetgum Springs with that guy?

"Tell dispatch we're done here and not far. They can send our engine home, but let's take the ambulance and check it out."

She nodded while he said goodbye to Miss Clara Dee, then they hustled back to the ambulance, cleared the move with the station, and headed a few miles west to Sweetgum Springs.

"Hey, isn't this where you found Frank?" Tash said, pulling Connor out of a deep reverie about...nothing. His head and heart had gone blank since he'd seen Sadie running after Nathan. He didn't understand it, he didn't like it, and he didn't want to think about it.

"Yeah," he said, but dispatch rang in again, saving him from a conversation.

"Second passing vehicle has reported the stranded SUV, a black Buick Enclave with Washington, DC, plates." She added the precise location, which he entered into the tablet on his lap, shaking his head when the dispatcher added, "Passengers again declined assistance. Woman appears to be injured."

Tash threw him a look and didn't say a word. Didn't have to. Then she threw the siren on and flattened the accelerator, always happy for an excuse to race like the wind.

"That's the vehicle," Tash said as they pulled up right behind the SUV hanging off the shoulder with no sign of driver or passenger. The vehicle had sunk into soft dirt nose first and tipped so the driver's side was at a forty-five-degree angle. He couldn't see anyone in or around it.

They both got out and hustled toward the vehicle.

As they rounded the back, he spotted a man he instantly recognized sitting in a muddy gully, a woman in his lap.

A blonde woman.

"Please leave us alone," the man called without turning around to see Connor.

Tash started to talk, but Connor held his hand up. "Call in and report that we're here. I'll talk to him."

At the sound of Connor's voice, Nathan turned, saw him, and exhaled.

"First responder, sir," Connor said, coming closer. "Lieutenant Mahoney. Is this woman injured?"

He hung his head. "Not...from the accident." His voice sounded weak and defeated.

Connor rounded him, looking down at the woman draped on his lap, cradled in his arms, realizing the man was actually rocking her.

"Can I look at her, please?"

Nathan shook his head, making Connor crouch

down on one knee to make eye contact. "I can help you," he said softly. "But you need to let me look at her."

"You could have helped," Nathan replied, the way he stroked the blonde hair reminded him of Sadie petting her cat when the world got to be too much. "But it's too late now."

"Too late?" He looked down at the woman, recognizing her, despite a tear- and mascara-stained face. "Let me examine her."

Just then, Tash came around the SUV, talking into her comm device. "Roger that, dispatch. Oh, I see LEO arriving now. Sheriff's here, Connor. Sir, can we please take a look at your friend?"

Connor stood, seeing a sheriff's cruiser pulling up. Instantly, he crouched back down and looked Nathan in the eye.

"Where is she?" he demanded.

Nathan stared at him, his hand still on Jane's head.

"Sheriff's here, Nathan," Connor said softly. "Tell me where Sadie is and maybe you won't get arrested."

"They ran off," he said, looking past Connor to the woods.

They?

As Tash and the sheriff came closer, Connor stood, knowing he wasn't going to get more from the guy, so maybe they would. As he did, his gaze dropped to the mud where he saw a round print that could only have been…a paw. A big dog paw…

They ran off.

Connor shot a look at the man on the ground, but he was finally relinquishing hold of Jane.

"Was Frank with you?" he demanded of Nathan.

The other man just looked up at him. "I don't know who that is."

He exhaled a sharp breath and grabbed his comm device, telling dispatch that another passenger could be in the woods. The other rescue vehicle from his station showed up, and everyone started to move in coordination, but Connor was itching to move.

He knew these woods, and so did Frank. The residential area where the little boy lived was a mile, maybe more, on the other side of thick woods with ravines, cliffs, and spring-fueled creeks with slippery rocks and unforgiving water. But it was all familiar to Frank.

"I'm going to go look for her," Connor said to Tash, who was taking Jane's blood pressure. Without waiting for a response, he jogged deeper into the woods.

None of it made sense—not her diving into Nathan's car and...*wait a second*. Why had she run from around the back of the guesthouse? Where was Frank then? There was no door back there. Unless you counted the dog door in the bathroom. Could Sadie fit through that?

If she was trapped in the bathroom.

He almost spit with fury and fear, picking up speed and heading instinctively in the direction where he'd found Frank. If he was lost, that area would be familiar to him. But if Sadie was lost...

"Sadie!" he called. "Frank!" He ran along a narrow track worn by deer and other animals, stopping to listen every thirty seconds, but hearing nothing but birds and...

Rustling. An animal. To his left.

"Frank! Come here, boy!" Unless it was a coyote or wolf or—

The familiar golden head poked through the bushes just like he had that first day. Only this time, Frank didn't look wary, he looked...victorious.

Proudly, he sauntered closer and dropped something he held in his mouth, then looked up, ready and waiting for praise.

"Frank." Connor practically fell on him with a hug. "Good boy. Where's Sadie? Take me to her!"

But Frank just looked down and barked, drawing Connor's attention to whatever he had. A filthy, muddy, navy blue...mitten.

He blinked at it, instantly recognizing it. "Wow, you found the mate. Good..." He looked up and past Frank, in the direction of the rushing creek where this mitten probably came from.

Without a second's hesitation, he sprinted off. "Sadie! Sadie!" His calls bounced around the woods, with nothing but silence in response.

He finally stopped at the foot of a steep hill, knowing that if he worked all the way around, he'd come to the creek and embankment where he'd found Dylan...and Frank. Could she possibly have gone that way? If so, then she'd reach the creek and not be able to cross.

"Okay." Connor was vaguely aware of the orders being delivered on his comm device and decided he would answer once he got up the hill. "Sadie!"

"I'm here." Her voice was weak, distant, but music to his ears. It shot strength and speed into him that he saved for the worst situations he faced. And losing her would be the worst of all.

He reached the top of the hill and looked left and right, getting punched in the gut when he didn't see her.

"Hey."

He looked down to see her about three feet below the ledge, clinging to a root, trying to dig her toes into the dirt to stay put.

"Do not move."

"Wouldn't think of it." Her voice was soft, her face pale and streaked with sweat and dirt, but she looked up with love and gratitude. "Just pretend I'm a kitten and save me, Lieutenant."

He was flat on his stomach in no time, reaching all the way over to clasp his hands around her wrists. "Hang on." Gritting his teeth, he wrenched her higher, pulling her toward him, holding her gaze as she inched closer.

Finally, she reached the ledge and rolled onto the dirt next to him, breathless. They just stayed perfectly still and stared at each other.

"I have a lot to tell you," she managed to say, somehow making him smile.

"Dying to hear."

"Let's just start with two really important things."

He nodded, finding the strength to reach over and brush dirt from her cheek, his heart folding in half from things he hadn't even known he could feel that now owned him.

"I think I'm in love with you," she whispered. "I know it's crazy and fast, but—"

He cut her off by coming closer to kiss her. "What's this 'think' stuff, Ear Girl?"

She smiled into the kiss and leaned back to look at him. "Yeah. I *know*."

"Good. Me, too. What's the other thing?"

"We need to get Frank to a vet, and whatever you do, do not throw away his poop."

"*What*?"

Chapter Twenty-six

"This is not like any Election Day I've ever seen." Sadie stroked Demi in the baby carrier that hung around her neck as she walked with Connor, greeting the locals with handshakes and hugs.

Frank trotted along a few feet ahead on his leash, a green-and-white shamrock-covered bandanna fluttering around his neck, his confidence in crowds growing every day. Of course, it was always better when they brought Demi, because he liked to show off for her.

"No ballrooms full of supporters and hotel rooms packed with open laptops analyzing exit polls?" Connor asked.

She shook her head, remembering those hotel rooms and exit polls and how it all mattered so much. And it did, and it should...for someone else. What mattered now was the well-being of this sweet little dog-forward town and the man who opened it all up to her.

"It's just different," she said. "I wasn't expecting a town square filled with booths and crafts and..." She gestured toward the center. "Green beer and tea, and that the polls are only open from noon to six."

"The Saint Patrick's Day timing for the election is just the luck of the Irish. The voting window is right out of Thad's famous charter." He gave her shoulder a squeeze. "My mom found the *History of Bitter Bark* book. Did I tell you? Thad said mornings are for working hard, and evenings are for family. Vote in the heart of the day, good citizens of Bitter Bark."

She laughed and leaned into the shoulder she loved to have against her cheek.

"Excuse me? Firefighter Mahoney?"

They turned at the woman's voice to see a couple with a little tow-headed boy between them, holding his parents' hands.

"Dylan!" Connor dropped right to his knees and extended his arms, but Dylan totally ignored him and reached for the dog.

"Fwankie!"

They all laughed, and Connor threw up his hands. "And now you see why Frank is running for mayor, and I'm just his sidekick." Standing slowly, he gave a quick hug to the woman and shook the man's hand. "Dave and Robin O'Keefe, this is Sadie Hartman, my—"

"Fiancée!" Robin exclaimed excitedly. "Oh, Sadie, what a story! Frank saved you and my son. It's just all we can talk about."

Sadie gave a quick smile to Connor, who'd let the story morph into another heroic Frank save in the woods. He never once tried to take credit for finding Sadie when she was hanging from a root, but put Frank front and center as the local hero.

"And you, young man," Connor said to the boy, "lost two mittens that day, and Frank wasn't going to rest until he found them both."

He gave a big smile, but Sadie doubted the child understood. She and Connor didn't completely understand, honestly, but they guessed that Frank had received so much praise for finding one mitten, he was incented to find the other when he got the chance.

"And that helped save Sadie, who is obviously a cat woman."

"That's Demi!" Robin cooed. "Frank's girlfriend. I read the feature story about them in the *Banner*. So cute!"

"And how's our famous gem-eater feeling?" Dylan's father asked, reaching to pet Frank, who stepped forward for the love, finally comfortable in the role.

"He's fit and ready to win tonight," Connor said. "And as far as we know, there's no more crystallized carbon in him."

As the couple chatted about the news, Sadie listened with amusement and maybe a little amazement at how it all got spun into a story with no villains and more than one hero. Nathan and Jane had come clean and publicly acknowledged that they had been hiding the lab-grown diamonds "for safekeeping" since Nathan's office had been experiencing some thefts.

It was shaky, but the news was overshadowed by Jane's announcement of her diagnosis, and her plans to travel the country as a spokeswoman for amyotrophic lateral sclerosis. With all the press coverage she received, Nathan persuaded the pharmaceutical company to let Jane participate in the final clinical trial. In exchange, she would help them navigate the process to get FDA approval, but only if they would invest more money into researching ways to lower the cost of the drug.

Satisfied that it was a win all around, Sadie did not contradict their story about hiding the diamonds with her. And how could she when Frank's famous eating incident became national news, and he stole even more hearts?

Even the diamond-growers association was thrilled with the press coverage, using the story to drive home their messages about the worth of the product.

"Hopefully, after all that," Connor said, bringing Sadie closer to him, "one of us will be beating Mitch Easterbrook tonight."

The O'Keefes glanced at each other, looking surprised at the comment.

"Haven't you heard?" Robin asked. "He's dropping out of the race. I think he's about to make an announcement on the steps of town hall."

"What?" Sadie gasped. "I can't believe it."

"I have a friend who is the caterer his wife uses," Robin said. "She told me Mrs. Easterbrook canceled everything they were planning for a victory celebration after the news broke. Even Mitch knows he can't beat a dog who poops diamonds."

"Or the woman that dog saved," Connor added.

"Well, one of us is going to win," Sadie said to them all. "And since we're a team, we all win."

"That's the spirit!" Dave gave her a high five. "If you want to hear Mitch try to turn this into something magnanimous that he's doing for the town, go listen."

They headed over to the small crowd gathered on the wide stone steps of the brick building.

Mitch was already speaking at a podium that had been set up at the top, the gathering of journalists around him looking a little larger than it had the first time Sadie met with them all. In some ways, they had managed to really lift Bitter Bark's profile.

"This decision wasn't an easy one, but my business is booming, and the people of Bitter Bark need me more to guide them through their dark days of grief with a strong hand and open heart. That's why when the polls open in ten minutes, my name will not be on the ballot."

No one seemed too unhappy about that.

"Who are you endorsing?" one of the reporters asked.

He shifted from one foot to the other. "I'll support whoever—or whatever—the constituents choose."

Connor curled his lip at the "whatever" comment and brought Frank closer for a good head rub. "Sore loser," he muttered when Mitch declined questions, and the crowd broke up. "I think I need green beer."

"And we need to vote," Sadie said. "Let's go in together when they open the town hall doors at noon."

As they started up the steps, Rose Halliday came right at them, her phone out as if she was ready to record an interview.

"Sadie! Connor! And of course, the dog of the decade, Frankendog."

Sadie sucked in a soft breath, but Connor just laughed at the name.

"You think I don't know that's what you named him?" Rose challenged, giving Frank a pet and getting a whoosh of his tail and a dog smile in response. "He wears it well," she said. "And this is a different dog than the one I met out there that day in Sweetgum Springs, Connor. He'll be a fine mayor."

"I don't know. He's got some tough competition, Rose."

The reporter beamed. "Listen, there's so much support for both of you, I wouldn't be surprised by a tie. Your engagement idea has charmed the town."

"Engagement *idea*?" Sadie gave a little smile. "You still don't believe us, do you, Rose?"

"Well, the thing is…" She turned and looked at the podium where Mitch was still shaking some hands. "He's ready to jump in when you two break up. A forfeiture is still on the table, as you know."

"Then take it off the table," Connor said. "Because there's no breakup in our future."

Sadie let the thrill of his words dance through her, but Rose tapped her phone and stuffed it into the bag on her shoulder with a dramatic flair. "Totally and completely off the record?" she asked.

"On or off," Connor said, "the answer's the same."

Rose looked from one to the other. "Strictly on a personal level, from someone who cares about this town," she said, "just tell me when. Because it's going to crush this town the day the 'mayor couple' splits up."

Connor and Sadie stood stone-still for a moment, then looked at each other, a million silent words passing between them. It had only been a month, but the idea of breaking up was unimaginable to her.

"Well?" Rose prodded.

Connor shook his head. Sadie smiled. And they each slipped an arm around the other's waist in a show of complete solidarity.

"Hope you're happy." Mitch threw the comment at them as he trotted down the steps past them.

"Ecstatic," Sadie said.

"Miles beyond happy," Connor added.

Mitch paused on the next step and turned back, mouthing, "Forfeit," at them.

"Oh, Mitch," Rose said on a slightly giddy laugh. "Give it up, will you?"

He didn't respond, but continued down the steps, leaving them all laughing softly until a flurry of people rushed by toward town hall.

"Polls are open!" Rose announced.

"Come on, Ear Girl. Let's go vote for each other."

For as long as Connor had been alive, with a few exceptions, he'd celebrated Saint Patrick's Day at Waterford Farm with every single member of his family and a ton of friends. Uncle Daniel had paused the tradition for a few years after Aunt Annie died, and last year, the whole thing had blown up in their faces when Katie Santorini's oldest son showed up, and the family tree had tilted under the weight of a new branch.

But Daniel and Katie had married, and judging from the fact that Yiayia had baked green bread and Santorini's had replaced ouzo with Jameson's, the Greeks could be as Irish as anyone else on this day.

Everyone gathered in groups in and out of the big house. About fifteen dogs ran around the pens with some of the staff trainers, who always helped out at these things. Sadie had gone inside with Darcy, Ella, and Cassie, who had kind of adopted her as one of their own.

So Connor looked around for Shane or Chloe, finding them with a group of cousins, in-laws, and extras, all gathered around Gramma Finnie and Yiayia, who held court in their rockers, each with a baby on her lap.

"Careful with Annabelle," Connor said to Gramma Finnie as he sat down on the hassock in front of their rockers. "She blows like Vesuvius when you least expect it."

"Nonsense, lad," Gramma Finnie said, situating the baby on her lap with the ease of a woman who'd rocked dozens of little ones. "You jus' need to know how to calm them."

"This one is always calm," Yiayia said, patting little Danny's head as she moved back and forth. "He's so good."

Molly beamed. "He's the best baby ever."

"Hey!" From the sofa, Pru gave her mother a tap with her shoe. "Don't rile up my sibling rivalry."

They laughed and talked some more, then Connor leaned over to Shane to say, "Don't leave without getting Sadie's—er, I mean Chloe's ring back."

"Don't need it anymore?"

"Not after the election."

"I'll pretend I'm not hearin' that, lad." Gramma Finnie made a sad face. "Agnes and I were so excited about another matchmaking victory."

"Oh, Gramma!" Pru stuck her nose in, of course. "They're not breaking up. Are you, Connor?"

"Not if I have anything to say about it."

Yiayia and Gramma Finnie exchanged a look. "We

did it!" They mouthed the words and leaned toward each other, their hands too full of babies to actually high-five.

"Really?" Pru practically shrieked.

"It's not pretend anymore?" Chloe asked.

"I should have bet more in the family pool," Shane mumbled with a half-smile.

"Who can blame you for not betting on me in the relationship department?" Connor asked. "I don't exactly have a stellar track record."

"Your track record starts now," Gramma Finnie said, inching her littler rocker forward. "From this day on, in sickness and in health, for better or worse…"

Shane snorted. "That's enough J-juice for you, Finola Kilcannon."

She tsked him, but kept her eyes on Connor. "I knew it the moment I met her," she said, her brogue thickening like it did when she got emotional.

"How'd you know?" he asked, dying for the answer.

She just tilted her head. "I remembered."

"Remembered what?"

"The two of you debating onstage…in high school. 'Twas obvious to any observer, lad, that you were meant for each other."

"Connor and Ear Girl?" Garrett snorted. "Sorry, Gramma. I was there. Wasn't obvious to anyone."

She shook her old white head. "She was just so lovely and serious. And you talked and joked and made everyone laugh."

"Like the idiot I was back then," he murmured.

"Back then?" Braden stage-whispered to Pru, who giggled.

But Gramma was deep in her memory of the moment, her blue eyes distant as she recalled a moment that Connor wished he could. "There was something in the way she looked at you, like she wanted to strangle you and kiss you at the same time."

Everyone laughed. "Perfect recipe for love," Shane joked.

"Then Margie told me she was comin' from Washington and..." Gramma lifted a shoulder and leaned her head toward Yiayia. "We worked our magic."

"The campaign manager idea was mine," Yiayia said. "Sorry, but it was brilliant."

"I like the way it all played out even better," Connor said, putting a hand on both women's arms. "Thank you, Dogmothers."

"Aww." Molly waved her hands at her face, air-drying tears she wasn't really shedding.

"Gramma, who's next?" Pru asked, up on her knees. "Say it's Declan. Please say it's Declan."

"Can it, child," Declan said from where he leaned on the porch railing.

"It's time for a Greek," Yiayia insisted, sitting up to point at the yard, where John Santorini was slowly making his way from the kennels to the porch, alone as he so frequently was. "My Yianni is next."

"Better find a geeky math lover for Spreadsheet John," Shane joked.

"Someone serious like him," Pru said.

"Who doesn't like to laugh," Shane said.

"And someone who cares more about the bottom line than anything," Alex, John's twin brother and partner at Santorini's, the deli they co-owned, chimed in. "But I have to say…" He put an arm around the beautiful blonde next to him. "You guys do good work."

Grace smiled at him and petted the light brown dog that snuggled between them.

"We're not perfect yet," Yiayia said. "But we're getting better."

From inside the house, they heard a few high-pitched shrieks.

"The results are in!" Ella bounded out with her unbridled energy. "The Bitter Bark mayoral results have just gone up on the town website."

Behind Ella, Sadie stood in the shadows of the kitchen.

"Do you know?" Connor asked her.

"Not yet." She came out with Darcy and Cassie, and a few others joined them, including John, who came up the steps, the poor guy clueless about what was about to hit him.

"Who wants to look?" Connor stood to reach for Sadie's hand and bring her right to the hassock where he'd asked her to marry him…the second time.

"I got it." Shane thumbed his phone as everyone gathered around, cracking jokes with nervous laughter.

"Wait," Sadie said. "Where's Frank? He should be here."

"He's in the kennels," John said, adjusting his glasses.

"I thought he was in the pen." Connor leaned back to look at all the dogs, but he didn't see the wild tail and stubby ears of the one he loved.

"Your orange cat found a safe spot in the back, and he went to join her." John ran a hand over his short-cropped beard and adjusted his dark-rimmed glasses. "Now that's an odd couple."

"I got the results," Shane announced, standing in the center of all of them and looking at his phone. "And...wow. *Wow*."

The group hummed with question, but Sadie and Connor just joined hands and looked at each other.

"Doesn't matter," she whispered.

"We've already won," he replied.

As he leaned over to kiss her, he winked at Gramma Finnie.

"All right, tell us without Frank," Sadie said. "I have to know."

Shane cleared his throat and started to read. "Dateline, Bitter Bark, North Carolina."

"Just give the results," Connor urged.

"It's a little more complicated than that," Shane said.

"You can say that again." Trace had his phone out, and Molly was reading over his shoulder, her jaw dropped open.

"Like I said." Shane shot a look at Connor. "Dateline, Bitter Bark, North Carolina. 'In a shocking and historic twist in what has already been the most unorthodox of mayoral campaigns in this town's one-hundred-and-fifty-three-year history, the winner of the office was not on the ballot.'"

"What?"

"Are you kidding me?"

"How is that possible?"

Shane waited for the outburst to die down before he continued. "'Not exactly on the ballot,'" he read. "'All the names were there in one form or another. Mercedes "Sadie" Hartman, Frank "the local hero dog," and Connor "Frank's Chief of Staff" Mahoney have all been actively campaigning for the office.' Third candidate Mitch Eastercrook wussed out at the last minute with his tail, not nearly as fine as Frank's, between his legs." Shane grinned. "I added that."

"Keep reading!" Sadie insisted over the noisy laughter, squeezing Connor's hand.

"Okay. Okay. 'In an election first, the winner was selected by write-in, achieving a historic eighty-seven percent of the vote. The next mayor of Bitter Bark will be, in truth, two mayors and a dog.'"

Another flurry of questions and comments stopped the reading, but Sadie and Connor just stared at each other as that sank in.

"A write-in?" she asked.

"As…a team?"

"That's exactly what it is," Shane confirmed. "Listen. 'The citizens of Bitter Bark overwhelmingly want Hartman and Mahoney as co-mayors, with Frank as the ceremonial mayor to appear at all events, support fundraising, and generally raise the spirits of the town. The humans are expected to handle budgets, pay raises, and other mayoral issues as co-mayors.'"

For a moment, there was dead silence, and then a cheer erupted so loud, the dogs in the pen started barking.

"Co-mayors?" Sadie whispered as if in shock.

"There's a little more," Shane said. "'At least fifty write-ins included requests to be invited to the wedding of the co-mayors, and several said that the job should be contingent on both mayors having the same last name.'" He held up a hand like he was taking an oath. "Swear to God, I didn't make that up."

All around them, the family cheered. The glasses clinked. The jokes erupted, and the congratulations rained down, and Annabelle cried at the noise.

But all Connor could do was look into Sadie's eyes and see the greatest victory he'd ever won. She bit her lip and put her hand on his cheek, her fingers trembling against his skin.

"I can't believe it."

"Neither can I."

"We both won."

"We sure did."

He took her hand in his and slid his fingers over the ring she'd been wearing since he'd given it to her right here in this same spot. "Take it off now."

She blinked at him, and some of the noise died down around them.

"Off?"

"Take that ring off, Sadie." He helped her, aware that now everyone was listening.

"Of course. It wasn't real." She slid it over her knuckle and handed it to him. He didn't even look at it, but raised it up for Shane. "Thank you, bro, for the loaner. We won't be needing that anymore."

"Oh." Gramma Finnie let out a soft whimper.

"Not at all?" Yiayia's disappointment was clear.

"No." Connor put his hands on Sadie's cheeks and held her face in front of his. "Because when I put a ring on this woman's finger, it will have taken Mother Nature a million years to create it, which is just about how long this love is going to last."

"Oh, my heart, lad, I canna take it."

Sadie's eyes filled. "Neither can I."

"I love you," he whispered. "Co-Mayor."

"I love you, too." She melted into his kiss while the family cheered.

After a moment, he inched back and gestured toward the kennels. "Let's tell Frank and Demi they'll be spending their days at town hall. And their nights…." He kissed her again. "Sadie, we're going to need a bigger bed."

Epilogue

"**A**nd that, according to Thaddeus Ambrose Bushrod, is the real reason this hickory tree is called a bitter bark tree." Connor looked around at the forty or so people gathered under and around that tree, many of them with children and picnic baskets. "Not because there was already a Hickory, North Carolina, but because our founder tried to eat the round, brown fruit and found it to be…" He glanced down at the book in his hand. "'As bitter a taste as hate and resentment, which no man shall harbor and be healthy.'"

The sentence had been underlined by the last person to read the book, Joe Mahoney.

Connor closed the book with a squeeze that he wished he could give his dad and a silent thanks for all the life lessons Thad—and Dad—taught him.

The whole crowd broke into applause and then continued their Saturday afternoon in the square, finishing picnics, walking dogs, and running to the playground.

Next to him, Sadie leaned in to give him a kiss on

the cheek. "Well done, teacher. I think Saturday Civics is a huge hit."

He nodded as no small amount of pride rolled through him. After he'd read *History of Bitter Bark*, as penned by Thad himself, the notes in the margins in his father's handwriting gave him the idea to pass some of this wisdom to the town. He still couldn't get over the irony that so many of his father's insights came directly from the man who'd founded Bitter Bark. Sure, Dad had put them in modern language, but the concepts were the same.

When he told Sadie how much he wanted to share the lessons, she'd joked that he finally cared about civics class, so the co-mayors launched Saturday Civics and invited local schoolchildren and parents— and dogs, plus one very beloved kitty—once a month to the square to learn the deep and colorful history of the town.

The program was young, but already a huge hit. Frank welcomed the families with a wagging tail that always got him treats. Sadie handed out flyers with the day's lesson and notes, and Connor stood at the base of Thad's statue and read a short chapter.

As the crowd thinned out and dispersed, Connor and Sadie cleaned up anything left behind. They usually took a stroll with Frank after Saturday Civics, sometimes stopping by Gramma Finnie and Yiayia's house to visit, sometimes getting some pizza to share on their favorite bench.

But today, Connor had a different plan. An elaborate plan. One that might take all day if it unfolded the way he hoped. But as Sadie walked toward him with that light blue sundress the same color as the Bitter Bark summer sky, he started to rethink that elaborate plan.

Better to get it done and start...celebrating.

"You got pretty dressed up for Saturday Civics," he noted, letting his gaze linger over every inch of her, from her stupendous hair down to the pink-tipped toes that peeked out of her sandals.

"It's our anniversary," she said simply.

Wait. She knew that, too? "Five months since we met at Bushrod's," he said. "I didn't think you remembered."

"Of course I remember." She reached him and wrapped her arms around his waist. "I've been looking for an excuse to wear this dress I bought from Yvette."

"Yvette? Oh, then I know what's underneath."

She bit her lip. "I did get something special to go with it."

He let out a little grunt. "Maybe we should just go home and..."

"Anything you want." She pressed into him and nibbled on his chin. "I want you to know they've been the best five months of my life."

He searched her face for a long moment, thinking about all he had planned, but...

"What's wrong?" she asked.

"I can't wait."

"For what?"

"I was going to start at Bushrod's and give you a little speech about finding you on the street."

"Start? Start what?"

He just lifted his brows. "Our anniversary celebration."

"Okay, Bushrod's. Let's go to the place where I

was lost." She lifted up on her toes and kissed him again. "And now I'm found."

"Actually, I was lost, Ear Girl. You were the one who pointed me in the right direction." Holding her tight, he looked around, mentally visualizing his map. "Then I thought we'd go to town hall and visit my dad's picture."

"Aww. I'd like that. The man who taught us both so much. Let's go now."

She tried to pull him in that direction, but he stayed still, not willing to leave this midsummer sunshine or the perfect feel of Sadie in his arms. "After that, I thought we could run up to the stairwell where we hatched the idea that changed our lives."

"And had our first kiss. Three of them, actually." She sighed. "Good times in that stairwell."

"Then I thought we'd drop by your grandparents' guesthouse and maybe climb a tree, since I never got to."

"A tree? Why?"

"Because…" He slid his fingers through her hair and lightly pushed some over her shoulder to see even more of her face. "It was my willingness to climb a tree that made you fall in love with me, or so you told this town."

She laughed. "It might have still been lust at that point, but yes."

"And then I was going to bring you right back here, to our pal Thad. So he could be our witness."

She studied him for a moment, curious. "Witness to what?"

He angled his head and gave her a look. "You really don't know?"

A soft flush rose on her cheeks, so he suspected she did know. They'd talked around it for months—both knowing it was a "done deal," but also that the deal hadn't quite been done. Yet.

He grazed her jawline with his thumb, lost in those golden-brown eyes. "I finally found it."

"Found...what?"

"The one."

"Aww." She squeezed him. "You're the one for me, too."

"No, not that one." He eased back, releasing his grip on her. "This one." He reached into his pocket and slowly pulled out the small box. "I had to do so much research to find the right one. It had to be perfect, with as many facets as you have and the same kind of sparkle."

"Oh, Connor." She stared at the box, then looked up at him. "Was it...grown?"

"Grown by the hand of God," he whispered. "And it took Him a million years, but that's how long it will last. It's the one. For you."

She put her hand over the closed box, her fingers trembling. Or maybe his were, because his whole body sort of vibrated with the rightness of this.

For a long moment, they said nothing, but looked into each other's eyes. "I've asked twice, Sadie."

"And I've said yes twice," she replied on a laugh. "I kind of thought we were already...well, we've certainly never gotten *un*engaged."

"But it was never as real as it is now." He glanced around, happy that all the people were distant and distracted with their own lives. He didn't want an audience. He didn't want family or townsfolk to applaud the moment. He didn't want anyone but the woman he loved with his whole heart and soul.

Wordlessly, he lowered himself to one knee and watched her shoulders shudder as she took in a soft breath. He took a mental picture of Sadie's beautiful face, memorizing the joy in her eyes and the certainty there, too.

Then he lifted the box lid and enjoyed her openmouthed gasp of delight when she saw the solitaire. "Connor! It's gorgeous!"

He grinned at the heartfelt reaction, watching her face tell the story he loved to read. Awe, surprise, delight, trust, and love. That was how they got from there to here.

He cleared his throat and looked into her eyes. "Sadie Hartman, you are the most beautiful, independent, brilliant, loving, sexy, funny, wonderful woman I've ever known. You changed my life and my family and my town and my outlook. I do not want to spend a single day of the rest of my life without you. And when one of us dies, it still won't be over."

"We'll be like Clara Dee and Henry?" she asked, her voice strangled by tears.

"Exactly. Waiting for the other one in heaven. I love you with my whole heart and soul. Will you marry me?"

She reached down and put her hands on his cheeks, gently guiding him back to a stand. "Connor Mahoney, you are the most amazing, caring, hilarious, sexy man I've ever known, and I will love you until the day I die and beyond."

"Is that a yes?"

"Oh my, yes. Yes. *Yes*." She held out her hand, and he slipped on the diamond that was as real as their love. She threw her arms around him, and he twirled her so her pretty blue dress fluttered in the breeze.

When her feet touched the ground, they kissed and hugged and turned to show old Thad. But at the base of the statue, Frank was stretched out in the sun, and Demi had her head on his paw, both of them staring at Connor and Sadie.

Frank swooshed his tail, and Demi sat up a little, as if showing off her glorious collar that had its own diamond solitaire, one that had truly come from the dog she loved. They'd decided it was okay to keep one of them, after all.

"So we do have an audience," Connor mused as they looked at their spoiled and beloved animals.

"Our kids," she joked.

"Let's have more," he said. "The kind that spit and drool and steal your sleep and make you crazy with happiness."

"Oh, Connor." She smiled up at him with nothing but love in her eyes. "Why do you think I bought that lingerie?"

"We should honor her somehow. Yvette Mahoney for the first child. Has a nice ring to it, don't you think?"

She laughed and held her hand out, letting Mother Nature's finest work glint in the sunshine. "Speaking of nice rings. This is…spectacular, Lieutenant."

"So are you, Ear Girl. So are you."

The Dogmothers are hard at work on their next match!
Watch my newsletter or reader group for updates
on John Santorini's love story...book five in
The Dogmothers series.

Want to know the minute it's available?
Sign up for the newsletter.

www.roxannestclaire.com/newsletter-2/

Or get daily updates, sneak peeks, and insider
information at the Dogfather Reader Facebook Group!

www.facebook.com/groups/roxannestclairereaders/

The Dogmothers is a spinoff series of
The Dogfather

Join the private Dogfather Reader Facebook Group!

www.facebook.com/groups/roxannestclairereaders/

When you join, you'll find inside info on all the books and characters, sneak peeks, and a place to share the love of tails and tales!

The Dogmothers Series

Available Now

HOT UNDER THE COLLAR (Book 1)

THREE DOG NIGHT (Book 2)

DACHSHUND THROUGH THE SNOW (Book 3)

CHASING TAIL (Book 4)

And many more to come!

For a complete list, buy links, and reading order of all
my books, visit www.roxannestclaire.com. Be sure to
sign up for my newsletter to find out when the next
book is released!

A Dogfather/Dogmothers Family Reference Guide

THE KILCANNON FAMILY

Daniel Kilcannon aka *The Dogfather*
Son of Finola (Gramma Finnie) and Seamus
Kilcannon. Married to Annie Harper for 36 years until
her death. Veterinarian, father, and grandfather.
Widowed at opening of series. Married to Katie
Santorini (*Old Dog New Tricks*) with dogs Rusty and
Goldie.

The Kilcannons (from oldest to youngest):

• **Liam** Kilcannon and Andi Rivers (*Leader of the
Pack*) with Christian and Fiona and dog, Jag

• **Shane** Kilcannon and Chloe Somerset (*New Leash
on* Life) with daughter Annabelle and dogs, Daisy and
Ruby

• **Garrett** Kilcannon and Jessie Curtis
(*Sit...Stay...Beg*) with son Patrick and dog, Lola

• **Molly** Kilcannon and Trace Bancroft (*Bad to the
Bone*) with daughter Pru and son Danny and dog,
Meatball

• **Aidan** Kilcannon and Beck Spencer (*Ruff Around
the Edges*) with dog, Ruff

• **Darcy** Kilcannon and Josh Ranier (*Double Dog
Dare*) with dogs, Kookie and Stella

THE MAHONEY FAMILY

Colleen Mahoney
Daughter of Finola (Gramma Finnie) and Seamus Kilcannon and younger sister of Daniel. Widow of the late Joe Mahoney. Owner of Bone Appetit (canine treat bakery) and mother.

The Mahoneys (from oldest to youngest):

• **Declan** Mahoney and…

• **Connor** Mahoney and Sadie Hartman (*Chasing Tail*) with dog, Frank, and cat, Demi

• **Braden** Mahoney and **Cassie** Santorini (*Hot Under the Collar*) with dogs, Jelly Bean and Jasmine

• **Ella** Mahoney and…

THE SANTORINI FAMILY

Katie Rogers Santorini
Dated **Daniel** Kilcannon in college and introduced him to Annie. Married to Nico Santorini for forty years until his death two years after Annie's. Interior Designer and mother. Recently married to **Daniel** Kilcannon (*Old Dogs New Tricks*).

The Santorinis

• **Nick** Santorini and…

• **John** Santorini (identical twin to Alex) and…

• **Alex** Santorini (identical twin to John) and Grace Donovan with dogs, Bitsy, Gertie and Jack

• **Theo** Santorini and…

• **Cassie** Santorini and **Braden** Mahoney (*Hot Under the Collar*) with dogs, Jelly Bean and Jasmine

Katie's mother-in-law from her first marriage, **Agnes "Yiayia" Santorini,** now lives in Bitter Bark with **Gramma Finnie** and their dachshunds, Pygmalion (Pyggie) and Galatea (Gala). These two women are known as "The Dogmothers."

About The Author

Published since 2003, Roxanne St. Claire is a *New York Times* and *USA Today* bestselling author of more than fifty romance and suspense novels. She has written several popular series, including The Dogfather, The Dogmothers, Barefoot Bay, the Guardian Angelinos, and the Bullet Catchers.

In addition to being a ten-time nominee and one-time winner of the prestigious RITA™ Award for the best in romance writing, Roxanne has won the National Readers' Choice Award for best romantic suspense four times. Her books have been published in dozens of languages and optioned for film.

A mother of two but recent empty-nester, Roxanne lives in Florida with her husband and her two dogs, Ginger and Rosie.

www.roxannestclaire.com
www.twitter.com/roxannestclaire
www.facebook.com/roxannestclaire
www.roxannestclaire.com/newsletter/